Murder On Skye

ALSO BY DANIEL SELLERS

DCI LOLA HARRIS SERIES
Book 1: Murder In The Gallowgate
Book 2: Murder In Lovers' Lane
Book 3: Murder On The Clyde
Book 4: Murder On Skye

Daniel Sellers

MURDER ON SKYE

DCI Lola Harris Series Book 4

Joffe Books, London
www.joffebooks.com

First published in Great Britain in 2024

Cover art by Nebojša Zorić

ISBN: 978-1-83526-830-8

For Katharine

AUTHOR'S NOTE

A number of places referred to in this novel are real, as are some institutions. The characters and events are fictional.

Please go to my website (www.danielsellers.co.uk) to sign up for my e-newsletter. You can also follow me on Twitter (@djsellersauthor) and on Instagram (@danielsellersauthor), or by following the hashtag:

#WhatWouldLolaHarrisDo?

PROLOGUE

Glasgow Chronicle, Thursday 6 June 2024, p. 1

CARTER CRAIG CAGED FOR LIFE

by Shuna Frain, news desk

Celebrity entrepreneur Carter Craig was today sentenced to life in prison for the murders of Alex Sanderson and Xena Mitchell in the notorious 'Orchid Nightclub Murders' in August 2021.

The sentencing follows Craig's conviction in May at the end of a lengthy trial, before which the accused was on remand. The defence argued that Craig was in Jersey at the time of the murders and that he did not leave the island for most of the month of August.

The prosecution presented a raft of circumstantial evidence and put forward a witness who claimed to have sold Craig cocaine in Glasgow the evening before the murders. They also demonstrated how Craig could have left Jersey and returned a day or two later using a private boat. It was enough to persuade the jury to return a majority verdict of guilty.

Passing sentence, the Rt. Hon. Lord McAndrew described Craig, 33, as a 'duplicitous and dangerous individual without remorse'. He sentenced Craig to serve a minimum tariff of thirty years, prompting cheers from the public gallery.

Craig stood emotionless in the dock, but stopped to cast his eyes over the jury before being taken away.

Continues on p. 2

* * *

Glasgow Chronicle, Saturday 8 June 2024, p. 6

PLAYBOY TO CONVICTED KILLER: SPECIAL FEATURE

by Tommy Singh, features editor

Craig's is a story for our times: a rise from humble beginnings to a life of celebrity and wealth that burned out fast in the glare of the media spotlight.

It was after his father's death that Craig's uncle by marriage, media magnate Duncan Gaunt, took him under his wing, setting him up in business and mentoring him as he built an empire of property, nightclubs and restaurants.

But it was the reality TV programme Glasgow Nights that brought him fame — and notoriety. Positioned as the wealthy playboy in the ensemble, he was lusted after by the young women on the show and became a kingpin and role model among the men. Many viewers took to his charisma and his brazenness. Others were repulsed by what they saw as his self-serving materialism and by what one reviewer called 'a distinct rumble of violence just below the surface'.

Craig's TV career ended abruptly, however, following a stint on Big Brother. He'd only been in the house a week before producers expelled him for bragging about how he'd forced a former girlfriend to have an abortion against her will, threatening to throw her down a flight of stairs unless she consented.

Continues

* * *

Glasgow Chronicle, Wednesday 17 July 2024, p. 1

CARTER CRAIG: SHOCKING DEVELOPMENT

by Shuna Frain, news desk

A shock announcement by Carter Craig's legal team has been met with dismay and calls for an urgent inquiry.

It is understood that the judge in the case, the Rt. Hon. Lord McAndrew, has received compelling evidence of jury misconduct throughout the trial.

Responding, the Crown Office said that any new evidence will be considered with due regard.

Continues

* * *

Glasgow Chronicle, Thursday 8 August 2024, p. 1

CRAIG RELEASED ON INTERIM APPEAL

by Shuna Frain, news desk

Carter Craig walked free from Glasgow's Barlinnie Prison this morning, following an interim application for liberation submitted by his legal team. This followed a sensational finding from an initial inquiry that his conviction was 'unsafe', given 'compelling evidence of juror misconduct' lasting several weeks.

The evidence consists of screenshots of a number of private conversations between four jury members on a well-known messaging app in which they discussed trial evidence and where one juror even disclosed new evidence she believed indicated Craig's guilt.

Three of the four jurors implicated have been arrested and charged with conspiring to pervert the course of justice.

The fourth juror, whom the other three claim was the ringleader, is missing, believed to be in hiding.

CHAPTER ONE

Monday 12 August

7.37 a.m.

'That Carter Craig lunatic's issued another of his "warnings",' Sandy said from the kitchen table, eyes on his phone.

'Has he?' Lola asked. 'What about this time?'

She wouldn't normally have any time for someone like Craig, but this morning she welcomed any distraction.

'According to the *Chronicle*'s website, he's launching a new campaign.' Sandy scrolled on. 'Reckons he's going to "clear his name and identify the guilty". Says he wants to "mobilise and direct anger against deep-state actors". Bloke's a twenty-four-carat nutcase. He's the one who should be mobilised against.'

Lola glanced at her own phone. Her Google search had completed, making her recoil. Sandy heard her sharp intake of breath.

'You all right?' he asked.

'Aye. Aye, I'm fine.' She swallowed and scrolled reluctantly down the various links, including NHS ones. *Lobectomy*, one said. *What to expect from my lung surgery.*

'What if I don't go and see him, Sandy?' she said, her voice shaking. 'What if I don't go and he gets worse?'

What if he dies?

'Then *go*,' Sandy said equably. 'It's your decision.'

'Aye, but . . . What would you do in my shoes?' she snapped. It was one of those times when she needed direction — for someone else to take responsibility. 'Can't you just tell me?'

Sandy appeared to give it some thought, pushing out his bottom lip. He hadn't showered yet and his hair was out at all angles, but his colouring — pale skin, near-black hair and deep-blue eyes — meant he looked good even at his scruffiest. She felt a pang of intense affection. Of love. They'd been together for five months now, and it was going surprisingly well. Sometimes it felt as if they'd been together for years.

Finally he said, 'Lola, you'd never forgive me if I told you what to think.'

Lola laughed weakly, but that was just what she did want. That was what she'd wanted ever since Kev had texted her out of the blue two days ago and told her that his brother Joe's cancer had come back, but in one of his lungs this time. She'd rung him back and that was when he'd suggested she might pay Joe a visit at the hospital.

Just when things were going right. Just when she thought she could be happy, Joe was back in her head again — the man she'd been involved with for almost thirty years, including during his marriage to someone else.

'Personally, I wouldn't go,' Sandy said now, then gave a rueful smile. 'But I'm hard-nosed. And I know I'd cope if the worst happened.'

'I could go,' she said, mainly to herself. 'I could slip in and see him. Just for ten minutes. That would be the right thing to do, don't you think?'

'Do that, then,' Sandy said.

'And what if he looks really ill? I don't know how I'll feel.'

It was going to be a long day. Her diary was relatively light, with two meetings and some admin relating to a case that was going to court, so she would have plenty of time to obsess about Joe and what she should do.

She groaned and started filling the dishwasher. Sandy was focused back on his phone.

'Craig's lawyers are spouting off too. Reckon they're gonna sue for millions.' He shook his head. 'Anyone with half a brain knows the guy's guilty. If you ask me, behind that bonnie face is a pure psychopath. And I tell you this: if I'd given evidence for the prosecution in that trial, I'd be running for the hills right now. Graeme Izatt was the SIO on the original case, wasn't he? Surely they're not going to let him lead any new inquiry. Guy's a grade-A idiot.' He glanced up at her. 'Sorry. You've got other things to think about, haven't you?'

'You could put it like that.' She turned the dishwasher on. 'I'll go for my shower.'

He put out a hand to stop her as she passed.

'Trust your gut,' he said. 'If you decide to go to the hospital I could come with you. But only if it'd help. I could wait for you outside, bring you home after.'

She stared. 'You'd do that?'

''Course.'

She bent to embrace him, emotion rising. He was warm, his pyjama T-shirt soft, and he smelled comfortingly of sleep.

But then her phone began to buzz and she pulled away.

'Hi, Anna,' she said, forcing brightness.

'Morning, boss. Just got a call from Control. Body of a young woman's been found at the north end of Kelvingrove Park. A young construction worker pulled her out of the river. Looks like murder.'

It seemed Lola wasn't going to have much time to think about Joe after all.

CHAPTER TWO

8.32 a.m.

Eighteen-year-old Kyle McDade was pale and antsy, his big wary eyes darting about the park as if he was in imminent danger.

'Dropped my bacon roll and everything,' he explained shrilly to Lola. 'Just piled into the water and hauled her out by her oxters, then I seen her face and fell on my arse. Stung my hands to fuck on they nettles.' His eyes moved towards the gloomy figure of Inspector Michelle Brown, the senior officer who'd responded to the 999 call. 'Yer woman said I should have left her where she was. Guess that's me in big trouble.'

'You did the right thing phoning us,' Lola said gently.

'Man, I thought I was gonnae puke when I seen that wire cutting into her neck like that. Fuck's sake.' He closed his eyes and covered his mouth with one hand. 'Look, can I go? Only, the boss is doing his nut cos he's already short-staffed and I'm an hour late. Probably fire me on the spot.'

'Not if he's short-staffed, he won't. Just explain you found a body and had to wait for the police.'

She called DC Kirstie Campbell over to make sure she had a note of the young man's details.

'On you go,' Lola told him, once Kirstie confirmed she had his phone number. 'We'll be in touch. Meantime, folk ask you about this, tell them to mind their own business. Including your boss.'

'Thanks, missus.' And he ran off.

The locus was at the north end of Kelvingrove Park, just beside the river walkway where it ran underneath Gibson Street. It was another scorching day, into the third week of a heatwave, and the park would normally be busy with people heading to work or dog walkers out enjoying the morning sunshine, but a whole section had now been cordoned off. Lola spotted Anna Vaughan in conversation with a man in a Glasgow City Council parks uniform. He looked hot and bothered, while Anna looked typically cool and elegant in a light linen outfit that perfectly suited her slender frame and blonde colouring.

Anna Vaughan had been temporarily promoted to DI while Lola was acting as DCI — a rank she'd held temporarily since last autumn. It had taken Lola months to back-fill her own role, which had had to be advertised. A number of DSs had applied, including Aidan Pierce, with whom Lola had a sticky relationship. Luckily Anna had applied too and had stormed the interview.

Lola, who felt anything but cool and elegant, tugged on a pair of overshoes and stumped over, pausing to consider the nettle-choked slope down to the river. Kyle McDade had made a mess of the embankment, scrambling into the water to pull the body out. If that was where it had been put into the water, then any evidence was likely now lost.

The police surgeon was emerging from the tent, stripping off her gloves. She saw Lola and lowered the hood of her white suit.

'Doctor Fleetwood,' Lola said, smiling.

'DCI Harris.'

Dr Amy Fleetwood was a friendly woman with fine, freckled features and a dry manner.

'Anything you can tell me?'

'Her throat's a mess. I'd say she was garrotted with the wire ligature that's still *in situ*. Been dead at least twelve hours. Can't say for sure until the PM, but I'd say she was dead before she went into the water.'

An Identification Bureau officer emerged from the tent behind Dr Fleetwood. 'DCI Harris,' the man said, words muffled by his protective mask.

'I know it's a stretch,' Lola said, 'but is there any sign she was dumped in the river here or further upstream?'

'That water's very low,' the officer said, eyeing the river, which still flowed, though sluggishly. 'She couldn't have floated far.'

'All right if I take a swatch at the body just now?'

'Fine by me. We'll be done fairly soon. I don't reckon you want to leave her lying about too long in this weather.'

Lola masked up and peered in through the tent's opening. She stared down into the bruised, blueish face, and caught her breath — but not because of the state of the victim.

She re-emerged into the sunshine and looked about for Anna. Lola spotted her a few metres away and beckoned her to join her at the opening to the tent and asked her to take a peep.

Anna leaned in through the opening, taking her time, then withdrew from the tent, eyes wide.

'It's the missing juror, isn't it?' Lola said. 'It's Kathryn Main.'

CHAPTER THREE

9.20 a.m.

'You're kidding me,' PC Howie Tait of Glasgow Central subdivision said when Lola got him on the phone. 'Aww, fff . . . How certain are you?'

'Fairly. It was the tattoo on her wrist that clinched it for me. The one described in the wanted–missing call.'

'The dolphin and heart?'

'That's the one. I took a photo of it. We could show it to the family for an early confirmation of ID. Who are the family, by the way?'

'A sister. Stays out at Anniesland.'

'We'll go together,' Lola said. 'Give me the address and my DI and I will see you there.'

* * *

9.43 a.m.

'Kathryn Main was a compliance officer for a bank,' Anna said as Lola drove the two of them along Great Western Road towards Anniesland. 'Her whole job was about following the rules. Why would someone so intelligent — and so careful — be so stupid?'

'No doubt she and the others imagined they were doing the right thing. They believed Craig was guilty and they were worried he was going to get off. Then they egged each other on and created their own echo chamber.'

Kathryn Main had been a juror in Carter Craig's trial for murder and one of the four who were now accused of conspiring to pervert the course of justice. In fact, she was believed to have been the ringleader.

'You don't think Craig killed her, do you?' Anna asked now.

'Why would he?' Lola said, more blithely than she felt. 'Yes, she tried to stick the knife into him, but ultimately she's the reason he was released. He's got every reason to be grateful to her!'

Craig had been tried for murdering business rival Alex Sanderson in an alley behind one of his nightclubs in Glasgow. Sanderson's girlfriend, Xena Mitchell, had been with him, so Craig had offed her too. His whole defence rested on a claim that he was out of the country for the month of August — a defence the prosecution managed to poke holes in, ultimately resulting in a majority guilty verdict, though unknowingly with the help of the corrupt jurors.

Lola didn't doubt that Craig's fans would be revelling in his latest vindication, and she worried what it might lead to. Still, she couldn't believe Carter Craig was behind the murder of Kathryn Main. Yes, he was a vicious individual, but he wasn't stupid. Except—

She started suddenly.

'Everything all right?' Anna asked.

'I need to check,' Lola said. 'But wasn't Alex Sanderson brought down before he was shot? Someone jumped on him and garrotted him from behind, possibly with a wire, though the weapon wasn't left at the scene.' She fell silent for a moment, frowning. 'Complicates things, doesn't it?'

* * *

Kathryn Main's sister Tara was badly shaken. She perched, pale and trembling, on the edge of a white leather settee in her tenement flat overlooking the busy junction at Anniesland Cross.

'Oh God, poor Kathryn,' she kept repeating, her breath coming fast and shallow. She gazed down at the photograph of the dead woman's tattoo, displayed on Lola's phone, staring with a kind of desperation, as if this was her last opportunity to connect with her sister.

'Try to breathe slowly,' Lola told her. 'Take your time and just sit for a minute.'

Lola was in one armchair, PC Tait in the other. Anna stood quietly by the window. Tait was young, and looked sick to his stomach. Until this morning he'd been hunting for a wanted woman. Now that woman had turned up dead.

Tara Main became calmer, but her hands remained clenched into fists in her lap.

'I never imagined something like this, even though she said . . . Oh God.' She turned to Tait, whom she'd met on several occasions while he looked for her sister. 'You said "signs of violence"? So someone did this to her?'

Tait cleared his throat. 'We don't know yet.'

'Then how can you be sure she was . . . that someone . . .'

Lola stepped in. 'I'm afraid there's evidence she may have been strangled.'

'Oh. Oh *God*—' Tara clamped a hand over her mouth.

'When did you last speak to your sister, Tara?' Anna asked.

The woman squeezed her eyes shut, then opened them and looked guiltily at PC Tait. 'Friday morning,' she whispered. 'She called me. It was the first time I'd heard from her since . . . you know. I begged her to come forward, but she said she was too scared.'

'You'll need to tell us everything you know,' Lola said.

'She said she needed help. She said she wanted to get out the country. That's how frightened she was.'

Lola asked gently, 'Who was she frightened of, Tara?'

The woman gaped at Lola as if she was completely mad. *'Who do you think?'*

* * *

'Kathryn Main?' Detective Superintendent Elaine Walsh's eyes were very round.

'The very same. We should have the formal ID later today.'

Lola was in the superintendent's room at Helen Street while Anna and Kirsty were still tying things up at the crime scene in the park. PC Tait had remained with the dead woman's sister. A family liaison officer would be there within the next hour, but till then the nervous Howie would have to do.

'And there's no chance it was suicide?'

'Don't think so, boss. It's possible to garrotte yourself, I'm sure — but how did she end up in the river?'

Elaine sat back, seeming utterly perplexed. They'd known each other for years and respected one another, though Elaine had had to rein Lola in more than once.

'So the sister says she was afraid of Carter Craig?' Elaine went on. 'But that doesn't make sense.'

'I know. Even if she was conspiring against him, he'd have taken it as a win.'

'I can understand her being afraid of us,' Elaine said, 'and of the families of Craig's victims — they're just about baying for blood. Find out exactly what Kathryn said to her sister, verbatim. Do we know where she was hiding out?'

'At a friend's empty flat in Falkirk. She vanished from there three nights ago — on Friday evening — according to the friend. Kathryn contacted her sister on the morning of the day she disappeared, saying she needed help to get out of the country. Craig was coming for her, that's what she said.'

Elaine chewed her lip. 'This has the potential to become messy very quickly,' she said. 'Craig is a horror. You know my eldest worships him? We've had words about it but, according to Simon, Craig's a hero: "the man who dares to speak truth to power", which is complete nonsense. He's a vile misogynist.'

Lola had seen clips of Craig's videos online, usually thanks to Sandy. His style of communication was that of a streetwise jock: affable, matey but with an undercurrent of violence. He made pronouncements with angry conviction that appealed in particular to teenage boys, decrying feminism, Islam, 'Big Pharma' and 'the mainstream media' — which seemed to include every broadcast channel but his own — and talking up 'traditional values', though never defining them.

'You'll need to tread *very* carefully if you interview him,' Elaine said. 'He's surrounded by advisers and lawyers. Knowing him, he'll probably try and film the whole thing for a new reality TV series. Fancy being famous?'

'Not particularly. I take it the MIT will be leading any new investigation into the nightclub murders?'

'So I understand.' Elaine peered closely at Lola. 'Graeme Izatt led the original inquiry and he's currently scrabbling around for new evidence to persuade the Crown Office to go to retrial. I'd say his ego is bruised. Why, what are you thinking?'

'I might just pay Graeme a visit,' Lola said. She explained the possible garrotte link. 'You'll know what's happened if you hear an explosion.'

Elaine smiled. 'I'll be round with my Marigolds on to scrape you off the walls.'

Lola got up.

'Before you go,' Elaine said, her tone softer now. 'What did you decide to do about Joe?'

She took a deep breath. 'I'm not going to go,' she said. 'It's for the best, for both of us.'

'And for you and Sandy, I expect,' Elaine said pointedly.

'There is that.'

'Sandy's a good guy,' Elaine said.

Five months later, Lola still thanked the gods who'd been smiling on her when she'd decided to go to a 'moon swim' with Anna at a remote loch near Eaglesham. Sandy had been there, though they hadn't spoken until they were in the pub afterwards. She'd agreed to go for dinner and drinks with him a week later. Then she'd made him dinner at her place, and he'd stayed the night.

Lola smiled. 'You don't need to tell me, boss.'

CHAPTER FOUR

5.12 p.m.

Lola had a natural distrust of anyone who worked in communications, having clashed with her own comms colleagues on numerous occasions — including during her last major case. She often found them territorial, risk-averse and generally less than helpful. But this afternoon she'd met a new officer from Corporate Comms, Saskia Kerr, who'd impressed her. She was young — in her mid-twenties, at a guess.

She listened carefully to what Lola told her, then produced a decent draft press release in under ten minutes. It gave minimal information, saying where Kathryn had been found and that her death was being treated as suspicious. It asked for information about the death, and to hear from anyone who had seen or spoken to Kathryn in the days before she was found.

'Where were you before here?' Lola asked her.

'A probation charity in Paisley for four years,' Saskia said. 'I went there straight out of uni. Talk about being thrown in at the deep end.'

'Often the best way,' Lola said.

They'd headed out to Kelvingrove Park together and Saskia had filmed Lola reading the statement for social media, standing on Gibson Street where it bridged the sluggish river.

Watching it back, Lola was impressed by how coolly she'd managed to deliver the words when in truth she'd felt thoroughly jangled. Joe's brother Kev had called her minutes before with an update. Joe's operation wouldn't be going ahead because he'd tested positive for Covid. The symptoms were mild, but they couldn't operate. Hopefully he'd be able to have the operation in a week or two.

'I'll let you know how he gets on,' Kev had said.

Taken by surprise, she'd thanked him, and immediately regretted it. The very last thing she wanted was daily updates about Joe.

The call had left her churned up and feeling cross with herself.

Luckily Anna had lots to report when she came in for a debrief, and Lola was glad of the distraction.

Tara Main, supported by a cousin, had formally identified Kathryn's body at the mortuary.

'She's given a statement,' Anna said. 'So has Tara's friend, the one who owns the flat in Falkirk where Kathryn was staying. We know from phone records that Kathryn rang her sister at ten fifteen on Friday morning in a panic. I've emailed you a transcript of the conversation as Tara remembers it. According to Tara, Kathryn was terrified Craig was "after her" — that's a direct quote. Kathryn called herself "stupid and gullible". But when Tara pressed her, Kathryn ended the call.'

'I'll read it later. Any other developments?' Lola asked.

'We're about halfway through door-to-door enquiries in the apartment buildings overlooking that stretch of the Kelvin,' Anna went on. 'No leads so far, though we're going to return to a particular block on Otago Street. The backyard virtually overhangs the river. Aidan's got an idea you could tip a body over the parapet right into the river. He reckons it could travel the hundred metres or so from there to where it was found, even with the water as low as it is.'

Lola raised an eyebrow. DS Aidan Pierce was the member of her team she trusted least. He was arrogant and hostile, and he seemed determined to undermine anyone who stood in the way of his career — including her. That said, he did sometimes have good ideas.

'I left him thinking how we could test his theory without looking like idiots,' Anna said. 'He's talking about finding a shop dummy.'

'Maybe you could heave him over the side,' Lola suggested with a dark smile. 'See if he floats.'

Anna remained poker-faced. She'd been briefly taken in by Pierce when she first moved up from London, but the scales had quickly fallen from her eyes.

'What about CCTV?' Lola asked.

'We've put in the request and the operations centre have identified four cameras that might be useful. They're all digital, so if we do spot something we'll be able to zoom in.'

'Good.' Lola clicked into a screen on her laptop. 'I asked to be notified of any calls in response to the appeal,' she said. 'Five in total so far, two of which look interesting.' She scrolled. 'One's from a woman called Tina Kline, K-L-I-N-E. Lives in a flat opposite the block in Falkirk where Kathryn Main was staying. Believes she saw Kathryn waiting on a corner on Friday evening. She saw her get into a "fancy car". She thinks it was red, but it was about ten thirty and the light was fading, so it could have been another dark colour. Would you go see her? Then get on to the CCTV people in Falkirk and see what they've got.'

Anna took down Tina Kline's details. 'You said there were two interesting calls, boss.'

'The second was from an Emma Spencer. Says she was a childhood friend of Kathryn's and that, from what she knows of her, nothing about her recent behaviour makes sense. She's offered to come in, so I'll talk to her.'

'Very good, boss.'

'Right. I'm going to talk to Graeme Izatt at the MIT. I want his blessing to talk to the relatives of Craig's victims — maybe one of them wanted revenge on Kathryn Main.'

'What about the other three jurors in the WhatsApp group, boss?' Anna asked. 'Shall I speak to them?'

'Yes,' Lola said, 'once the door-to-door is out of the way. I want insights into what could have motivated Kathryn to act so out of character.'

Her phone was buzzing.

'Graeme, how nice.'

'Heard you're after me,' the familiar voice barked. 'I'm free for the next hour if you want to drop in.' He added ominously, 'And there's something I want to ask you.'

* * *

6.34 p.m.

'But why the hell would he go after Kathryn Main?' Izatt wanted to know. 'It was her flaming shenanigans that got him released, for God's sake! If anyone wanted her dead it would be Craig's victims' families — or me!'

'Could be a petty kind of revenge because she dared to try to stick the knife in,' Lola suggested. She didn't really believe it herself.

They were in Izatt's office, Lola sitting placidly in a chair while he paced behind his desk, scraping his fingernails along his whiskery jawline. Izatt was ageing badly, with his skin greying to match his hair and his eyes looking bloodshot — though at fifty-one he was only four years older than Lola. He had the appearance of a man permanently enraged that his talents weren't properly recognised. It didn't help that he always looked like he'd slept in his clothes. Lola privately thought he could help himself if he paid some attention to his personal grooming and started treating his colleagues as a resource rather than a threat.

'The fact is,' Lola said calmly, 'Kathryn told her sister she was scared Craig was coming after her. She died just three days after he got out of Barlinnie. Plus there's the method: the wire was still embedded in her neck. Isn't that how Sanderson was attacked before getting shot?'

'That's right. This must be him. I know it, just like I know he was behind the nightclub murders.'

'We've got the wire used on Sanderson stored in evidence, haven't we?' Lola asked. 'I'd like to see it, and the PM photos too — just to assess any similarities in the wounds.'

Izatt groaned and threw himself into his chair. It sagged under his bulk.

'I want to interview Craig as well,' Lola said. 'We could see him together if you prefer.'

'All right,' he groaned. 'I'll set something up with Craig's lawyers. And yes, I want to be there.'

'I'll talk to Sanderson's family too.'

Izatt groaned. 'I can give you a contact for the brother. But go easy. He's furious with us, to put it mildly. Talking about suing us. Upset him and you might find yourself accused of victimisation. What a fucking mess. That's Craig's whole reason for being, by the way. He's a virus. He infects things and people and destroys them from the inside.'

'Do you think there'll be a new trial?' Lola asked. She felt a twinge of sympathy. 'Or will they dismiss charges and request a brand-new investigation?'

He dropped his hands and looked at her. 'New trial's on a knife edge. The Crown Office aren't confident of a conviction. They weren't overly confident last time. If a section of the jury hadn't decided to go rogue, there was a good chance Craig would have got off — or the charges found "not proven". I'm supposed to be providing new evidence to help make the case. Well, guess what — there isn't any. At this rate we're heading for "all charges dismissed" and a new inquiry — except Craig's the only suspect, as far as I can see.' He began to eye Lola beadily. 'I need more people,' he said. 'Which brings me to that request of mine.'

'Go on,' she said, steeling herself.

'I need a DC or two, just for a few weeks.'

'A DC or *two*? Pushing your luck, aren't you?'

'I'm desperate, Lola. I'm on my own here.'

She thought about it, but not for long. 'No to my DCs. But how about a DS?'

'You mean . . .'

'Aidan Pierce.'

Izatt's eyes became slits as he thought about it. Pierce's reputation went before him, but Izatt had always defended him, claiming to see value in Pierce where others were unable to. Lola had never understood it.

'He'd kill to get into the MIT, Graeme. You never know, it might be the making of him.'

Izatt winced. 'What about the other one? Anna. She's good, isn't she?'

'Sorry, Graeme. Anna's a temp DI. It's Pierce or no one.' She made a face of mock concern. 'Not worried you won't be able to handle him, are you?'

His chin went up a touch. 'I can handle him.'

'Good,' Lola said. 'I'll talk to him. And if he's game, you can have him for as long as you like.'

Izatt had the look of a man who'd just signed up for a warranty he hadn't meant to take out.

Lola stood. 'Let me know about a meeting with Craig,' she said. 'And drop me a note with a contact for Sanderson's brother. Bye, Graeme.'

CHAPTER FIVE

6.42 p.m.

Madeleine Wicks had tried phoning her niece several times, but each call went to voicemail. She'd texted too, pleading with Aileen to call her — *just so I know you're all right!* Maddie could see Aileen had read the messages, but there was still no response. So, as soon as her meeting in Edinburgh was over, she drove to Aileen's place in Partickhill.

Aileen and her sister, Evie, had inherited their parents' ground-floor, main-door flat. It had its own tiny, fenced-in garden at the front, where shrubs and roses grew thickly, like a fairytale thicket protecting the occupants from the menacing world outside.

Maddie drove past looking for a parking space — and saw the gate to the little front door standing ajar. Then she spotted Aileen across the road, loading bags into the boot of her tiny car.

She found a space and reversed her Mercedes slickly in, then was out of the car and down the street in a flash.

'Aileen, there you are!' she cried.

Aileen spun round and froze, her eyes wide with alarm.

'I've been trying to contact you all afternoon. Oh, darling, don't look like that — I was *worried!*'

Aileen's shoulders sagged and she let the bag she was holding slide to her feet. Maddie was shocked by her appearance. She looked paler and thinner than usual. Her long fair hair hung lankly and her eyes were dark hollows.

'I didn't have time to answer while I was working,' Aileen began. 'And then I needed to come home and get my things together.'

Maddie embraced her niece, who received the gesture limply, then pulled back so she could look Aileen in the face. 'You're going to Skye, aren't you?'

Aileen hunched, eyes down. 'I need to see Evie. I need to know she's safe.'

Maddie eyed the tired old Renault and bit her lip. The idea of Aileen driving two hundred miles north along tricky roads filled her with dread.

'Must you go tonight?'

Aileen nodded and hugged herself as if she was cold, which was ridiculous given the balmy evening. 'I booked a room for the night in Portree, but . . . I could probably cancel it and go tomorrow instead. I'm so tired.'

'I think that would be wiser, darling. Oh, and *look* at you! When did you last eat?'

'I'm not hungry.'

'Now, listen,' Maddie said, speaking with authority, 'let's get your things locked safely away, then I'll take you to Byres Road for some dinner—'

'I don't want to.'

'But darling, you have to eat.' She sighed. 'A takeaway, then? Your choice.'

Aileen's pale green eyes searched the street, as if looking for an excuse. Finally, stiffly, she said, 'Okay, then.'

Twenty minutes later they were inside and an Indian was on its way. Maddie sat at Aileen's kitchen table while Aileen fussed about, refusing to rest.

'It's horrible, isn't it?' Maddie said. 'The idea of Craig being free and on the streets. But we need to face it. I suppose we should have seen it coming.'

'I did,' Aileen said, turning from the cupboard where she'd taken it upon herself to rearrange spices.

'Yes.' Maddie recognised the accusation in her niece's response and relented a little. 'You did.'

Some of the tension in Aileen's shoulders seemed to leave her at her aunt's admission. Maddie saw, not for the first time, a trace of her late sister in the wan face. Aileen, like her mother, was headstrong. Once her mind was made up, little could change it. She'd retreat into a shell of silent sullenness and remain there until her oppressor gave up and went away. Only occasionally would she flare up, with a flash of anger that could be savage.

'Did you hear about the juror?' Maddie asked her tentatively. 'The one who was missing? It was on the news. They found her this morning. Dead.'

Aileen nodded. She didn't make eye contact.

The news had featured a clip of a detective speaking from the bridge on Gibson Street. Her name had seemed familiar. Then she'd remembered: she was a friend of one of Maddie's clients, Sorcha, who'd talked about her warmly. Maddie had made a mental note of the name on the screen: DCI Lola Harris.

'They're not saying much about it,' Maddie went on, 'but it sounds to me like it could be murder.'

'She was strangled,' Aileen said, unblinking. 'With a wire, then dumped in the Kelvin.'

'That wasn't on the news!' Maddie's skin crawled.

'I've a friend who lives in the block overlooking the area. She heard it from a neighbour who'd spoken to the man who pulled the body out of the water.'

'Hence the dash to Skye?' Maddie was quiet for a moment. 'Darling, Evie is safe. Craig doesn't know where she is. He doesn't know anything about—'

'Doesn't he?' Aileen interrupted. 'The break-in at the flat, remember? That was only a few months afterwards.'

'We don't know he was behind that. We *don't*. There are break-ins all the time.'

The doorbell rang. Their food was here. Maddie laid it out and, while they ate, talked determinedly only about work, about the battle she was waging with the owners of a hotel her firm was designing, about their unreasonable demands and the extra miles, plural, she felt she'd already gone. Aileen was an interior designer too, though just starting out, and with only a couple of projects on her books. Maddie asked her how things were going. Aileen shared, but not much. They were on coffees when Maddie finally broached the subject properly.

She leaned in and peered closely at her niece, forcing her to meet her gaze. 'Have you given any thought to what we discussed before? You *know* what I'm talking about.'

Aileen recoiled.

'Well?' Maddie pressed.

'The answer's no. Besides, there'll be another trial before long. Hopefully he'll be convicted properly this time.'

'Will he?'

'What do you mean?' A flash of anger in her eyes. Of fear too.

'I saw my friend Charles,' Maddie said quietly. 'He's an advocate and he knows people in the Crown Office. Darling, he said there's a good chance there won't be a new trial.'

Aileen's lips parted. Her lower lip trembled.

'You know it was in the balance last time. Charles says the only reason they got a majority verdict of guilty was because of what those jurors did . . . I'm sorry, but I think we have to be realistic. They just don't have enough evidence.'

Maddie could see Aileen panicking behind that still exterior, taking deep breaths that narrowed her nostrils.

'But you do,' Maddie went on. 'You could give them what they need to put him away for good. We could talk to the police together. I might know someone who could advise us.'

'Who?'

'A friend of a friend. She's a police detective. Her name's Lola and she's meant to be very nice.'

'"Nice"?'

'Yes, darling. What's wrong with nice?'

Maybe nice wasn't the word. She'd seemed compassionate. Yes, that was it. Empathetic too.

'Maybe she could tell us if it would be enough. Who knows, it might not be, but at least we'd have *tried*.'

'And what if it is enough?' Aileen asked.

'Then we talk to Evie. It would have to be her decision.'

Aileen eyed her for several seconds. 'But would it? Wouldn't they try to force her?'

Maddie said, 'Darling, it's a chance to put Carter Craig in prison for a long, *long* time. Not just for Evie, but for all those other people whose lives he's destroyed. It might be the only chance left.'

CHAPTER SIX

Tuesday 13 August

9.15 a.m.

DS Aidan Pierce listened in silence, watching Lola with suspicious eyes. But he was interested, she could tell. Behind the insolent mask there was excitement.

'It's a great opportunity and might be your way into the MIT,' she breezed.

They were in one of the small meeting rooms. It was air-conditioned and almost as icy as their working relationship.

'Maybe I'll speak to DCI Izatt first, so I understand the scope of the role,' he said.

'That's fine, but I can tell you now, the "scope" is Carter Craig.'

She caught a twitch of an eyelid.

'Is that a problem?'

'No.' He sat up, squaring his shoulders inside his beautifully tailored jacket. 'Why would it be?'

Lola shrugged and fixed a smile. 'Talk to DCI Izatt today. You can tell me what you've decided this afternoon. No later than that, please.'

Pierce sauntered back to his desk. Lola's phone buzzed. Her visitor was in reception.

* * *

'I didn't know if you'd want to see me,' the woman said as she went breathlessly ahead of Lola into the interview room. 'It's not as if I can tell you what happened to Kathryn.' She dragged out a chair. 'Oh, it's so lovely and cool in here. Honestly, I can't tolerate this heat. We're just not made for it, are we?'

'Have a seat, Ms Spencer.'

'Thank you.'

The woman sat and swept her long hair back from her face, pulling it into a scrunchie. Emma Spencer was a pleasant-looking woman in her late thirties, with an open face and light-blue eyes. 'It's so nice to sit down too. I haven't stopped. Oh, and thanks for this.' She reached for the cup of water Lola had brought in for her from the cooler.

Emma was a solicitor, specialising in family law but currently on maternity leave. Her mum had agreed to take the baby for the morning. She seemed keyed up, so Lola let her gabble on for a minute to expend some energy.

When she spotted an opportunity, Lola said gently, 'When you called you said you'd been friendly with Kathryn some years ago.'

'Yes, that's right.' She nodded and took a deep breath. 'We grew up on the same street, you see. Well, till Kathryn's mum moved away when Kathryn was fourteen or fifteen. She was a year or two older than me. We didn't keep in touch, but I always liked her.' Her face crumpled briefly and she dived into her bag for a tissue. 'Poor Kathryn.'

'When did you see her last?'

'In person?' Emma asked when she'd got herself together again. 'Oh, ages ago. Maybe ten years ago, and only by accident. She was at Braehead, she and her sister Tara. I was there

29

with my husband. We said hello. I said how well she looked. She told me she was working at the bank. Not in a branch — in the head office. Something to do with compliance, though not very senior. We said all the usual things — how we should meet up. Then she added me on Facebook. I quite like that. You're sort of in touch, but there's no obligation. Anyway she sent me such a nice message when Noah was born.' She stopped, eyes on the table, then took out a tissue and blew her nose. 'I'm sorry . . .'

'It's okay,' Lola said. Then, after a pause, 'Were you surprised when you heard what had happened at the trial?'

'Oh God, yes, *completely*! I was *gobsmacked*. I mean, the first I heard about it was when she was missing, that she was wanted by the police! I couldn't believe what I was hearing.'

'Why?'

Emma Spencer frowned hard at the table, chewing her lip as she seemed to think how to phrase her answer. She looked back at Lola. 'Kathryn was a mouse,' she said. 'She was a lovely person, but crushingly shy. Or she was when I knew her. She tried not to be noticed, you know? She'd even sit sort of hunched up to make herself small. She went along with things and didn't make a fuss, even when you knew she wasn't really enjoying it. If you'd told me she was on a jury then I'd say she'd have kept quiet. Oh, she'd take it seriously — of course she would — and she'd put her point across. But tamper with due process? Break the rules? She worked in compliance, for goodness' sake. I mean, judges are very clear about standards of behaviour when juries are being sworn in. What she did — it's unthinkable.'

'Kathryn followed the rules?'

'The Kathryn I knew. But they said in the media she was the ringleader. *She* started the messaging after hours. *She* set up the WhatsApp group.'

'All the evidence points to that, yes,' Lola said.

'If it really is true, then I think she must have had a very good reason.'

'The other three jurors in the group say Kathryn believed she had evidence of Carter Craig's guilt.'

'Perhaps she did.' Emma seemed about to add something, then drew back.

'What is it?' Lola asked gently.

The woman watched her for a few seconds. 'I know it sounds crazy,' she said, 'but what if someone was manipulating her, pushing her from behind? Using her to feed the jury evidence that could convict Craig? Only it backfired, didn't it? It backfired horribly. Now Craig's free and Kathryn's dead.'

CHAPTER SEVEN

11.36 a.m.

Blair Sanderson had ignored all Kirstie's calls, then blocked her number, so Lola had decided they should turn up at the café he ran with his girlfriend in Shawlands.

From what she'd gathered, Blair was the gentler of the two Sanderson brothers. His older brother, the late Alex, had been a nasty piece of work, running several illegal enterprises, including a protection racket in Glasgow's East End, and employing vulnerable young people to transport drugs around the city. He'd begun selling drugs to members of private clubs in the city centre, including at Carter Craig's Orchid House nightclub. For that incursion Craig had sent round his thugs to give Alex a battering, leaving him with a broken arm, a broken shoulder bone and missing teeth. Alex had retaliated by obsessively targeting Craig, drawing on mutual contacts and following every lead until he unearthed a video showing Craig verbally abusing and physically attacking a woman. According to the prosecution at Craig's trial, Alex Sanderson had used the video to try to extort money from him, saying he was merely recouping lost revenue after Craig ran him off his patch. And it was this that sealed Alex's fate. Craig had supposedly offered Alex a deal, inviting him to the Orchid House and telling him to come in by a side door — but strangling and shooting him in the alley outside. Him and his girlfriend Xena.

Alex's brother Blair had form. He'd spent time in prison for violent assault in his early twenties, but since getting out had gone straight. He owned two cafés, one in Dennistoun and this one in Shawlands. The Shawlands café was called Radio Days and it was styled like an American diner. Lola and Kirstie were greeted by the smell of bacon and maple syrup. An unhappy-looking woman in her thirties with badly dyed blonde hair came out from behind the counter to seat them. There were other customers seated at tables. Lola told her quietly they were police and wanted to speak to the owner. An older woman with curly grey hair and wearing a light-green blouse eyed them beadily from a nearby table.

'He's busy in the kitchen,' the blonde woman said. 'It's nearly lunchtime.'

'I know that,' Lola said. 'But this is important.'

The woman looked cross but led them behind the counter and through an orange beaded curtain. Lola glanced behind her and saw the woman in the green top still eyeballing them.

Blair Sanderson had his back turned. He appeared to be chopping salad. It was hot and noisy. Bacon sizzled and an extractor fan whined. Sanderson jumped when his girlfriend spoke. He wheeled round, knife in hand, a big man with a red, freckled face. He was in his late thirties but already balding.

'What's this, Gabs?'

'Police,' Gabs said. 'Something "important".'

'Oh yeah?' Sanderson put down the knife. 'What do you want?'

Lola introduced herself and Kirstie and held out her warrant card. 'We'd like a word, Mr Sanderson. All right if I call you Blair?'

He reached for a cord and turned off the noisy fan.

'Depends.'

'It's about the death of Kathryn Main, who was a juror in Carter Craig's trial.'

'You *what*?' He began to laugh but then his top lip curled in an ugly sneer. 'You think I had something to do with that that stupid cow's death?'

Lola sensed the girlfriend shifting uncomfortably behind her.

'We're questioning a number of people,' Kirstie said stiffly. 'Purely routine. I did try to call you.'

Sanderson studied her, his nostrils flaring.

'You didn't answer my colleague's messages, so we're paying you a visit,' Lola said.

'Go see to the customers, Gabs,' Sanderson said. 'Here, take these.' He handed her two containers, one with sliced onion, the other with jalapeños.

The young woman took the containers huffily and pushed off, leaving the three of them in the little kitchen.

'So, you think I did for her?' Sanderson said, leaning against the work counter, arms folded and smirking now. 'Why?'

'How did you feel about what she did during the trial?' Lola asked him.

He eyed her cautiously. 'I wasn't impressed. Obviously.'

'You were quoted in the *Chronicle* attributing Carter Craig's release directly to her actions.'

'I stand by what I said.' He shrugged. 'There's plenty of folk agree with me. Judge said she'd face jail time for what she done — her and the other three wallopers. And so they should. Craig's free because of them. Three years we waited for a trial. *Three years.* And for what — Craig set free? I don't call that justice.'

'Did Kathryn Main get what was coming to her?' Lola asked softly.

He blinked and she saw his Adam's apple bob. 'Never said that, did I?'

'Where were you between five p.m. on Sunday evening and seven a.m. the next morning, Blair?'

He stared at her in dismay, then shook his head and gave a dark laugh. 'You hear this, Gabs?' he asked his girlfriend, who'd come quietly back into the kitchen. 'They think I killed that juror.'

'That's bullshit,' the young woman said. 'He never went near her. Blair wouldn't harm anyone.'

'It would help if we knew where you were, sir,' Kirstie said coolly. 'For purposes of elimination.'

Sanderson folded his arms defensively but then seemed to relent. 'Sunday, we were at your mam's, weren't we, Gabs? Then we stopped at the shops on the way home.'

'What time would that have been?' Kirstie asked.

'Oh . . . sixish.'

'Which shops?'

'The big Asda in Govan. Her mam stays in Ibrox. We stay in Paisley, so Asda's on the way.'

Lola heard the beads shift behind her. The older woman with the curly mop and green blouse had come into the kitchen.

'Why don't you lot leave him alone?' the woman said nastily to Lola. She had a gruff smoker's voice.

'And you are?' Lola asked.

'Leave it, Mam,' Sanderson said. 'They're just asking questions.'

'What are you saying to him?' the woman asked. 'Don't you think we've all been through enough?'

'Are you Nina Sanderson?' Lola asked. She introduced herself. 'We're investigating the death of Kathryn Main, the juror—'

'I know who she is,' the woman growled. 'Stupid little bitch saw that whole trial collapse. I'm glad she's dead.'

'Mam!'

'Shut it, Blair!' She turned her snarling face back to Lola. 'You accusing him of offing her, is that it? He's a good boy. Wouldn't hurt a fly.'

'Mrs San—'

'As for me though? I *would*. I'd have finished her off myself for what she done. So why don't you come questioning me?'

'All right,' Lola said, ready to play the woman's game. She told her the times they were interested in.

'I was in the hospital waiting for my old neighbour to die,' she answered with a note of glee. 'Sat there the whole night, her and her sister, bar the odd trip to the loo. Poor cow didn't pass till just gone six. After that we went home in a taxi.'

'Very well,' Lola said.

'That it? Don't you want the ward number? Not going to go harass them nurses to confirm it?'

'I think we're satisfied for now, thank you very much, Mrs Sanderson.'

'Mam, just go and finish your lunch,' Blair said to her.

The woman eyed him, then scowled once more at Lola and pushed through the beaded curtain.

'Sorry about that,' Blair mumbled. 'Go see if she's all right, Gabs.'

'Just a moment,' Kirstie said to the young woman, frowning. 'Is your name Gabrielle?'

'Yeah, why?' Gabs said shiftily.

'Are you Xena Mitchell's sister?'

'What if I am?'

Lola stared at Kirstie in amazement at her making the connection. 'Two brothers, two sisters?' she said to Sanderson. 'Is that how it was?'

Blair nodded. 'Alex'd been seeing Xena for a few months when they had a party at theirs. I went, Gabs was there with her sis and the rest's history. Your colleagues knew that,' he added defensively. 'It's never been a secret.'

'I see.'

They got the rest of the pair's alibi, but it was thin: from Asda they'd returned to the flat they shared in Paisley. Blair had gone to bed for an hour. Then they'd made dinner — pizzas and loaded potato skins — and watched films till eleven, or thereabouts. Then they'd gone to bed. Blair had got up at five thirty to get to the wholesaler's.

'It wasn't him,' she told Kirstie when they were back in the car. 'The man's angry, but he believes in justice. He waited three years to see Craig in court.'

'I tend to agree, boss. And the girlfriend?'

'She's altogether the more brutal of the pair, I'd say. I wouldn't want to go up against her or Blair's mum in a fight.' Finger on the ignition, she studied Kirstie with interest. 'How did you make the connection, by the way? Did she and her sister look alike?'

'It's her name — Gabrielle is the best friend of Xena in *Xena: Warrior Princess*.'

Lola stared. 'Her mum's favourite TV show, do you reckon?'

'Maybe. Then when Blair mentioned Ibrox I remembered that's where Xena's mum lived, so . . .'

'You're a born detective,' Lola said, and Kirstie smiled one of her secretive smiles.

CHAPTER EIGHT

1.31 p.m.

Carter Craig's private gym was in the basement of a Victorian tenement building on the south side of Kelvingrove Park, less than half a mile from where Kathryn Main's body had been found. Lola and DCI Graeme Izatt were met at the door by a tall and slender, cool-eyed woman with pinned-up dark hair, dressed from head to toe in black.

'This way, please,' she said in a vaguely foreign accent.

Izatt went first.

Lola heard voices from somewhere in the basement, the thump of heavy bass playing and the clank of gym equipment. The air was thick with sweat and deodorant. A man laughed raucously and another joined in. They were spirited away from the noise, down a dark corridor.

'In here, please,' the woman said, holding open a door into a large room. 'Mr Craig will join you shortly.' She retreated.

The room was bright but with no natural light. A large board table stood in the middle of the room and two black settees faced each other in a corner. Lola helped herself to water from a cooler.

'Want some?' she asked Izatt.

'No.'

He was nervous. His breathing was quick and shallow and he looked unhappy. She suspected it was because this was Craig's territory. He caught her eye and gestured discreetly to a camera in a corner of the ceiling. He'd warned her they'd be monitored, recorded too, probably, and to avoid speaking when they thought they were alone.

She pulled a chair out from the table and sat, then checked her phone. No signal. She took out her pad and pen, and waited.

Izatt was pacing now.

'Sit down, will you?' she said. If they were being watched then it was important not to show any nerves.

Izatt sat, just as the door opened and a small sweaty-faced man in a pin-striped suit hurried in with a briefcase.

'Good afternoon!' the man said, his pink cherubic lips curving into a smile. His white-blond curls emphasised his oddly angelic appearance.

He mopped his forehead and cheeks with a hanky then gave Lola a hot, damp little hand. 'Stephen Kitchener,' he said primly and bowed. 'A member of Mr Craig's legal team.'

She shook it. 'DCI Harris,' she said.

'Very good. And you must be Mr Izatt,' Kitchener said, turning. 'We haven't met previously.'

Izatt rose. 'Craig "refreshed" his team, has he?'

Kitchener beamed with pleasure. 'I am new to the effort, yes.'

He laid his briefcase on the table, unclipped it and began taking out papers.

'Mr Craig asked me to apologise for the slight delay. He has just been dealing with some urgent business. He is currently showering.'

Lola glanced at Izatt. His hands were balled into fists.

Kitchener beamed and continued to arrange his papers. One in particular appeared to catch his attention and he peered closely at it, murmuring to himself before nodding with satisfaction and laying the paper down.

Men's laughter reached them from the corridor, then the door flew open and Carter Craig filled the doorway.

'Good afternoon, friends,' he called in his rich baritone, throwing the door shut behind him. 'Sorry to make you wait.'

He was still flushed from his workout and shower. His broad shoulders strained against his grey tracksuit. He tossed a sports bag onto one of the settees, then, towering over the table, reached a big hand out to Lola. She ignored it.

'Afternoon, Mr Craig.'

He grinned, revealing perfectly even white teeth. Lola looked at him and thought she could understand why so many women found him irresistibly attractive. His features were fine, with high, prominent cheekbones, a straight brow and a square, lightly whiskered chin. His large, almond-shaped eyes were a startling teal blue and his gaze seemed to have a hypnotic quality. Only thirty-three, he was completely bald, his scalp tanned and shining. There was something repulsively engineered and polished about him.

'What can I do for you?' he asked, giving Lola another polished smile as he lowered himself onto the edge of the settee opposite her. He leaned forward like a keen counsellor.

'Kathryn Main was found murdered yesterday,' Izatt said simply. 'My colleague here is investigating.'

Craig frowned and looked about the room, then bit his lip and shook his head.

'Sorry,' he said. 'Can't place her.'

'Kathryn Main was a juror in your trial, Mr Craig,' Lola said evenly. 'It's thought she was the ringleader of the group that communicated online. She went missing shortly after her behaviour was discovered. Yesterday she turned up dead in the River Kelvin.'

'Dear oh dear.' He looked and sounded genuinely sorry, but then the corners of his mouth tweaked upwards into the smallest of smirks.

'May I ask,' the lawyer came in, 'if your visit is a mere courtesy to share this unfortunate news with my client, or whether you have another reason?'

Ignoring him, Lola said, 'Kathryn Main shared less-than-flattering information about you with her fellow jurors, Mr Craig. By their own admission, it influenced them. What did you make of her actions?'

A small shrug. 'To be honest, I was . . . *amused* when it transpired I was being released because of what she'd done. She did her level best to see me put away.' He frowned with mock concern. 'Kill herself, did she?'

'She was murdered, Mr Craig.'

The lawyer and his client exchanged glances as if in surprise, but Lola saw through the act.

'She was strangled with a thin wire,' she went on. 'Perhaps you recognise the method.'

'The method . . . ?' Craig said, furrowing his brow. 'Oh, yes! They said that was how I immobilised Alex Sanderson before I shot him.' He gave her a pitying smile. 'So you think you've identified a link. Bit obvious, don't you think?'

Lola asked, 'Did you kill Kathryn Main, Mr Craig?'

She heard the lawyer's tiny intake of breath but kept her eyes on Craig.

Craig surveyed her blandly, his beautiful eyes unblinking. She had the sudden unnerving impression that this wasn't a human being before her, but an automaton, perhaps generated by AI, with no conscience at all.

'Doesn't matter what I say, does it?' Craig said softly and a little sadly. 'You'll believe it or you won't. Doesn't seem to matter that there's never a scrap of evidence.' He turned his attention on Izatt. 'Isn't that right, Graeme?'

Izatt scowled at Craig from under his messy grey eyebrows but said nothing.

Lola said, 'Where were you, Mr Craig, between five p.m. on Friday evening and seven a.m. on Monday morning?'

Craig's eyes narrowed and he bit his lip as he pretended to think about it. 'That's quite a window,' he said. 'I'm a busy boy these days. Can't rightly say off the top of my head.'

'Can't you?' Izatt snapped, earning himself a sharp glance from Lola.

'I'd need to give it some thought, that's all I'm saying, Graeme.' Craig smiled, but there was no warmth at all now.

'Maybe a trip to the nick would help jog your memory,' Izatt said.

'Oh, I doubt that,' Craig said, more coolly still. He looked to his lawyer. 'I'm sure we can put together some information for our friends here, Stephen, don't you think?'

'I'm sure of it,' Kitchener said, with one of his cherubic smiles.

'Today, please,' Lola said and rose. 'DCI Izatt?'

Izatt glowered but got up too.

'Thank you for your time, gentlemen,' she said.

* * *

2.13 p.m.

Izatt contained his fury till they were outside and down the street.

'He's going to run rings around us again, isn't he?'

He chuntered on. Lola took the opportunity to check her phone and found a text message from her friend Sorcha, from the Covid Divorce Club, which Lola had joined as a kind of support group. *Strange request,* Sorcha had written. *My interior designer saw you on the news and wants some advice. V. special circumstances!!! Okay if I give her your number?*

It *was* a strange request. Lola had no idea who Sorcha's designer was but, judging by her spectacular Dowanhill townhouse, the woman must be very talented.

Happy to talk to her, she wrote. *But give me her number and I'll call her later. What's her name?*

Thanks so much, Sorcha replied. *Her name's Maddie Wicks and she's lovely but in need of a quiet chat. I don't know any details, I'm afraid. Xx*

CHAPTER NINE

3.34 p.m.

Madeleine Wicks's design studio was in a converted mews building in Park Circus, the peninsula of grand, blond-sandstone townhouses and apartments that jutted into the green swathe of Kelvingrove Park like the prow of a ship heading west.

'Oh, I was *so* happy to hear from you,' she said, grasping Lola's proffered hand in both of hers. She had big rings on her fingers, covered with gemstones, and wooden bracelets clacked on her wrists.

On the phone Madeleine Wicks had sounded intense and excitable, but in person she seemed sensible enough. She was certainly appealing, her appearance, gestures and speech exuding her personality. She was fifty-ish, of medium height and generously proportioned. Her hair was a mass of dark curls, attractively highlighted with natural grey and clamped in place here and there with wooden clasps.

'Follow me into the consulting room.' She turned in a swirl of velvet and silk and led Lola along a corridor, past a room where three young women worked at computers surrounded by samples of fabric and wallpaper. Then they were going down a set of stairs into an office at the back of the building, overlooking a cobbled lane. There was a raised work table in the middle of the room with six stools around it. Huge books of fabric and wallpaper samples were stacked high at one end.

Maddie talked about Sorcha and what great friends they'd become, and how Sorcha had blossomed since leaving that 'dreadful' man.

'Of course, *we* all knew what he was like even if she didn't. Well, maybe she did. She's talked warmly of you in the past. When I saw you on TV yesterday I recognised your name and called Sorcha right away. She said I could trust you.' She paused and peered at Lola with eyes that were a beautiful cornflower blue, and fringed with long dark lashes. 'I hope I can.'

Lola gave a neutral smile. She was, however, prepared to be open-minded. She was in a good mood, having just read an email from Aidan Pierce accepting the secondment to the MIT. *I'll let DCI Izatt know*, she'd replied, murmuring a cheerful 'good riddance' as she saw the email fly from her outbox.

'Take a seat, won't you?' Maddie said, gesturing to one of the high chairs around the work table. 'Now, do you want a coffee? One of the girls will make it. It's from a proper machine.'

'I'm quite all right. And . . . I don't have a lot of time, Ms Wicks.'

'No, of course.' She took a seat opposite Lola. 'And please, it's Maddie. Let me tell you all about it.'

She launched into a slightly confusing story about her sister's death and how Maddie had promised her she would keep an eye on her two daughters.

'And as I said on the phone,' Maddie continued, 'it's the younger of the two, Evie, who was attacked by Craig three years ago.'

'And she chose not to report it?' Lola asked gently.

'It was her decision, not that I agreed with it. This was when Evie was seventeen. She was rather wild, I'm afraid. She'd go to clubs and take drugs sometimes. She'd met Craig at one of these clubs a few months earlier and become infatuated. God only knows why! The man's a brute. She saw him a couple of times, but you know his reputation. A different girl every night. But then one evening, he called her out of the blue. It was very late but he sent one of his people to pick her up. He took her somewhere they could be together. They had sex. It was consenting, so Evie says, but then afterwards his whole demeanour changed and he attacked her. Tried to choke her, called her all sorts of names and threw her against the wall, then shoved her to the floor and kicked her. And then he raped her. Evie is adamant she didn't consent that time.'

'I'm very sorry,' Lola said.

'She blamed herself, I'm afraid. Awful, isn't it? Wouldn't even see a counsellor, though her sister Aileen and I tried our very best to persuade her. And then . . .' She paused, took a deep breath and looked Lola hard the eye. 'And then, a few weeks later, Evie found out she was pregnant. She kept the baby. He's two now.'

Lola had half expected the revelation, but it still chilled her. 'How likely is it that he's Craig's child?' she asked.

'Evie is certain. Remember she was only seventeen. She'd slept with one other man, but that had been months earlier.'

'Why have you come to me, Maddie?' Lola asked, sensing they'd reached the crux.

'Because the night it happened was the same night those people were killed in the nightclub. Saturday, the twenty-first of August 2021. He attacked Evie, high on whatever he'd taken, then he went to that nightclub and committed murder.'

Lola stared. She wasn't speechless very often, but she was now.

'Craig's alibi was in question throughout his trial,' she said after a minute. 'You're telling me you knew he was in Glasgow that night?'

'That's exactly what I'm saying.' The woman lifted her chin to show she wasn't ashamed of what she'd done. 'To have made Evie come forward would have been horribly cruel. It would have put her through enormous trauma, not to mention actual risk of harm. I mean, Craig is a very violent individual. We couldn't risk anything happening to Evie, nor to the child. I'm sure you understand that.'

And Lola did. But it didn't make it any more palatable.

'Evie had some mild bleeding shortly after she found out she was pregnant, around six and a half weeks.' Maddie spoke steadily, holding Lola's gaze with her wide blue eyes. 'She had an early ultrasound. Combined with what Evie could tell them about her cycle, the doctors confirmed the date of conception as within a five-day period, with the twenty-first bang in the middle. The hospital has records. A DNA test would prove Hamish is Craig's child.' She leaned forward. 'He was there in Glasgow the night of the murders — *and Hamish is the proof.*'

Lola let it sink in, then asked, 'Does Craig know about the child?'

'We don't believe so. We can't imagine how he would have found out. We were . . . very careful. There was a scare early on: Evie moved in with Aileen for a time and somebody broke into the flat one day when both girls were out, only nothing was taken. As a result we decided to move her away from Glasgow.'

'And where is Evie now?'

Maddie swallowed and seemed to waver for a moment. 'This must be in absolute confidence,' she said firmly.

'Of course.'

'On the Isle of Skye. She lives there with her father's uncle and his second wife, on a croft on a remote peninsula in the far west of the island.'

Lola's brain was racing and she took a few moments to collect her thoughts.

'Craig claimed he was in Jersey for the month of August. How would we prove Evie didn't go to Jersey herself?'

Maddie said, 'Evie was at work that day, here in Glasgow. The restaurant manager and her colleagues would confirm as much. She'd worked there every day that week. She was about to start a college course and she had a part-time job in a restaurant on Bath Street. She worked long shifts there Wednesday to Friday, and during the afternoon and until about eight p.m. on Saturdays. One of Craig's people collected her from the restaurant after her shift. And the next morning she turned up, battered and bruised at Aileen's, asking for help. Aileen took her to A & E at the Queen Elizabeth hospital. They made up a story that she'd fallen down some stairs, drunk. I don't know if the medics believed her. But they X-rayed her and patched her up. She needed two stitches on her chin.' Maddie pointed to the left side of her own jaw. 'Just here. The hospital will have the records of that too. The next morning, the Monday, she registered for college. She was desperate to do the course — it was in textile design.' She smiled. 'We're all designers in our family. Evie was at the college for the next two days, though she said she felt horribly self-conscious, what with her injuries.'

Lola forced herself to steady her breathing as she reviewed the facts in her mind.

'You've explained why you haven't come forward before,' she said. 'What's changed?'

'Aileen and I thought — hoped — Craig would be convicted and go to jail for a long time,' Maddie said. 'But now he's free, isn't he? I have an advocate friend who's convinced there won't be a new trial. Even if there is, there's nothing to say Craig won't get off again. But our evidence *could* convict him, couldn't it?'

'I would need to take advice on that. I take it Evie doesn't know you're here?'

'No. At this stage I'm just exploring options. Evie is one of life's innocents. She's naive. And if she encounters something that frightens her, then she simply turns away from it. Aileen doesn't know either. She's gone to Skye to see her sister today, to reassure herself she and Hamish are safe. We've talked repeatedly about whether to come forward, and last night I asked her to think it through again. Aileen's stubborn

— she can be feisty too — but I think she'll give it some consideration. However . . . if you tell me the evidence doesn't hold weight, then we'll forget it, but with clear consciences because we'll have *tried*.'

'And what if I tell you it does hold weight?'

A pause. 'Then I'll talk to Aileen again. I'll persuade her we should talk to Evie.'

'Let me talk to my boss,' Lola said. 'I expect she'll want to seek a view from the Crown Office. If they think the evidence is valid, we will need Evie's permission to see any records.'

The woman nodded. 'Very well.'

'Then, if we believe there's a case to be made, we'd need to seek a statement from Evie herself — and talk seriously about the possible consequences.'

'You mean because we've withheld evidence? That is what we've done, after all.'

'Not that,' Lola said. 'Evie is a victim too. No, I was talking about a new trial. Evie would be a key witness — she would need to testify that she saw Craig that night. And the child's DNA would be the key evidence. I think we would need to think very carefully about how to move forward.'

'Meaning what?' Maddie asked.

'Well, we'd take every step we could,' Lola said, 'but it would mean the boy was a threat to his father. Hamish could be in danger.'

CHAPTER TEN

3.52 p.m.

The heat that was cooking Scotland's Central Belt was less fierce on Skye. In Glasgow, the grass was yellow and the ground dry and cracked, while the air hung soupily in the streets. Here, it was pleasantly warm. The landscape was a vibrant green woven with wildflowers tipping in a stiff breeze. Aileen drove with her windows down, enjoying the fresh clean air.

She'd been coming to Skye since she was a child but its vastness still amazed her. It had taken an hour to drive from the bridge to the town of Portree. She'd stopped there for a supermarket salad, and now she was on the last leg: the forty-five-minute drive further west towards the Duirinish peninsula and one of the remotest communities on the island.

She'd called Evie before she left Glasgow to say she was going to visit. The excitement in her sister's voice confirmed what Aileen had suspected: that Craig's release had either passed her by or at least made no perceptible impression. That was good in one sense, but it still grated. Once again Aileen felt as if she shouldered the burden for the two of them.

'How long can you stay?' Evie had wanted to know.

'A day or two. I'll see.'

'It'll be so lovely!' She'd made a giddy squealing noise. 'I'll tell Jessie and we'll make the room up.'

The road beyond Dunvegan was narrow and winding with blind bends, and busy with tourists, some of whom seemed less than confident about using passing places. More than once she had to reverse to let someone edge nervously by.

As she drew close to Glendale she rehearsed once more how to break the news that Craig might not face a new trial. She still hadn't decided whether to tell her that a juror from his trial had been found dead, murdered using a method Craig had been accused of using in the past.

Maddie wanted her to talk to Evie about providing evidence against Craig, but Aileen's instinct remained firmly against that. While it would be reassuring to know Evie understood the threat, she couldn't put her and Hamish — especially Hamish — at risk.

Despite Aileen's relief at being on Skye, by the time she reached Glendale her thoughts were in turmoil and her stomach clenched tight. The final stretch of road wound north for seven miles close to cliff edges towards the isolated community of Skaravaig on its exposed plateau overlooking the Atlantic. Great-Uncle Donny's cottage — a long, one-and-a-half-storey whitewashed cottage with a red tin roof — was reached before the village. After seven long hours of driving, she'd arrived.

And there was Evie, running down the rutted driveway to meet her as she refastened the gate, yelling with excitement as she flew to embrace her big sister.

Aileen looked over Evie's shoulder up the long track and saw white-haired, ruddy-faced Uncle Donny standing by the doorway, his second wife Jessie behind him just inside the croft. Jessie was holding blond Hamish on her hip and saying something to him while her long grey hair lifted in the wind. Hamish raised a hand and waved. Aileen waved back.

Evie seemed happy. Hamish was safe. Nothing bad could reach them here.

* * *

Jessie had baked scones. They ate them with whipped cream and raspberry jam on the patio at the front of the croft, overlooking the little garden and the rotary washing line that turned as clothes and sheets lifted in the breeze.

Evie sat beside Aileen, with Hamish on her knee. Hamish was fascinated by his aunt, reaching for her hair with jammy fingers and repeating, 'Want play, Ay-ay!' *Ay-ay* being the closest he could get to Aileen's name. Aileen took him on her knee at one point, bouncing him as he giggled. She pressed her face into his blond hair and spent minutes gazing into his beautiful, tilting blue eyes. His father's eyes, of course . . .

The croft was on the west side of the peninsula, looking out over the Atlantic. The views were breathtaking, across acres of green hills and an eternity of blue sea beyond. Half a mile to the north were the fifteen or so houses of Skaravaig, and beyond the village, higher up the sloping ground and closer to the cliff edge, was the St Columba Centre, a sort of well-being retreat with its own accommodation in a modern wood-and-glass building. The peninsula was an idyll. It seemed impossible that danger could reach Evie and Hamish here. Still, Evie's determined innocence, her brazen naivety, continued to bother Aileen.

Jessie talked at length, telling stories about some of the neighbours, and saying more than once how very few tourists they saw up here. Glendale seemed busy by comparison, she said — Portree a metropolis! 'The peninsula is quite the safe haven,' she said. She reminded Aileen about Theresa Macleod, who managed the community shop and café. For years she'd run a domestic violence charity in Inverness, and still offered sanctuary in her home on the peninsula to women fleeing their abusive partners. Theresa sometimes brought the women to the croft for tea and cake. Aileen had no doubt Jessie was telling the stories deliberately, and for her benefit. While Evie appeared uninterested in her sister's motives for visiting, Jessie understood entirely.

Evie used the name Daisy here on Skye. It was her middle name, and they'd thought it wise to use an alias, just in case Craig ever thought of tracking down the Evie Mackinnon he'd briefly known in Glasgow. Donny and Jessie used the name easily, and Evie responded to it. It was as if she was another person. Aileen didn't think she'd ever get fully used to it.

The scones finished, Evie took Hamish down onto the lawn, near the ever-turning washing line.

'Daisy's very happy here,' Uncle Donny murmured.

'So it seems,' Aileen remarked.

She began to say more, but then couldn't find the words.

'What's wrong?' Jessie asked, studying Aileen's face.

She took a deep breath. 'I just don't know what she's thinking,' she said. 'I used to be able to read her, but now I can't. I can't tell whether she's worried about Craig and burying it, or whether she just . . . hasn't understood.'

'She understands he was released,' Jessie said. 'And why.'

'Does she?'

'Oh, yes.' Jessie nodded. 'We talked about it. Not for long, but we did. We thought it best to address it, didn't we, Donny?'

Uncle Donny nodded.

'But she doesn't seem . . . well, *bothered.*'

'But that's what you wanted, isn't it?' Donny said mildly. 'Isn't that why you and Madeleine wanted her to come here — so she could live happily?'

'Yes,' Aileen said.

'Daisy's so childlike,' Jessie said. 'And that's a good thing in so many ways. Look at her with the boy.'

Aileen watched Evie chasing Hamish on her hands and knees as he careered away towards the fence then turned and shrieked with laughter when she caught his ankle.

'And, of course,' Jessie said, 'she understands this is only a blip.'

'"Only a blip"?' Aileen stared. 'What do you mean?'

Jessie shrugged and said lightly, 'We know it won't be long before there's a new trial.' She smiled. 'And this time Craig will be sent away for good.'

* * *

4.51 p.m.

Aileen suggested a walk into the village, just the two of them. Evie didn't like that. She wanted Hamish to come as well, but Aileen insisted. She'd come all this way — surely they could spend an hour together, the two sisters?

And so Evie had relented and Jessie took the boy back into the house. Uncle Donny stood on the step of the croft to watch them leave, and waved when they were through the gate.

Ten minutes down the lane, they passed the top of a rutted driveway, which snaked away through huge rhododendrons to a half-glimpsed ruin of a house. Aileen could just make out the broken rafters that poked up through a gaping hole in the roof.

It was another ten minutes before they reached the next house and the village. Very few of the houses on the peninsula were holiday homes. People had lived here for generations, working on the farms mainly. There was a tiny church and a community shop that doubled as a café. Children had to travel to Glendale for primary school. Hamish would start there in two years' time. The secondary school was in Portree, which was a hike, but local transport was reliable, except when the weather was at its worst.

Beyond the village, on the slope of land below a range of looming crags, the St Columba Centre gleamed in the afternoon sun. Aileen had never visited it, but Jessie had told her there was a small staff of maybe five or six, including a couple who lived in, and it could host fifteen or so guests. You could book in for any period of time, and there were bursaries funded through some foundation or trust or other. They ran classes, in everything from Gaelic song to tapestry weaving, and there was yoga and tai chi too. This afternoon, she could make out eight or nine people in a field to this side of the building. As one, they dropped into a crouch and made slow, sweeping movements with their arms.

'Do you ever go up there?' Aileen asked Evie.

'Once. They did a baby yoga afternoon. It was lovely. I asked them about work. Cleaning, anything, but there's nothing just now, so I work here.' She pointed to the café as they approached.

Inside, three tables had been squeezed close together against a picture window, in among boxes of tins and crates of potatoes, apples and oranges. Two of the tables were occupied, one by a grey-haired lady who recognised Evie and pulled her into conversation. Aileen went up to the small counter and ordered coffees from a diffident lad in a green shirt, and waited for them to be made.

She brought the steaming mugs to where Evie was in conversation.

'This is Gracie,' Evie said by way of introduction.

'And are you on your holidays?' Gracie asked. She smiled warmly, the skin around her eyes wrinkling like crepe, her cheeks a deep weathered red.

'No,' Aileen said tightly. It always shocked her how nosy some strangers could be. 'Just a short visit.'

'Och, that's a shame. Well, if you're here again, pop in. Mine's the last house, the wee bungalow right where the road ends — number twelve. Daisy knows the place.'

The woman eventually went back to her pot of tea and her view of the sunny, breeze-ruffled fields. Following her gaze, Aileen spotted a table and chairs in a little garden.

'Let's sit outside,' she said and led the way through a door at the back of the store.

She felt better once it was just the two of them again. Safer.

'Craig's out of prison, and we need to talk about what it means.'

Evie wrinkled her nose. 'I don't see why it matters.'

'Don't you?' Aileen stirred her coffee, darkening the cap of milky foam as resentment swelled inside her.

'He doesn't know about Hamish. Even if he did, we're safe here.' Evie smiled, as if that was an end to it.

'And you're happy for me to do the worrying for both of us?' Aileen asked. 'Is that what you mean?'

Evie recoiled. 'Why are you being like this?' she said, frowning and wriggling her shoulders as if to shrug the harsh words off.

Aileen felt angry words forming in her mouth and knew she should stop them, but she wanted so badly to spit them in Evie's face, just to see her reaction.

'I think it's time to take things a bit more seriously,' she said.

'Why? And what "things"?'

'Craig's free. He's dangerous.'

'I *know* that!' Evie half shouted. 'It was me he attacked, remember?'

'That's not what I meant,' Aileen said. 'I mean he's dangerous *now*. I know you're here and you feel safe, but . . . what if something changes?'

'Nothing's going to change. Why would it?' Evie blinked fast and her lips twitched. Aileen knew she'd got through, if only a little.

'Because . . .' she began. 'Because . . .' But she faltered, staring into her mug. Did she need to tell Evie about the murdered juror? Or that Maddie had warned there might not be a second trial? Evie felt safe here. She'd only accuse Aileen of being cruel, of trying to frighten her — of wanting to punish her.

'No,' she said finally. 'You're right. Nothing's going to change.'

Evie smiled and turned to gaze dreamily towards the cliffs and the silver-blue band of sea.

* * *

Aileen was in the kitchen with Uncle Donny, just the two of them, putting away the washing up, when he brought up Evie's future.

'Jessie and I won't be around forever,' he said, drying a dish. 'There'll come a time when she'll need to make a decision.'

'I know,' Aileen replied. Through the kitchen window she could see Jessie deadheading roses along the fence at the back of the property. Evie was reading to Hamish under the shade of a wind-bent apple tree.

'Maybe when the young one's started school,' Uncle Donny said. 'She might think about going back to college herself. She's welcome to be here, of course she is — I don't mean that. But . . . she can't hide away forever.'

She took her time before asking, 'Does she ever talk about what happened to her? I mean, about what Craig did to her?'

'Oh, no. Jessie's tried from time to time. She worries about Evie, about the long-term impact. We both do. But you know your sister — she runs deep.' He smiled. 'Like you.'

Confirmation that her uncle and his wife worried too should be reassuring. But instead, now Aileen had to worry about them as well.

'She has a friend here at least,' Donny confided. 'Someone she does talk to.'

'Oh?'

'Theresa, who owns the shop and café. She's taken Evie under her wing. She says Evie is welcome to keep working at the shop but she thinks Evie needs to grow her horizons too, especially when Hamish starts at the nursery. There are jobs in Portree — though, of course, she'd need to learn to drive.'

Aileen looked out into the garden again, at her happy sister, reading away to young Hamish, clueless to the anxiety she caused to just everyone around her.

'I'll work something out, Uncle Donny,' Aileen told him.

CHAPTER ELEVEN

Wednesday 14 August

9.37 a.m.

'So . . . the child's DNA would be the evidence?' Elaine Walsh asked. 'It seems incredible.'

'Perhaps,' Lola said, 'but, combined with the scans that are on record, it would prove Craig wasn't on Jersey when he said he was.'

The superintendent eased herself back in her chair and frowned. 'But Maddie Wicks's niece hasn't agreed to testify?'

'Not yet. They haven't even asked her. It seems like everyone hoped they wouldn't have to — that Craig would go down for the nightclub murders. But now everything's changed.'

'And how hopeful is Ms Wicks that Evie would testify if asked?'

'Hard to say. She wants to know whether the evidence is likely to work. If it is, I think she'll have a go at persuading her. Which is why I came to talk to you.'

Elaine eyed Lola carefully. 'But not to Graeme Izatt — whose case this is?'

'No,' Lola said, maintaining a neutral expression. 'Not to Graeme.'

Elaine sat up. 'I'm happy to put in a call to the Crown Office,' she said, then added, eyeballing Lola, 'but if their response is positive, you'll be taking this lead straight to Graeme and handing it over, won't you?'

'Yes, boss.'

'I mean it, Lola!'

'I know you do, boss.' She gave her best good-girl smile.

'How are you getting on with the Kathryn Main inquiry, by the way?'

'Slowly. Our main lead is the red car that collected her at the flat in Falkirk. There's something deeply out of character about Kathryn's behaviour at the trial. According to her family, neighbours and an old friend who came to talk to us, Kathryn was a shy and retiring sort.'

'So someone put her up to it?'

'Very possibly. Anna's talking to the other three jurors who shared messages. If Kathryn was the ringleader, then it's possible one of them will know what was motivating her.'

'Any clue as to how the body got into the Kelvin?'

'There's a block of tenements on Otago Street,' Lola said, recalling the briefing Anna had emailed her this morning. 'The close and the ground-floor flats have direct access into a yard out back, and there's a parapet overhanging the water. One of the flats has been empty for the past three months, but it was broken into towards the end of last week. IB are going in this morning to look for fibres, hairs, anything they can find.'

'And was Craig behind her death?'

'If he was then it was indirectly. His solicitor has submitted an alibi this morning. At a glance, it looks . . . watertight. It's possible someone did the murder for him, but the question remains: why? Yes, he's vengeful, but why do something so blatant, especially while his appeal is still pending?'

'Could someone be setting him up?'

'The thought had crossed my mind.'

Elaine checked the time on her phone and sat up.

'I've a meeting in ten minutes,' she said. 'I'll call the Crown Office quickly just now. Hopefully they'll come back to us by the end of the day. Where is she, by the way, this young woman and her child?'

'On Skye, living with relatives.'

'Try to find out the precise location, just in case — but keep the intel under wraps.'

Lola understood. People like Craig had friends everywhere.

* * *

10.12 a.m.

Joe's brother Kev had texted her for the second day running with an update on Joe's health. The latest message said he was still testing positive for Covid and was headachy and tired but feeling 'a wee bit better'. He detailed what Joe had had to eat.

She read it in a state of stunned bafflement. Kev knew she and Joe had gone their separate ways. Was this a misguided attempt to reconcile them?

Joe and I don't see each other anymore, Kev, she drafted in response. *No need to send reports on his health.*

Then she deleted the words, which were harsh. Kev loved his brother and this was one way of coping with his illness.

After a minute's deliberation, she wrote, *Glad he's doing better. Appreciate the updates but don't feel you need to send. Thanks. L.*

She sent that and got a plaintive thumbs-up emoji a few minutes later.

Feeling jangled and cross, she went into the email from Carter Craig's solicitors and read again the detailed account of his movements between 5 p.m. on Friday and 7 a.m. on Monday.

According to the schedule, Craig had been at his uncle's castle home in Perthshire from early afternoon on Thursday — the day he'd been released from jail — until the Friday morning, when he'd travelled to London for a meeting with a litigation lawyer, followed by a party in Soho. He'd spent the weekend in London, staying at a high-end hotel in Belgravia, and meeting friends and dining out. He'd then flown back from London on a private jet, landing at Glasgow airport just after 6.30 p.m. on Sunday. From there he'd been chauffeur-driven to dinner at a Michelin-starred restaurant in Glasgow's West End with his current girlfriend, a model called Lorelei West, and then on to a club in town, where a famous New York rapper was 'performing for friends'. From the club he and the model had been driven the sixty miles to his uncle's place in Perthshire, arriving there after 3 a.m. Craig's uncle was a multi-millionaire businessman and the house and grounds had their own security staff who should, the solicitor's note stated, be able to confirm comings and goings.

Every contact provided would need to be interviewed, but Lola had no doubt that the alibi would stand — as Izatt had said it would.

And still there was the problem of the motive.

But if not Craig, then who else would have wanted Kathryn Main dead? Blair Sanderson despised her, yes, but he was smart and seemed in control of his emotions. What about his and Alex's mother? Or his girlfriend, Gabrielle — the late Xena's sister?

Anna and Kirstie had spent the past two days mapping Kathryn Main's life as best they could and Anna had sent Lola a note of their progress, which she read through now. A friend from Kathryn's university days had echoed the description of Kathryn provided by her childhood friend, Emma Spencer. Likewise Kathryn's neighbours in the modern block of flats where she lived in Maryhill, her work colleagues and most of all her relatives: her sister, Tara, and an aunt, both of whom were in a state of shocked disbelief.

Her flat, according to Anna's report, evidenced a quiet life spent among books and classical music, or watching DVDs of black-and-white Hollywood films. It was well but unshowily furnished. Kathryn had used social media, but intermittently, and had fewer than fifty friends on Facebook.

She had, according to every account, been quiet and shy, principled and dutiful, and not in the least disruptive or malicious. Her behaviour in the jury made no sense.

Anna had interviewed Tina Kline, the Falkirk woman who believed she'd seen Kathryn getting into a car on the Friday night she disappeared, and subsequently consulted Falkirk council's CCTV operations centre. And there, on a recording from the Friday evening, it appeared: a smart red BMW, sliding into the little estate just before 10 p.m., where it collected a woman who could be Kathryn Main from the roadside. From there it headed out of town, south towards country roads and unmonitored darkness. The camera had recorded the plate but it was false, which to Lola's mind only confirmed the car's significance. She'd already had it added to the public call for information, though nothing had yet come back.

At the end of Anna's report was a note saying she'd interviewed one of the three jurors who'd communicated with Kathryn during Craig's trial and would see the remaining two this morning. She'd update Lola at lunchtime.

Lola used the next half-hour to learn more about Carter Craig, and everything she found confirmed for her that he was a narcissist, obsessed with his image and managing every aspect of his online persona. She was amused to learn that his name was a fiction. He'd been born Colin McQueen but changed his legal name in his late teens and spent the next decade filling out the character he'd created for himself.

He had a house in Milngavie, to the north of Glasgow, called the Frontier, which she found easily on Google Maps. It was a sprawling white modern place. There was a swimming pool in the grounds and at least three unidentifiable cars in the expansive driveway.

She read more about his past.

His father had died when Craig was six. His mother, Elizabeth, had been left high and dry and had appealed to her sister, Rebecca, who'd married the millionaire media owner Duncan Gaunt. The Gaunts took mother and son into their home and provided them with an apartment in one wing. By all accounts, the uncle was fond of his nephew but disregarded Elizabeth, especially when Rebecca died of cancer aged only forty-seven. It was Duncan Gaunt who'd furnished Craig, on his twenty-first birthday, with enough capital to start his own property empire. Craig had drawn on the network of privileged young men he'd met at the private school Uncle Duncan had paid for him to attend. The school was Greykirk in Perthshire.

Greykirk. The name rang a bell. And then it came to her. She quickly checked Craig's date of birth.

'My God,' she murmured, then, glancing round the office to check she wasn't about to be overheard, picked up the phone and dialled.

'Oh, it's you, is it?' Izatt said nastily.

'Yes, there's something you need to know.'

'Is that right? Only, I've a bone to pick with you first!'

Her skin prickled with apprehension.

'Just what the hell are you playing at?' he barked.

'I'm sorry?'

'I've just had a call from the Crown Office about new evidence you've dug up that could convict Craig. Something to do with a kid. Planning to keep it from me, were you?'

CHAPTER TWELVE

12.13 p.m.

'Graeme, calm down!' Elaine snapped at last. 'Please, try and get a hold of yourself. In my view, Lola acted correctly. She was asked for advice and took appropriate steps.' She added pointedly, 'I agreed it was important to check the likely validity of new evidence before doing anything with the information. Lola fully understood the need to pass any actual evidence your way — didn't you, Lola?'

'Yes,' Lola muttered, sitting on her own fury.

They were in Elaine's office, though the room's ice-box temperature didn't seem to be cooling Izatt's rage.

'I want to know the kid's name and whereabouts,' he said. 'The mother's too. I can't *believe* you've withheld this information from me. If I hadn't got that phone call, I'd have been in the dark while you were laughing at me behind my back.'

'Nobody is laughing at you,' Elaine said tersely.

Elaine, true to her word, had made a call to the Crown Office and detailed the hypothetical new evidence. It seemed the request had been passed on and one crucial detail left out: that the answer to Elaine's question should come back to her.

Instead, because it had been noted against the Craig inquiry, the responding officer had picked up the phone and dialled the senior investigating officer named on the file: Graeme Izatt.

'And we don't even have details of the people involved, do we, Lola?' Elaine went on. 'The question I posed was purely hypothetical at this stage.'

But Graeme was not in listening mode.

'I can't believe there's a woman out there who could have testified she was with Craig that night — *and* offered DNA evidence to support her testimony!'

'Craig raped her, Graeme,' Lola said.

'So she alleges.'

'Oh, come on!' Lola yelled at him.

'Folks, please!' Elaine snapped. 'I take it the answer was positive, though?' she asked Izatt now. 'The evidence would be valid in the eyes of the Crown Office?'

'With a high probability of success, so I was told, sitting there with egg on my face — thank you very much!' He turned to Lola. 'I want the name of the person who came to you with this story. And I want to know where the woman and the kid are. I know it's Skye but I want the location.'

Lola looked sharply at Elaine, who seemed taken aback. The superintendent bit her lip and winced at Lola. She'd promised not to give the Crown Office any details, but one had clearly slipped through.

'You can't force someone to give evidence, Graeme,' Lola said, regaining her composure. 'The whole family are terrified of Craig, and with good reason. He's a monster and the child's a threat to him.'

'We'll look after them if we have to,' Izatt threw in.

'It's going to take patience and persuasion,' she said, 'and kindness.'

'Kindness, my arse.'

'All right, compassion and respect, if you like!'

'What about showing Craig's victims some "kindness"?' he demanded. 'What about showing some to *me*?'

'Graeme . . .' Elaine warned.

Izatt made a dismissive spluttering noise.

Lola said firmly, 'I'll speak to my contact and tell her what the Crown Office have said. Then it's up to her to talk to the young woman.'

'*We* need to talk to her,' Izatt said. '*I* need to.'

Elaine came in, 'And do you think that'd work, Graeme?'

He squared his shoulders, frowning.

Elaine tapped her pen on her desk. 'Let Lola talk to her contact,' she said. 'Let's hope the contact can persuade the young woman to come forward. Beyond that . . . well, enough lives have been ruined already. It's not our job to ruin more. Do we understand each other?'

* * *

12.31 p.m.

'Hang back a moment, Lola,' Elaine said, when Izatt was out of the door.

Lola sat back down and waited for the dust to settle.

'I must apologise,' Elaine said, looking cowed. 'Clearly I must have mentioned Skye on the call to the Crown Office. I'd meant to say she was in a remote island location.'

'It's okay. So long as word doesn't get out.'

'Talk to your contact as soon as you can,' Elaine said. 'Let's move things on and hopefully our role will be concluded.'

Lola remained where she was, wondering how to voice her concerns.

'What is it?' Elaine asked.

'If my contact does manage to persuade her niece to come forward, I'd feel responsible for what happened to her and the child. I'm not sure I could just hand them over to Graeme.'

Elaine watched her. 'And I think I'd share your concerns,' she said at last, then glanced towards the door as if Izatt still loomed there. 'Let's take things one step at a time, shall we?'

Lola found Graeme Izatt by the doors to the stairwell, jabbing irritably at his phone. She took a deep breath and went over to him. He heard her and looked up with big angry eyes.

'Remember I called because I had something to tell you?' she asked quietly.

He grunted.

'It's very simple: Carter Craig and Aidan Pierce went to the same school. Greykirk in Perthshire.'

He looked ashen. 'You've got to be fucking kidding me.'

'I might be wrong about the dates but I'm pretty sure Aiden's thirty-three. They'd have been in the same year. Graeme, he should have told you that.' She smiled pityingly. 'You're going to have to talk to him.'

* * *

2.34 p.m.

Maddie Wicks received the news that the evidence could be valid coolly enough, but all the time fiddling with the wooden bangles on one arm. Lola didn't tell her that Graeme Izatt had got wind of the information. Hopefully she would never need to know.

'I see,' Maddie said at last. 'So now I have to act.'

They were in the consulting room at the back of her Park Circus studio again. It was stuffy despite the open window giving onto the lane. Lola could hear voices outside, and the smell of cigarette smoke found its way into the room.

'Meaning what exactly?' Lola prompted.

'Meaning I have to persuade Evie,' Maddie said. 'But I have to persuade her sister, Aileen, first. I can't say the prospect fills me with much joy.'

'Will Aileen be resistant?'

'Most likely.'

'We could talk to Aileen together if you like. Lay the facts before her. Make sure she feels she's part of the discussion.'

66

'Let me think it through,' Maddie said.

'Take all the time you need,' Lola said, though in her mind Izatt was nagging away. 'Call me if you have any questions.'

'I will,' Maddie said. 'And thank you. Sorcha was right: you're so kind. If anyone could help Evie, I'm sure it would be you.'

CHAPTER THIRTEEN

3.42 p.m.

Anna and Kirstie had now interviewed the three jurors who'd been part of Kathryn Main's WhatsApp group. One of the interviews had thrown up an intriguing lead and Anna suggested Lola might want to talk to her too. They arranged to meet at Cowcaddens and go to the woman's flat together.

Lola got there early, so called Graeme Izatt to relay Maddie Wicks's response.

'How much bloody time does someone need?' he snapped. 'I'm not buying this. Give me this woman's name and I'll have a word.'

'No, Graeme.'

'Lola, this might be my only chance to get that bastard!' He sounded shrill and shaky. 'Don't you get that?'

'I get it,' she said. 'Did you talk to Pierce about his old school chum, by the way?'

'Yes, and a big thank you for sticking that particular spoke into my wheel. Turns out Pierce was two years above Craig, or Colin, or whatever he was called when he was supposedly a normal human being.'

'Two years? But they're the same age.'

'It's to do with when their birthdays fall, plus Pierce got put up a year because he was gifted.'

'"Gifted"?' She rolled her eyes. No doubt Pierce had used that word himself.

'He's a brainy lad, Lola.'

She rolled her eyes. 'You're welcome to him, Graeme.'

She hung up just as Anna pulled into a parking space further along the road.

Susan McKenna's flat was on the sixteenth floor, with views across the heat-hazed city.

'You must think I'm a right bloody idiot,' she said, sitting down on her sofa and lighting a cigarette. 'Don't blame you if you do. I *am* an idiot. I thought it was the right thing to do. We all did. And now that creep's back on the streets and I'm looking at jail time.'

Susan was a big woman in her late thirties with lots of curly brown hair. Her skin was bad and she looked downright miserable. The windows stood open because of the heat, and noise from the M8 rumbled loudly below. She was a care assistant in a nursing home, she told them, though she'd been suspended by her employer thanks to being charged with a crime: namely, conspiring to defeat the ends of justice.

'Half my family won't even speak to me,' she told Lola, taking a long drag on her cigarette. 'My brother's boys, though — they think I'm ace. Indirectly managed to get their hero off "fake charges", didn't I? Anyway, you don't want to listen to me moaning on. You wanted to ask me more about Kathryn.'

Anna began. 'Earlier, Susan, you said Kathryn struck you as a "lonely soul", that you thought she was in her element in the jury — as if it was "a big social thing" for her. That's right, isn't it?'

The woman frowned.

'Yeah, I did think that,' she said after a few moments. 'She brought buns in one day. I remember thinking it was a shame.'

'She was making friends?' Lola asked.

'You could say that. She confided in me one day that she didn't have any friends. Not really. She had her sister, but other than her . . .'

'How did the WhatsApp group come about? Did Kathryn suggest it?'

'It was the second week of the trial. I'd given her my phone number — she was going to send me a link to some drink she had. Fermented something or other. Good for the gut and helps you lose weight. I wasn't that interested but she kept on about it and she seemed really sad and I thought, well, what's the harm? So I gave her my number and she sent me the thing. Then a couple of nights later — like, really late on — I get this message saying, *He is guilty, isn't he? We can't let him get away with it.*' She swallowed a mouthful of tea. 'And I — well, I'd had a drink, hadn't I? I replied, *Yeah, I reckon he is.* And we got to chatting like that, and there's me thinking — it's okay, it's all encrypted. Besides, I love true crime stuff. Always have. She said she'd been messaging two of the other jurors, Carole and Damien. That they felt the same, and what could we do about it?' Another, deeper drag of her cigarette.

'Next thing, she's messaging to say the other two wanted us to have a group chat and it'd be fine because it was encrypted. So I said okay, and Kathryn set it up. She made us swear to keep it under wraps and only ever talk about it over WhatsApp — never in person. And then she told us she had evidence Carter Craig was guilty as sin. Said it was from a friend who was terrified Craig'd come after her and her daughter. We discussed it for hours that night and the next — how to get the other jury members to go along with us. We managed it, didn't we? Drip by drip, we made sure they understood.' She bit her lip.

'Who was Kathryn's "friend"?' Lola asked carefully. 'The one with the daughter.'

'I don't know.'

'Only, you said Kathryn told you she didn't have any friends.'

The woman's eyes widened. 'Yeah, that is weird, isn't it?'

'Did she mention the friend's name?'

A shake of the head. 'No. She said the friend had asked her to keep everything confidential.'

'Could she have been talking about herself, do you think?' Anna asked. 'You know, the way people sometimes say, "I'm asking for a friend," but really it's for them?'

She thought about it. 'No. I don't think so. The way she talked, I'd swear the friend was real. She described how upset she'd become, talking about Craig and what he'd done to her daughter.'

'And what had he done?'

'Raped her. Kathryn had seen evidence. Photos of bruises where he'd held her by the throat.'

'Did you see the photos?'

'No. Kathryn had seen screenshots of conversations between this girl and Carter Craig too. Really nasty stuff, Kathryn said.'

'How old was the daughter?' Lola asked.

Another frown. 'Not sure. Grown up, I think. Why are you asking me about this?'

'We'd like to trace the friend and her daughter. Did Kathryn tell you anything about this friend that might help us identify her? Her first name, where she lived, how she knew her?'

A slow shake of the head. 'I'm sorry.'

'You're sure it was a woman and her *daughter*, not a niece?'

She caught a little look of curiosity from Anna.

'Daughter, I'm sure of it,' Susan said.

Lola signalled to Anna that it was no good. Anna went through the motions of asking the woman to get in touch if she remembered anything. Susan seemed to relax as her visitors made to leave. Then she said, distractedly, 'This talk of Kathryn being lonely — you know . . . there was something else weird.'

'What's was that, Susan?' Lola asked.

'It was early in the trial, so I didn't connect it till now.'

Lola experienced a tiny zap of adrenaline.

'I don't think I'd even talked to Kathryn at that point. We didn't really start chatting till the second week. Yeah, that's right. It was maybe the second or third day, right at the end of the afternoon session, and I was thinking, *Oh God, we're going to be here for weeks. My boss is going to kill me.* Anyway, I remember how this woman beside me seemed so excited, and she *waved* to someone in the public gallery. Gave a big smile and waved. I turned to look but there were loads of people, all getting up to go, putting their jackets on and stuff. I heard her tell someone she was going out for an early dinner.'

'And this was Kathryn?'

'Yeah, though I didn't know her name at the time.'

Lola glanced at Anna, whose eyes were avid. She turned back to Susan.

Susan's demeanour was different now. No longer someone ashamed of her behaviour, but someone who was actively helping.

'Did you see anyone wave back in response?'

Susan shook her head. 'Sorry.'

They asked more questions to try to pin down the day and date.

'Can you look on a kind of register or something?' Susan asked.

'You don't sign in to access the public gallery,' Lola said. 'You don't even have to show ID. You go through security, and that's that.'

'There might be CCTV footage from the public areas,' Anna said. 'It depends how long it's kept for. Usually it's thirty-one days, I think. If we do find a recording showing people leaving that court then we will ask you to take a look and see if you recognise anyone.'

Lola said, 'You might spot someone who attended more than once. A face that became familiar.'

'I'm not sure I would,' Susan said, dismayed now. 'You tend to focus on what's going on in court. The judge and the advocates and the witnesses. And the accused, of course.'

It was indeed a long shot. But CCTV might hold the answer — and not just the CCTV inside the High Court building. There would be cameras outside, and ones belonging to local businesses. One of them might well have captured Kathryn Main leaving the court in the company of her mystery friend.

* * *

4.50 p.m.

When they were riding down in the lift, Anna said, 'Why did you ask if it might be a niece Kathryn's friend was worried about?'

'It was just an idea,' Lola said evasively.

As they were crossing the car park Anna said, 'If someone — this mystery "friend" — was playing Kathryn to secure Craig's conviction, are we really suggesting that person then killed Kathryn to shut her up? I mean, Kathryn did what she wanted.'

'But the plan failed,' Lola said. 'Craig got out of jail. Maybe the so-called "friend" got scared she'd be in the firing line too. Solution: kill Kathryn.'

'Using an MO Craig was believed to have used when he attacked Alex Sanderson?'

'In hopes of setting Craig up?' Lola suggested, aware how feeble it sounded.

'It just seems so . . . far-fetched.'

'Why don't you look in the files. See if you can find any case that resembles the one Kathryn's friend described to her: where Craig attacked a young woman and injured her throat. We might find her that way.'

Lola's phone was ringing. It was DC Kirstie Campbell.

'Just heard on the grapevine, boss. Do you remember Martin "Mack" McBurney? He was the prosecution witness who claimed he sold Craig cocaine the weekend of the nightclub murders. Well, he was found dead round the back of his flat in Dennistoun an hour ago — though he'd been dead a few hours. Garrotted with a wire. DCI Izatt's freaking out about it.'

'My God,' Lola said. 'He's picking them off one by one, isn't he? Thanks, Kirstie.'

She was about to tell Anna the news when Anna answered a call of her own. She came off it a few moments later, eyes alight.

'That was Inspector Michelle Brown, boss. She and her officers are at Kathryn Main's flat, responding to a call of a suspected break-in. A neighbour heard someone moving about upstairs and called it in. Kathryn's sister Tara is there now. She says stuff's been moved but she can't tell if anything's been taken.'

'A break-in in the middle of the afternoon?' Lola asked.

'Hardly a break-in,' Anna said. 'According to Michelle the locks on the door and windows are all intact. She reckons whoever was in there must have had a key.'

CHAPTER FOURTEEN

5.22 p.m.

Graeme Izatt heaped instant coffee into a mug with a shaking hand, then sloshed hot water from the kettle and scalded his hand.

'For fuck's sake!'

He swore and ran it under cold water, then put another splash of cold into the coffee and took a mouthful. It tasted horrible, but it would get him through the next hour.

He was at the end of his rope and unsure what to do or where to turn next. The Craig case had pushed him to the absolute limit of his patience. He'd spent the last few weeks scrabbling around for new evidence and found none. The juror who'd done her best to get Craig sent down had washed up dead in the river; and now Mack McBurney, who'd claimed to have sold Craig drugs the night of the nightclub murders, was dead too, a wire embedded in his throat.

Izatt was convinced Craig was behind McBurney's death, but his solicitors had already provided yet another beautifully curated alibi for the past twenty-four hours.

Izatt didn't know if he wanted to weep or laugh hysterically.

This on top of one of his own colleagues, Lola bloody Harris, doing the dirty on him, taunting him with the possibility of evidence that even the Crown Office believed might be enough to convict Craig — then taking it away. She hadn't even had the courtesy to let him talk to this mysterious 'contact' of hers.

Well, he had a plan of his own. And that clever lad Aidan Pierce was going to help him bring it to fruition.

He swallowed more hot coffee and winced. His indigestion was getting worse. He ate another two orange-flavoured indigestion tablets, to add to the four he'd already taken since lunch. They barely touched the sides these days. He was sure he was getting an ulcer.

His phone bleeped. A message from Aidan.

Stuck Craig in room 3. He's acting cool enough. Solicitor's on his way. Suggest we make a start in fifteen minutes but it wouldn't hurt to leave him to dwell on things a bit longer.

Good lad, Izatt typed. *Looking forward to it.*

CHAPTER FIFTEEN

5.12 p.m.

Kathryn Main's flat was on the top floor of a low modern block just off Maryhill Road. Her downstairs neighbour, a tiny, frightened lady in her sixties, had heard a soft bang and footsteps above her just after 3 p.m. and called 999. A car got there within four minutes, a second joining it a minute or two after that, but by then the intruder had gone.

Inspector Michelle Brown and her officers had found the door standing open, but with the lock intact. Inside there were signs that drawers and belongings had been disturbed. They'd called Tara Main, and she'd come straight round. Tara was still there, looking confused and bereft.

'I don't know what's been taken,' she told them tearfully. 'Things have been moved but I can't tell if anything's missing. I was just going through her bedroom drawers. All her jewellery's still there, not that she had very much. What's going on?' the woman pleaded. 'It's Craig, isn't it? It's got to be. He's playing games with us all, and there's nothing anyone can do.'

Tara returned to the bedroom, while Lola and Anna remained in the living room to await the arrival of their IB colleagues. A minute later Tara gave a shout, then came hurrying through.

'I think I know what's missing,' she said, a hand to her forehead. 'Of course, Kathryn could have taken it with her to Falkirk, but we can check that, couldn't we?'

'What is it?' Lola asked.

'It's the necklace. The one with the moonstone. Sterling silver and a beautiful milky stone. She loved it. I remember she said she kept it by her bed because — well, it was supposed to bring "inner clarity", whatever that means. I can't believe I forgot about it. She was so proud of it. It meant so much to her.'

'And why was that?' Lola asked, her skin prickling as she sensed what was coming.

'A friend gave it to her,' she said sadly. 'That's what Kathryn said: "It's a present from a new friend."'

CHAPTER SIXTEEN

9.32 p.m.

Arriving back in Glasgow was like returning to summer. Even this late in the evening, the air was warm and the streets were buzzing. People sat drinking and eating in pavement cafés on Hyndland Road.

Aileen was exhausted from the drive, and from carrying the emotional baggage she always brought home from a visit to Evie.

They'd had a nice day, walking in the fields above Skaravaig with Hamish, taking turns to carry him when he got tired. They'd eaten sandwiches in the shadows of the crags. The view from there was incredible, looking down over the shining Atlantic, but Aileen had been a bag of nerves the whole time because beside the cliffs was a precipice with a sheer drop to rocks and the crashing waves. Hamish had seemed determined to run about, careering in circles. 'He won't go near the edge!' Evie had kept saying. 'He's too sensible.' Aileen had sat, shivery and tense, and been relieved when it was time to go.

She found a space to park right outside the flat — something that was never guaranteed — and performed her usual ritual of sitting quietly in the car and surveying the building and the street for signs that anything wasn't quite right.

The gate in the low fence surrounding the private garden stood slightly ajar, but that could be down to the postman. Everything else seemed in order.

She unloaded the car and unlocked the front door — and realised the burglar alarm wasn't set. She stood, her key still in the lock of the half-open door, staring at the box, her mouth suddenly dry and her heart thumping. Quickly she turned on the light in the hallway, then listened.

You just forgot to set it, that's all.

But she never forgot. *Never.* She was obsessive about security. Had been even before what had happened to Evie.

Then she saw there was no post on the hallway floor. Not even a flier. If nothing had been delivered, who had left the gate ajar?

But the lock wasn't damaged, so no one had come in, at least not this way.

'Is somebody there?' she called, her voice shrill in the silence.

The flat seemed too quiet, too still, as if it was holding its breath. She listened, her mouth dry and her hands all pins and needles.

You're hypersensitive right now. You're imagining things.

But fear got the better of her, and she backed out into the garden, pulling the door closed.

From the safety of her car she called Maddie.

* * *

9.55 p.m.

'I'll go in, you stay out here.'

Maddie was in high spirits, which Aileen found grating.

'I don't mind coming in if you're with me,' Aileen said.

'No, okay, darling. Anyway, mob-handed is probably best.' Maddie pushed open the gate and stepped up to the front door. Key ready, she turned, all smiles, and asked in a stage whisper, 'Ready?'

Aileen nodded.

Maddie went ahead into the hallway. 'So far so good,' she murmured over her shoulder, then yelled, 'Come out, come out, wherever you are!'

Aileen winced but kept pace as Maddie reached the first door on the right, into the living room. She turned the handle and flung the door open, flicking on the light and peering in.

'All clear! Kitchen next?'

The kitchen, at the rear of the flat, was empty too. Flooded with light, the place lost all menace. Aileen began to feel silly.

'Utility room,' Maddie said, stepping across and checking inside. 'All good! And the back door seems secure to me.'

'Thank God,' Aileen said, heaving out a breath, which was quickly followed by a sob.

'Oh, darling, you must have got a fright, that's all.' Maddie pulled her niece into her arms. Aileen wept stupidly for a minute. 'We'll do the bedrooms and the bathroom, not forgetting the hall cupboard, then I think you deserve a glass of wine!'

They went through the remaining rooms and found no sign of anything untoward.

'But I didn't turn the alarm on,' Aileen said when they returned to the kitchen. 'I've never forgotten to do it before.'

'You've got so much on your mind, that's all,' Maddie said. She'd retrieved a half-full bottle of Pinot Grigio from the fridge and was now looking for glasses.

'Next cupboard to the right,' Aileen said absently.

'I'm driving but I can have half a glass,' Maddie said, and poured. 'Now, sit down, darling. Tell me about Evie.'

Aileen sat, looking sulky.

'Well?' Maddie prompted.

'She's happy, I think.'

'Is she? Well, that's good.'

'Yes.' She took a sip of the ice-cold wine. 'But it's not healthy. It's like she's in a bubble. As if she's shut off any notion of risk. She won't talk about Craig at all. Uncle Donny's worried about her — about what she'll do when Hamish is older. About where she'll live, whether she'll get a job. She works six hours a week in the community shop. It's not enough to live on.'

'If Donny and Jessie are worried about money, I could help,' Maddie said. 'I have offered in the past. Evie and Hamish are a shared responsibility.'

'It's not the money. It's Evie's well-being he's worried about and I can see what he means. It's as if she only exists in the present, without any past or future. That can't be healthy, can it — for her or Hamish?'

'No, darling. No, it can't.'

They sat in silence for several seconds.

'But we can't *force* her to face what happened to her, can we?' Aileen said.

Maddie was watching her strangely, as if she was on the point of speaking but was scared to do so.

'What is it?' Aileen asked.

'I wondered if you'd talked to Evie about the possibility of coming forward. Of making a statement.'

'No. It didn't feel right.'

'I see.' Maddie was chewing her lip and her face was flushed pink. 'Oh *lord* . . .' She took a swig of her wine and her eyes moved about the kitchen as if looking for a crutch.

'What?' Aileen asked, her chest suddenly tight.

'The thing is, I had a word with someone about it.'

'Who?'

She reached for Aileen's hand, but Aileen withdrew it sharply.

'The friend of a friend I told you about. She's *very* discreet. I explained the situation and she took advice, or rather her superintendent did. The upshot is: the Crown Office think it would be enough.'

Aileen tried to swallow. She pushed back from the table and started to get up, but her legs didn't seem strong enough to support her.

'Just imagine the closure it could bring to see that man locked up for good,' Maddie said, 'and knowing it was Evie who put him there!'

'You shouldn't have done it,' Aileen said, holding on to the marble kitchen counter with one hand, anchoring herself there. 'Not without Evie's permission.'

'Oh, I didn't give the detective any details. Give me some credit!'

'But now they know the evidence exists they'll start looking for it! You were wrong, Maddie. You had no right!'

Maddie stared, mouth open.

'You've betrayed me. You've betrayed Evie!'

'I *haven't*! Listen, all I did was ask for advice. The detective said I'd done the right thing. At no time did she put any pressure on me. Darling, nothing's changed! The only difference is that now we know it could work.'

Aileen's thoughts were in full cascade now, a torrent of fear, anger and panic.

'What did you say to her exactly?'

'Just the bare bones.'

'No names?'

'No!'

'But she knows we're related, that Evie's your niece?'

'Yes, well, she had to understood why it was so important to me—'

'So, she could find out.'

'Well, yes. But there's no reason to think she'd try. Honestly, she's a very nice person—'

Aileen rolled her eyes.

'Aileen, don't do that.' Maddie got clumsily to her feet, sending her chair screeching backwards and knocking the table so that her wine glass toppled, smashing and sending wine everywhere. 'Oh no, I'm sorry!'

'I think you should go.'

Her aunt froze, hands out, and stared at her. 'What?'

Aileen was a block of ice. 'I said, I think you should go now.'

'Darling—'

'Just *leave*!'

* * *

10.42 p.m.

Aileen threw the rest of her own wine down the sink, then set about picking up the shards of glass, not caring if she cut her fingers. She could still hear Maddie's pleas ringing in her ears.

She was still shaking fifteen minutes later as she emptied her travel bag in the bathroom. Her reflection in the mirror over the sink made her start. Her face was emaciated, with dark hollows for eyes. She brushed her teeth facing the other way.

She took an antihistamine to help her sleep, then retreated to the back bedroom, which was always the coolest room in the flat, though tonight it felt stuffy too. The room's single sash window could be opened a few inches, then locked in place with two bolts. Only a cat could get through the gap. She tugged the sash, which was usually stiff in its runners, only to find it rose easily, and further than it should, as if it had been oiled. She looked and, in a split second, understood that the bolts had been unscrewed from the frame.

She let go and jumped back as the sash banged heavily back into place.

She backed away, feeling cold fingers all over her skin.

She was right. Someone had been in the flat.

She had to get out. To get into her car and drive.

CHAPTER SEVENTEEN

10.50 p.m.

Lola's phone buzzed and she saw Elaine Walsh was calling.

'Oh, good, you're still awake,' Elaine said, sounding tense.

'What's wrong?' Lola asked.

'Are you at home?'

'Yes, and it's just me. Sandy's away upstairs.'

'Okay,' Elaine said, hesitating for a moment. 'I hope you're sitting down.'

'Oh God. Why, what's happened?'

'Graeme Izatt interviewed Carter Craig about Mack McBurney's murder,' Elaine told her. 'Aidan Pierce was with him. Things got heated and Craig taunted Graeme about his inability to lay anything on him. Then he started laying into Aidan. Apparently they were at school together. I didn't know that — did you?'

'Yes, I did. And I told Graeme. Aidan swore to him they hadn't known each other. Are you telling me they did?'

Elaine hesitated. 'It seems Aidan lost his temper.'

'Which he's done before,' Lola pointed out.

'The upshot is, Aidan told Craig we're in possession of new evidence relating to the nightclub murders.'

Lola's entire body locked with tension.

'He told Craig a woman has come forward saying Craig raped her that evening, and that she had a child as a result of the rape.'

'Oh no, please tell me this isn't true.'

'I can't. He revealed she lives on Skye and said she's considering giving a statement.'

Lola took a moment to gather her thoughts.

'And how did Craig respond?' she asked.

'He shut up, according to Graeme. He tried to bluff but seemed "cagey and nervous". Graeme took that as a sign they'd hit home.'

Lola felt utterly winded.

'I can't believe Pierce did that,' she said. 'And Graeme didn't even try to stop him? At least he had the decency to call and tell you what had happened.'

'Oh, that's not why he called me.' Elaine gave a dark laugh. 'As far as he's concerned Pierce "played a blinder". No, the reason he called was to get me to force your hand and reveal the name of the contact. He's told Craig he's got the evidence — so he means to have it.'

'That can't happen,' Lola said calmly, though inside she was screaming. 'It can't. Not without the contact's permission anyway. Listen, Elaine, I want to know exactly what was said during that interview. I'm going to ask Izatt for the recording.'

Elaine sighed. 'Well, you can. But Lola, the things Craig said to Aidan — they weren't nice at all. You need to tread sensitively.'

'Why? No one "treads sensitively" around me!'

'Lola . . .'

She breathed. 'All right. Sorry, boss.'

'Have you spoken to her since we heard back from the Crown Office?' Elaine asked now.

'Yes, but it's a long game,' Lola said. 'It requires tact — which Graeme and Pierce both lack.'

'I agree with you there, but Graeme wants a meeting first thing in the morning,' Elaine said. 'We should go in with a line we're both content with. I've got your back on this, Lola, but I'm worried. Graeme said Craig seemed to make the connection. He said he could see him piecing things together.'

'Meaning what?'

'Meaning Craig likely knows exactly who the young woman is — even if Graeme and Aidan are still in the dark.'

* * *

11.05 p.m.

'What's wrong?' Sandy asked, appearing in the kitchen. 'Is it Joe?'

'Joe? No! It's work. I've got a tricky meeting first thing. Look, you go up,' she said. 'I need to think.'

'Want to talk it through?'

'No, but thanks.'

He kissed her, making her smile, and took himself off to bed.

She made tea, then sat at the kitchen table and wondered whether to call Maddie Wicks and warn her. But warn her of what? That Craig knew Evie might testify against him? That he might be about to seek her out — her and the child?

Neither Pierce nor Izatt gave a toss about the young woman — a victim herself. They saw her as a means to an end: a triumphant conviction. She wondered if Izatt would bring Pierce to the meeting in the morning. She imagined his smirking face as Izatt no doubt tried to browbeat her into handing over Maddie Wicks's name and number.

Just then her phone buzzed into life, making her jump. She saw the caller's name and felt a surge of dread as she answered the call.

CHAPTER EIGHTEEN

Thursday 15 August

12.32 a.m.

'I can't thank you enough for coming,' Maddie said, taking Lola's arm and pulling her into the house before closing, locking and bolting the door behind her. 'It's an imposition, I know, so I really am very grateful.'

Lola nodded sheepishly, wondering how long it would be before that gratitude evaporated.

Maddie Wicks lived in a terraced town house in Strathbungo, a mile or so from Lola's place, on one of the elegant but narrow avenues off Pollokshaws Road. The hallway was wood-panelled and dark, but stunningly lit. A great curving staircase dominated the space, illuminated from below so that the shadows of its iron balustrade were thrown high up the walls and across the ceiling.

'Aileen is in the back sitting room,' Maddie told Lola breathlessly. 'She's calmed down a bit, but she's still very frightened.' She lowered her voice further. 'She's furious with me for speaking to you. She feels I betrayed her. She's convinced that my telling you is connected to the break-in, which is nonsense, of course.'

'I wonder if you and I could have a word first,' Lola said. 'Is there somewhere we could talk?'

Maddie seemed taken aback, but quickly recovered. 'Yes, come into the kitchen.'

But before they had taken more than a step, a quiet, flat voice spoke from further down the shadowy hallway: 'Hello.'

'Oh, Aileen!' Maddie said, masking her surprise with forced brightness. 'This is DCI Harris. She's the nice detective I told you about.'

'Hello, there,' Lola said, steeling herself.

A young woman stepped silently forward.

'My niece, Aileen Mackinnon,' Maddie said.

The young woman — she could only be in her mid-twenties — looked to Lola like a novice nun. A particularly pious one, but with repressed anger behind her eyes. She wore a light-grey shift dress over a white long-sleeved top. Her fair hair was parted in the middle and fell long and straight almost to her waist. She watched Lola with distrustful pale green eyes.

'Nice to meet you,' Lola said carefully.

'Craig knows about Evie, doesn't he?' Aileen Mackinnon said.

Lola didn't speak.

'He knows about Evie,' she repeated, a tremor of anger in her voice now. 'Maddie told you everything and you told Craig. And now he's coming for her.'

'Aileen, no!' Maddie went to her and took her gently by her thin arms. 'It's not Craig. It's not possible.'

'Is there somewhere we could sit down?' Lola asked quietly.

'Yes,' Maddie said. 'We'll go into the kitchen.'

'I'll know if you're lying to me,' Aileen said, eyes first on Maddie then on Lola.

'Oh Aileen, don't!' her aunt cried.

Lola followed the two women down the hallway and into the vast kitchen. Maddie invited her to sit on one of two benches either side of a sturdy table in the middle of the room. Aileen eyed her warily, but settled on the bench opposite. Maddie fussed about, filling the kettle and then asking about drinks.

'So, you believe somebody broke into your flat?' Lola said to Aileen once the kettle had begun to boil and Maddie had come to join them.

'Not "somebody". *Craig.*' Her eyes were such a curious colour. Like dull jade. 'Who else would want to come in but not take anything? He did it for one reason only: to find out where Evie is.'

'Why don't you tell me what happened earlier this evening?' Lola asked.

Aileen relayed how she had been suspicious from the moment she saw her gate standing ajar and that she'd called her aunt when she saw the burglar alarm was off.

'Once we'd given the place a good checking over,' Maddie came in, 'I told Aileen that you and I had spoken about Evie and what had happened to her.'

'And look what's happened!' Aileen snarled.

Maddie turned to Lola with exasperation. 'Would you explain to my niece that this business at the flat is nothing to do with our conversation?'

But something in Lola's expression caught Maddie short.

'I'm afraid there's something you both should know,' Lola said, clenching her fists in her lap.

'What?' Maddie asked, eyes wide.

'My superintendent took advice from the Crown Office on the anonymous scenario I relayed to her. But unfortunately the response went back to the detective who led the original inquiry into the nightclub murders.'

Aileen closed her eyes, like a saint readying herself for more pain. 'Go on.'

'It seems he interviewed Craig this afternoon and put the allegation to him.'

Maddie stared.

'See, I was right!' Aileen cried, then turned furiously to her aunt. 'You broke our confidence and see what's happened.'

Maddie gripped the edge of the table, her eyes darting as she struggled for words. 'But — why would your colleague do that? Didn't he realise how sensitive this was? I trusted you. You told me I could, but you were wrong — or lying.'

'Maddie, please,' Lola said. 'I regret this bitterly. It should not have happened.'

'No, indeed!'

'The detective in question has been under huge professional and personal pressure to find new evidence that could convict Craig,' Lola said.

Maddie closed her eyes, then opened them and turned to her niece. 'Oh, darling, I'm so sorry.'

'Did he tell Craig about the baby?' Aileen asked Lola.

'I'm afraid so.'

'And what did Craig say?' she asked steadily.

Lola hesitated, but decided that the young woman deserved the unvarnished truth. 'He denied it, apparently.'

'I bet.' Aileen lifted her chin and peered down her nose at Lola, all piety gone.

The kettle came to a boil and Maddie got up and went to it.

'I want to put things right if I can,' said Lola, following her.

'It's too late,' Aileen said from the table. 'He knows now, and he won't stop until he's found Evie and Hamish. Hamish is a threat. God knows what he'll do.' She eyeballed Lola. 'But if anything happens to that child it will be your fault.' She turned to her aunt. 'Yours too, Maddie.'

'Darling, don't!' Maddie seemed to sway.

'Put the kettle down,' Lola said sharply. 'Here, on the side.'

Maddie seemed not to realise she was holding it. She blinked several times, then did as Lola instructed.

Lola felt a wave of weariness come over her. She returned to the table and sat, meeting the young woman's contempt head on.

'I'll arrange for officers to go to your flat and check it for fingerprints. They'll advise you on how to secure the place, but I would suggest you stay here or somewhere else until you can have the locks changed.'

Aileen watched her without blinking.

'And then what?' she asked. 'He'll still be free, won't he? But now he'll have a new goal, to get rid of my sister and her little boy.'

'We won't let that happen,' Lola said.

'Won't you?' Aileen raised an eyebrow. 'Is that another of your promises?' She turned sharply to her aunt. 'Did you tell her where Evie is?'

'I said they were on Skye,' Maddie said, wincing.

'And did you pass that on to your colleague?' Aileen asked Lola.

'Yes,' she said simply. 'And I understand it was mentioned to Craig during the interview.'

'*Oh God!*' Maddie cried.

'God can't help,' Aileen said. 'Nobody can. They'll never be safe again, not while Craig's alive.'

Lola considered very carefully how to ask Aileen her next question. 'Is there something in your flat — papers, postcards, anything — that could indicate to someone where Evie is staying?'

'No. I'm very careful.'

'Do you think that's why he broke in?' Maddie asked.

'If it was Craig,' Lola said, 'or someone working for him, then yes, it's possible. Right now, I suggest we go back to your flat, the three of us. I'll ask colleagues to meet us there.'

Aileen nodded silently and got to her feet.

'I'll drive us,' Maddie said to her niece. The sense of shared purpose seemed to warm the atmosphere between them, if only a little. 'Then I'll bring you back afterwards, darling, and you can stay here. Now,' she said, 'give the chief inspector your address and she can meet us there.'

CHAPTER NINETEEN

7.57 a.m.

Lola had got home from Aileen Mackinnon's West End flat just after 4 a.m. She'd arrived at a kind of truce with Maddie Wicks, who'd finally seemed persuaded that Lola's actions had been well intended. Aileen had remained cold with her, though had begun to ask about witness protection should her sister ever agree to testify.

She'd climbed into bed, careful not to wake Sandy, then lain for a miserable couple of hours, unable to sleep as her thoughts raced and her skin became clammy with anticipation of the breakfast meeting with Izatt.

Now, sitting in Elaine's room, waiting for him to arrive, no doubt in a state of great glee, she felt more drained than she ever had in her life.

Elaine was eyeing her with concern. 'What have you got on after this?' she asked.

Lola frowned as she thought about it. 'Progress review meeting with the team and planning next steps in the investigation.'

'I suggest you have that meeting,' Elaine said, 'and once everyone's clear on what they're doing, *go home and go to bed*. Do you hear me?'

Lola nodded her weary assent.

Elaine glanced at the clock on the wall and Lola realised she was nervous herself. 'He'll be here any minute,' Elaine said. 'Leave the talking to me. Understand?'

A minute later, there was a rap at the door and Izatt barged in, hair everywhere and his old grey suit a crumpled mess, but with seething triumph written all over his face.

'Good morning,' Elaine said coolly as he took a seat.

'Same to you,' Izatt said, then turned to Lola, smirking. 'Got that info for me, have you?'

Elaine spoke for her: 'What information would that be?'

'Details for the witness DCI Harris here is concealing.'

'I'm not concealing any witness,' Lola said, earning herself a sharp look from Elaine.

'As good as,' Izatt said. 'Craig knows about her now — should have seen his face.' He chuckled. 'That means we've got to produce her — unless you want to make us look even more stupid than we do already.'

'The young woman in question is a victim of rape,' Elaine said coldly. 'It is her choice whether she wishes us to bring charges against Craig.'

'What happened to her is irrelevant to my inquiry,' Izatt said. 'This girl's the key to convicting a killer. She's morally obligated.'

Lola caught Elaine's eye and looked away, fighting the urge to tell her colleague exactly what she thought of him.

'Give me her name,' he said to Lola now. 'Aidan and I will talk to her. Help her to see that this is no time to be selfish. You won't be involved, so there's nothing for you to be squeamish about.'

'The young woman's family have declined to provide details,' Elaine said, her voice all the more icy. 'It is possible that in time DCI Harris here will gain their trust and be in a position to speak to her herself.'

'What?' Izatt snapped. 'This is nothing to do with *her*!'

'On the contrary,' Elaine snapped back, equalling his vigour, 'DCI Harris was *trusted* to provide advice. Unfortunately,' she went on stiffly, 'information meant for her found its way to you. You then chose to exploit it by providing it to the alleged offender!'

Izatt's top lip curled and Lola felt a twinge of satisfaction.

'I was within my rights as the SIO to put an allegation to the suspect. I—'

Elaine stopped him with a hand. She leaned back in her chair, narrowing her eyes as if to study him properly for the first time.

'You might consider your actions righteous,' she said. 'I am appalled by the lack of sensitivity with which you and your DS misused the information you'd come by — and which, I might add, was unconfirmed.'

'DS Pierce is as frustrated as I am!' Izatt said.

'And hopefully regretting his error,' Elaine said.

Lola took the opportunity of Izatt's brief, stunned silence. 'I want to know exactly what was said at the interview, Graeme. I assume the transcript won't have been prepared yet. Will you send me the link?'

He groaned and rolled his eyes.

'I think DCI Harris has the right, don't you?' Elaine said.

'Fine.' He was fizzing now, teeth bared and his fists clenching and unclenching.

'DCI Harris here will remain in close contact with the young woman's family,' Elaine went on. 'She will endeavour to win their and the young woman's trust. If she can, she will seek a statement from the young woman that *could* then constitute new evidence to dismantle Carter Craig's alibi for the nightclub murders.'

Izatt bridled in his seat, virtually baring his teeth he was so angry.

'Graeme, I ask you in the strongest possible terms,' Elaine went on, 'not to do anything further that might jeopardise the safety of this young woman or her family. If necessary, I'll speak to your boss about this. Now, do I make myself clear?'

* * *

Leaving Elaine's office, Lola felt tiredness wash over her. One meeting to get through, then she could rest. Luckily, it seemed Anna and Kirstie had plenty of tantalising leads to keep her awake with.

'Another juror answered the appeal yesterday late afternoon,' Anna said, once they were installed in the meeting room downstairs. 'He wasn't one of the four who shared messages, but he remembered seeing Kathryn outside the court building as they were leaving one evening, hurrying away in the company of another woman. He remembered it because he tried to say goodnight to her and Kathryn had seemed awkward. She just gave him a half-smile and went off with this woman.'

'Description of the woman?' Lola asked.

'Not great, I'm afraid. She was older than Kathryn. Blonde, he thinks. Says she was well dressed and had a silk scarf round her neck. The scarf might have been orange or pink, he can't be sure. He only saw the woman that once.'

'Does he remember when it was?'

'The first week of the trial, but he isn't sure what day.'

Lola nodded. 'So it could be the same night Susan McKenna saw Kathryn waving to a "friend" in the public gallery?'

'Could be. Of course, it could be entirely innocent. Do you think we should make an appeal for the woman to come forward?'

Lola thought about it. 'Not yet. Let's talk to all of the jurors from the trial. See if anyone else saw Kathryn and the woman. Any luck with the CCTV?'

'Marcus and Jonno are going through the footage from a convenience store in the Saltmarket and from a pub on King Street. It's grainy and not zoomable. Both sources are in colour though.'

'So we might spot a red or pink scarf.'

'Exactly. Or a red BMW.'

'Indeed.'

'Talking of which,' Anna said, 'a witness from a flat on Otago Street claims she saw a red BMW driving down to the side of the block of flats we're interested in — the block where the backyard overhangs the Kelvin.'

'When was this?' Lola asked.

Anna turned to Kirstie.

'The Friday evening, around eight,' Kirstie said, looking pleased.

'IB were looking at one of the ground-floor flats,' Lola said, recalling. 'There'd been a break-in, hadn't there?'

'They haven't uncovered anything, but another neighbour thinks he heard odd noises from the flat on the Saturday. It fits.'

'This is excellent.' She could feel her blood pumping nicely and was tempted to forgo a trip home to bed. 'Who owns the flat?'

'It's rented out by an agency on Great Western Road,' Anna said. 'We can find out who owns it.'

'I'll look into that,' Kirstie said.

'Good. And what about the moonstone necklace, the one from Kathryn's "new friend"?'

'No sign of it at the Falkirk flat where Kathryn Main was hiding out,' Anna said. 'Tara Main has a photo of it on her phone from a message Kathryn sent her. I've got the screenshot printed out.' She went into a folder. 'Here.'

Lola took the sheet of paper, which showed a screenshot from an iPhone in full colour.

The thumbnail photo showed a bluish, opalescent round stone in a silver setting, and part of a delicate silver chain.

Isn't it beautiful? Kathryn had texted.

Wow! And that's a present?? Tara had replied.

I said how much I liked it and she said I could have it! I couldn't believe it.

'I've got the full-size image on record,' Anna said. 'Digital forensics are checking the photo for a geotag but, going by the rest of the text conversation, Kathryn was at home when she took the snap.'

'Worth a try,' Lola murmured.

'It's another thing we could add to the appeal for info,' Anna said.

Lola nodded, and chewed her lip. Appeals relating to hard evidence like this could produce the goods, and quickly, but there was a risk in showing your cards too early. You also risked looking all at sea, firing out appeals on multiple leads, none of which might go anywhere. But this was a concrete item, one they had reason to believe Kathryn had received from the new friend during the early weeks of the trial.

'Let's put it out there,' Lola said. 'Talk to Saskia in Comms. You'll like her. Give her a high-res image and let's see what comes back. Any luck tracing a case that might tell us who Kathryn's "friend" is?'

'We've had a look,' Anna said. 'We haven't spotted anything yet that fits the bill.'

'Okay. Where are you up to with checking Craig's alibi?'

'Hmm. It checks out as far as we can tell. I've spoken to his uncle's PA-cum-housekeeper. She's horribly officious. Seems determined to keep us from the uncle at all costs, though she claims she herself was in the house and can verify Craig's arrival and departure. I've made it clear that we want to speak to the uncle direct and so I'm waiting for "an appointment".'

'I'd like to come,' Lola said. 'Let me know when you get the nod.'

The meeting over, Lola went back upstairs with Kirstie, while Anna headed off to meet Saskia from Corporate Comms.

Graeme Izatt was sitting beside Aidan Pierce at Pierce's desk. Pierce was remonstrating with Izatt quietly. Izatt raised his voice, then quietened again. He turned his head and looked at Lola. Lola got a glimpse of Pierce's face. It was sullen and red. He was unhappy about something. Izatt himself looked less than pleased, but appeared to be making some kind of case to the DS.

Suddenly Pierce got up and stalked away from his desk. Izatt returned to the hot desk he was using and began clattering at his keyboard.

A second later, Lola saw an email from Izatt's account appear in her inbox. The subject header was *Int. recording — G. Izatt, A. Pierce, C. Craig, S. Kitchener (sol.)* and the date.

'Thank you kindly,' Lola called across the office.

Izatt rose from his seat and tucked his loose shirt back into his trousers. He wasn't happy about sharing the recording. She hadn't expected him to be. Clearly Pierce was unhappier still. She looked forward to hearing what exactly had pushed Pierce to lose his temper and tell Craig about the young woman on Skye. But it could wait. Right now, she needed sleep.

She realised Izatt was watching her. She returned his gaze with raised eyebrows, ready for any further nonsense he might throw at her.

He rose and sauntered over.

'The answer's still "no",' she told him, zipping her bag.

'Your new fella,' Izatt said, taking her aback.

'Sorry?'

'It's Sandy Johnson, isn't it?' He was leaning close and smiling unpleasantly, with one hairy eyebrow arched. 'Ex-police? Went off to work for his brother? Lives out East Kilbride way?'

A chill went through her as if she was turning quietly to stone.

'What about him?' she said, hating that her voice sounded tight.

'Just wanted to double-check,' Izatt said quietly.

Then he smiled. Pierce was coming back from the kitchen, a mug in hand. He glowered at Lola.

'Goodbye, Graeme,' she said, and made quickly for the door.

CHAPTER TWENTY

4.17 p.m.

Lola came back to work feeling relatively fresh after three hours' sleep. She took her laptop to a meeting room and settled down, teeth gritted, to listen to Izatt and Pierce's recorded interview with Carter Craig.

Proceedings got underway, with Izatt talking at length. No surprises there. In time, he explained that they wanted to ask questions about the death of Mack McBurney and asked Craig what contact he'd had with the drug dealer. Craig answered softly, pleasantly enough, denying everything. The solicitor, Stephen Kitchener — the one Lola had met at Craig's gym — came in at points.

Izatt asked about timings, pushing Craig and becoming angry, while Craig remained impressively calm. Pierce stepped in, pointing out a small contradiction in Craig's answers about his whereabouts, earning himself a sharp retort from Craig: a crack in the friendly veneer that Izatt was quick to pounce on.

The questions trailed off and the solicitor suggested, very mildly, that he couldn't see where the interview was going. He asked for it to be terminated.

IZATT: *Not so fast.*

KITCHENER: *Oh?*

IZATT: *The August alibi from three years ago. Still reckon it's watertight, Craig?*

KITCHENER: *Mr Izatt—*

IZATT: *Well, Craig? Do you?*

CRAIG: *That's a settled account. You know it is.*

IZATT: *Is that right?*

CRAIG: *Especially now McBurney's dead, wouldn't you say?*

KITCHENER: *Mr Izatt, if you have new information, then kindly present it to us, otherwise—*

IZATT: *More than new information, sir. New evidence.*

KITCHENER: *'New evidence'? Kindly explain.*

IZATT: *You were in Glasgow the night of the nightclub murders, weren't you, Craig? You were with a certain young lady.*

Silence.

IZATT: *What's wrong, Craig? Remembered something, have you?*

CRAIG: *Don't know what you're talking about.*

A muttering on the recording. It was indistinct, but it sounded like Pierce.

CRAIG: *What did you say to me?*

PIERCE: *I said, she's about to make a statement that you raped her that night.*

A pause, then Craig began to speak, before Kitchener shut him up.

KITCHENER: *Mr Izatt, this is news to us.*

CRAIG: *Look at the state of you, Aidey. Think what you could have been.*

Izatt cleared his throat and began to speak, but then shut up, as if in response to some gesture from Pierce. Lola's skin prickled. This was it: the crunch point Elaine had referenced.

CRAIG: *Damaged your confidence, didn't it, what old Leo did to you?*

IZATT: *Leo? Who's Leo?*

There was a commotion, the sound of chair legs scraping.

PIERCE: *Shut it, Craig. Remember where you are.*

KITCHENER: *Really! I must protest at the—*

CRAIG: *Humiliating, wasn't it, Aidey?*

IZATT: *What's he talking about, Aiden?*

PIERCE: *You're the one being interviewed, Craig, not me.*

CRAIG: *Has Aidan not told you about what happened to him at school, Graeme? The shame was real, wasn't it, Aidey? The burning shame of it.*

Lola winced.

PIERCE: *Shut your mouth, Craig.*

IZATT: *Aidan, sit down!*

Craig spoke more quietly now, a relentless soft mocking.

CRAIG: *All because he was so sad about his mummy dying. Tragic story, Graeme. He went and talked to creepy Mr Breedlove. And, oh, how 'Old Breeder' wanted to comfort little Aidey!*

As much as Lola disliked Pierce, Craig's taunting was horrible to hear.

PIERCE: *Fuck you, Craig.*

CRAIG: *Leo Stewart got the photo, didn't he, Aidan? Of Breeder's hand on your leg. And you were smiling, like you were enjoying it. Remember?*

PIERCE: *That's bullshit, Craig.*

He sounded shrill with panic.

CRAIG: *Oh, I don't think it is.*

PIERCE: *[Indistinct]*

CRAIG: *Sorry, Aidey. What was that?*

A roar of rage from Pierce. A clatter of chairs, then more than one raised voice.

PIERCE: *You're going back to jail, Craig!*

Kitchener intervened, then Izatt was speaking quietly and urgently, possibly to Pierce. Lola couldn't make out his words.

PIERCE: *The girl you raped — guess what? She got pregnant and she had the kid. Your kid. Pair of them are living up in Skye. The kid's DNA will prove it's yours. That and the scans will show you were in Glasgow that night.*

Silence, then:

CRAIG: *You're talking shit.*

KITCHENER: *The tone of this interview is most irregular.*

The solicitor sounded shaken. Silence for a few seconds, then it was broken by a triumphant Izatt.

IZATT: *You remember, don't you, Craig? You remember the girl. You know who DS Pierce is talking about. I can see it in your face! Dear oh dear. Bit of a nasty shock, eh?*

KITCHENER: *Who is this girl? What are you talking about?*

IZATT: *What's the matter, Craig — cat got your tongue?*

Lola couldn't listen to any more and stopped the recording. Her stomach churned. Pierce's recklessness was bad enough. But it felt wrong — prurient — to have heard his humiliation at Craig's hands. This was Izatt's fault and her anger at him was only intensified: she'd warned him Pierce and Craig had been at school together, but he'd been so blasé.

Had Pierce been so keen to work with Izatt as a way to get back at someone who'd tormented him at school? If so, why hadn't he been ready for Craig's verbal attack?

No wonder Pierce had seemed angry when Izatt sent Lola the recording. He'd be stewing now, waiting for her reaction once she heard it. Possibly expecting her to use his error against him, or even to make reference to his humiliation at school. But she would never do that. She groaned as she realised she would have to find a way to reassure him of the fact. As if things weren't complicated enough already.

Her phone buzzed: it was Anna, checking if they were still meeting. She glanced at the clock and realised she'd lost track of time. She put her laptop away and headed upstairs.

* * *

'The big news is,' Anna said, 'after much battle with the house-keeper, I've got us an appointment with Craig's uncle, Duncan Gaunt, tomorrow morning at ten fifteen.'

'Trying to intimidate us with the quarter-hour, is he?'

Anna stared, clearly missing the reference.

'*The Prime of Miss Jean Brodie*,' Lola said. 'Scottish classic.'

'Noted, boss. The address is Clunie Castle,' Anna said. 'It's in Perthshire. A ninety-minute drive, according to Google.'

'That's fine.'

'Oh, and I'm seeing Craig's girlfriend, or, to be more accurate, the woman he happened to be with on Sunday night. She was in London till today, so I've only spoken to her on the phone. I'm seeing her at her flat by the river at six thirty. I don't reckon I'll get much from her but, based on the phone call, I'd say it might be entertaining.' She eyed Lola. 'Don't suppose you fancy coming?'

'Aye, why not?' Lola said drily.

'Something interesting on the missing necklace,' Anna said now, 'from one of Kathryn's colleagues at the bank. She describes Kathryn "showing it off" in the canteen one day, in a way she'd never seen her behave before. Blushing and giggling the whole time — "almost as if she was in love".'

'Blimey.'

'Kathryn told the colleague the name of the friend who'd given it to her. She can't remember exactly, but thinks it could have been Liz or Lucy — that it started with an L. She said Kathryn let the name slip, then seemed embarrassed and withdrew into herself.'

Lola stared, brain scanning her recent memories. She leaned forward and tapped at her laptop for Wikipedia's entry on Carter Craig.

And yes, there it was.

'Craig's mother is Elizabeth McQueen, born Elizabeth Fraser,' Lola said. She and Anna watched one another. 'That's interesting, isn't it?'

'I'll find her, boss.'

Lola's phone was ringing. It was DC Kirstie Campbell.

'I thought you should know,' Kirstie began, sounding uncomfortable, 'but Carter Craig's making a live broadcast on his website. You might want to tune in and watch from the beginning. Only . . . he's mentioned your name.'

Kirstie emailed a link to the site and Lola clicked on it gingerly, turning her laptop screen so Anna could watch too.

Craig appeared onscreen in a gymnasium, possibly the one she'd visited beside the park, crouching in expensive fitness gear, talking down into a camera that was propped on the floor. The broadcast appeared to be coming to an end, with a call for his fans to be 'good to one another' and a heartfelt promise that he was 'there for each and every one of you', just the way his fans were for him.

His demeanour was one of good-humoured exasperation, that told viewers that he was the good guy and spoke from the heart. 'Peace out,' he said and made the V sign.

'Scroll back to the start,' Anna said and Lola dragged the bar.

'Hey, everyone,' Craig began, waving and beaming for the camera. 'How's it going? Sweet, I hope. Stuff going down here. The usual shit, and I'm looking for your good vibes. Oh man, it's hard being me sometimes!' A winning chuckle that turned Lola's stomach.

'I've been out of the big house a week and the feds have had me in already. Oh, I was lawyered up, no fear, but they're trying to lay *two murders* on me. I mean, *what the fuck*?'

'You think his lawyers advised him to say all this?' Anna murmured.

'God knows. I reckon PR opportunities supersede legal advice these days.'

'My old friend Mr Izatt — remember him? — had me in over the death of someone called Martin McBurney, a purveyor of one of Scotland's finest lines in cocaine — "lines", geddit? He was the poor sod they dragged into court to give spurious evidence against yours truly. So a druggie got the sharp end of someone's frustration. Well, guess what?' He leaned down, leering into the camera. 'I've got a solid alibi. Which, no doubt, Mr Izatt is currently trying his best to dismantle. He's also trying to pin another death on me . . .'

Lola steeled herself.

'Remember the poor bitch who did her best to get me put away for life — Kathryn Main? And remember how badly that turned out for her? Well, they fished her out of the River Kelvin earlier this week. So, of course, who's suspect number one all over again? And Mr Izatt has a few more questions for me, along with a colleague of his. DCI Harris, first name Lola. I know — sounds like a fucking poodle!'

Lola gasped and exchanged outraged stares with Anna.

'Now answer me this: why would *I* go after the woman who got me off my conviction and released from jail?' He paused and sat back on his haunches, frowning and looking down and to one side, as if in deep thought. 'Isn't it almost as though someone's *setting me up*? Going after folk who've apparently "wronged" me to fit me up. Question is, who would do that? Try putting that point to the feds, though, and you get blank stares.'

A couple more minutes of mock humility and self-justification and they reached the end of the broadcast.

Lola closed her laptop. 'Well, isn't that delightful? What did he say, "a name like a poodle"?' In spite of herself, at the sight of Anna's mortified expression she started to giggle. 'What was the purpose of that whole broadcast?'

'To bait his fans, I imagine.'

'To what end? Does he want his followers to come after me and Graeme?'

'I guess he's done it before. He's named DCI Izatt in the past, hasn't he?'

'I think he has.'

'I seem to remember Graeme getting a load of abuse outside the High Court one time. I'll ask him if anything else transpired.'

The idea of being targeted by Craig's supporters made her skin prickle.

'Maybe you should take advice, boss.'

'I'll talk to Elaine.'

Anna was frowning now, as if she was wrestling with some new idea.

'What you thinking?' Lola demanded.

'I was just wondering — I know Craig's vile, but what if he's *right*? What if someone is trying to fit him up?'

'D'you think?'

'It's possible, isn't it?'

'Anything's possible.' Lola frowned as something interesting occurred to her. 'That was a live broadcast, wasn't it?'

'I think so. Why, boss?'

'Just thinking something through.'

Craig had talked in his broadcast about the police's allegations that he was behind the murders of Kathryn Main and Mack McBurney, but he'd neither mentioned nor dismissed the new evidence he and his lawyer learned about today. Why not?

Because he knew it was true and didn't want to raise the topic?

In which case, the broadcast was pure deflection. It meant Craig was really rattled.

* * *

5.47 p.m.

Lola swallowed her revulsion and phoned Graeme Izatt to ask if he'd seen Craig's broadcast.

'Yeah,' he said, sounding determinedly blasé. 'Ignore him. There was no specific threat. He's done it to me millions of times. He's a prick.'

'Did you report it up the way, or . . .'

'What's the point? Just be sensible. He doesn't scare me.'

She sighed, unhappy.

'There is a way to stop him, Lola,' Izatt said now, sounding snide. 'I've told you to give me that information.'

'No, Graeme,' Lola said. 'Not after what happened in that interview. I've got to protect that young woman's interests. I've listened to the recording, by the way. Not your finest hour — nor Aidan's.'

'Now, the lad's upset, Lola, so—'

'Aye, well, I can understand that.' She sighed. 'Look, Graeme. What he did was wrong, but I'm not going to pursue it. I didn't know he'd lost his mum so young.'

'He's not a bad lad, Lola.'

'I have to go,' she said, unwilling to get into it. And she cut the call.

Her sister Frankie had tried to call while she was on to Izatt. Lola rang her back.

'Is he for real?' Frankie half yelled down the phone. 'Who the fuck does he think he is?'

'He's Carter Craig and the world's his oyster,' she replied cynically.

'That's scary stuff, Lola. His fans are everywhere.'

'How did you hear about it?'

'Neighbour's son worships him. He'd seen it. Told his sister, who told his mum. The mum, Sandra, came over just now. She knows who you are and what you do for a living. I can't believe you're sounding so calm about it.'

'It happens,' Lola said, then added, quoting Izatt, '*There was no specific threat!*'

'Will you stay at Sandy's for a bit? You can come here, you're more than welcome.'

'I'll be perfectly fine,' she said. 'Now, I've got to go. I'm busy.'

Next it was Sandy phoning her, and she went through a similar routine with him. Except Sandy was battle-hardened and more sanguine than Frankie, telling her to keep her chin up.

'I'll see you later,' she said, feeling shivery as she said it. She still hadn't decided whether to tell him that Izatt had asked if she and Sandy were together: the way he'd insinuated he knew . . . something. The thought of it made her feel sick.

CHAPTER TWENTY-ONE

6.32 p.m.

'Oh, hiya,' sing-songed the young woman who opened the door to Lola and Anna in a high-pitched Liverpool accent. She hung off the doorframe and inspected them, literally, from head to toe — finding their outfits depressing or disappointing or both, judging from the look in her heavy-lashed eyes. 'You'd better come in.'

She let go of the doorframe and slinked majestically away from them, towering in her six-inch pink stilettoes, her long, curling ash-blonde hair shimmering as she went. She was wearing pink hot pants, a slinky silver top and a lot of jewellery: rings, earrings, bracelets, a necklace. Her arms, legs and even her tanned, exposed belly were tattooed, mostly with what looked like some kind of Indian script. How old was she? Late twenties? It was hard to tell.

This was Lorelei West, one of Craig's many girlfriends and the one who'd been with him the Sunday night and Monday morning when Kathryn Main had been strangled and put into the river.

The flat was a duplex penthouse, at the top of the tallest new block at Glasgow Harbour, and open-plan, with windows on all sides and everything gleaming white: kitchen units, leather settee, rugs. Lola wondered what Maddie Wicks might make of this design — this neutral, negative space.

Lorelei led them into her kitchen area and posed beautifully by a breakfast bar on which nothing stood. Lola looked about. There was no microwave, no cookbooks, no utensils. Just gleaming white floor-to-ceiling cupboards. She wondered which cupboard hid the fridge, and whether there was anything in it all, apart from still, cold air.

Lola had assumed they'd been brought into the kitchen so there could be an offer of coffee or water. No offer was forthcoming and Lola realised they'd been brought here so they could be impressed.

'This is lovely,' she said.

''S'not mine, you know? Me dad bought it. He owns used car garages, an' that. He and me mam've got places all over. It's dead handy, but not if you need dinner bringing in. They can never find the place and then security's dead tight, so you end up having to trek down in the lift. It's a right pain.'

'I can imagine,' Lola said, nodding with as much sympathy as she could muster.

'What do you for a living?' Anna asked.

'I model stuff. But I'm getting old — I'm going to be thirty in a few years — so I might retire.' She paused and turned. 'I quite fancy being an actress, or maybe a detective. I like all that — *CSI*, *Silent Witness*. But I'm not sure I'd fit in.' She eyed their outfits with renewed disdain and sighed. 'What you here for anyway?'

'It was me who called,' Anna said. 'I said I wanted to meet you face to face so we can talk about your Sunday evening through to Monday morning.'

'Carter said you'd want to check alibis,' the woman said cheerfully. 'You think he topped some woman, don't you? He

111

didn't though. He was with me. I'm his alibi, he says.' She smiled happily to herself and played with a curl of hair. ''S'quite exciting, really.'

'Not if you're the dead woman's grieving family,' Lola said stonily.

Lorelei let go of her hair and looked miffed. 'He said you'd be horrible to me. Said you'd try to bully me. He was gonna send one of his lawyers round, but I can't stand lawyers. The way they look at you, like you're dead thick.'

'Could we sit down?' Anna asked politely.

'Yeah, go for it. There's the settees—' she pointed to a square of very low, white leather couches — 'or we could go up to the mezzanine. There's a kind of table thing.'

They elected for the 'table thing', and followed Lorelei as she tottered her way up a flight of floating glass stairs that gave Lola the heebie-jeebies. All around them, through the acres of glass, was Glasgow, giving views north-east towards the spike of the university tower, to the south to Ibrox and the stadium. Close by was the sluggish brown river and, at the other side, the shipyards of Govan. Lola had grown up less than half a mile from this glass box, in a poky tenement. There hadn't been much money, but there had been love, and arguing, and colour and warmth.

Lorelei led them to a long glass table, with ten glass chairs pulled up to it. Lola hauled one out, surprised at its weight.

'So, what d'you wanna know?' the woman asked when they were all sitting. She posed even in her seat.

Anna asked her questions.

'Yeah, I was already at the restaurant when Carter arrived from the airport,' Lorelei said. 'You're gonna ask me its name, aren't you? Well, I don't know it, but it had tablecloths. The food was all right, but I didn't eat much . . . What time did we leave? I couldn't tell you. Honest. I was drinking and thinking I'd like to get to me bed, really, but Carter had organised this thing in town, at one of his clubs . . . No, I don't know the name of it. There was a rapper, from New York. He wasn't very nice. Had his hands all over me. And then we left, and it was really late. Don't ask me when . . . Yeah, we went to his uncle's castle. I like it there. It's really nice, but . . . a bit old-fashioned. The shower's not great and I don't like his uncle or that woman. Give me the creeps, the pair of them.'

'What woman?' Lola asked.

'Don't ask me her name.'

Lola returned Anna's dry glance.

Anna asked for names or descriptions of people Lorelei remembered from the restaurant and the club, and from the castle, when they'd arrived and when they left the next morning.

She gave what answers she appeared capable of, long lashes fluttering.

'How often do you see Carter Craig?' Lola asked.

'Oh, not often. He's not really my boyfriend, like I said to you on the phone.'

Anna nodded.

'But he likes me and we're good together. I think he's a bit of a shit, really. But he's so rich! And so many people are scared of him. I like that. Big man there to protect me.'

Lola couldn't stand much more and signalled to Anna to give it up.

'He said I should show you these photos,' Lorelei said in a new, more urgent tone.

'Oh?' Lola said.

'Here,' the woman said, holding out her phone.

'What are we looking at?' Anna said, taking the phone and scrolling steadily through what looked to Lola to be a series of heavily filtered selfies of Lorelei and Carter Craig.

'One taken at least each hour all through that evening and into the early hours of the morning,' Lorelei said quietly and coolly — a very different woman from the airhead she'd appeared to be so far. 'Each one will be timestamped and geotagged too. They show exactly where Carter was, and when, all that night.'

'Don't delete these,' Anna said, handing the phone back. 'We may need them. But I'm sure you're aware of that already.'

The woman smiled.

'I might go for a sleep,' she said at the door. 'All these questions. You've really worn me out.'

* * *

6.57 p.m.

'I might go for a sleep too,' Lola groaned as they crossed the car park.

She checked her phone. Elaine Walsh had tried to call her. Lola rang her back.

'About Craig's broadcast,' Elaine said, 'the advice from Comms is to do nothing. If you get cornered, you've nothing to say. You don't roll your eyes, you stay calm and in a good humour.'

'Got it, boss.'

'Apart from that, how are you feeling? I know how horrible this must be.'

'I'm okay. I'm getting on with things.'

She had a sudden urge to confide in Elaine about Izatt's insinuation about Sandy. To ask if the superintendent had heard anything herself. And if she hadn't, then at least to receive a kind word.

'Well, you know where I am. And Lola, one hint of trouble, one unfamiliar car outside your house — media or otherwise — you call it in. Craig's a game player but his followers love him. It just takes one to go a step too far.'

'Thanks, boss. Have a good evening.'

CHAPTER TWENTY-TWO

7.22 p.m.

Lola found Sandy stretched out on the settee, feet up, watching TV, his flat, lightly haired midriff showing.

'Everything all right?' he said, twisting and sitting up.

'Aye, I think so,' she said, dropping her bag by the armchair.

He rose to embrace her and she had to deliberately relax in his arms, so great was the tension in her body.

She felt as if adrenaline was pumping through her veins, with nowhere to go. She still felt guilty about the fact Craig had found out about Evie and her son. This was mixed with anger at Izatt and his snide reference to Sandy. And under it all was the fact Carter Craig had named her publicly. She wasn't scared, but it was unsettling all the same.

Kev had heard about it — Joe too, according to the barrage of anxious texts.

I'm fine, Kev, she'd texted back, sitting parked in her drive a couple of minutes ago. *These things happen. Tell Joe not to worry.*

If you're sure, Kev had replied, quick as a flash. *He still cares for you, Lola.*

Which she *really* didn't need to know.

Sandy studied her closely and frowned. 'You don't look all right. Is it Craig's threats? Has something happened?'

'Oh, that!' she joked. 'Och, that's water off a duck, that is.'

He pulled her into a hug.

'What does Izatt say about it?' he asked.

'Oh, he doesn't give a stuff.' But mention of Izatt's name had reminded her again. She should tell Sandy, she knew she should. But she couldn't face it. What if she told him and he lied and she saw through it? She pulled out of the embrace.

'I need a shower,' she said, to hide her discomfort.

'Fine,' he said, frowning. 'Then we'll need to talk about dinner. Do you want to go out, or . . . ?'

'I don't mind,' she said.

He studied her face. 'There's something else, isn't there? What is it?'

She eyed him, her heart racing and her fingers prickling. *Oh God . . .*

'It's Izatt,' she said.

'What about him?'

'You knew him, didn't you?'

'In passing,' Sandy said, 'and a long time ago. Why?'

'He asked about you, that's all.'

'Did he?' Sandy pushed out his bottom lip and shrugged. 'That's . . . nice.'

'He wasn't being nice. Graeme's never nice.'

'Oh?' He studied her closer still.

'I'm probably being silly.'

Lola turned and went into the kitchen. He came after her.

She poured a glass of water and took a drink, then leaned against the counter. Sandy mirrored her, leaning against the table, his expression open, wanting to help.

Don't go there, Lola.

Too late.

'I pissed him off. Actually, *he* pissed *me* off, then Elaine tore him a new one. Anyway, Graeme had a go at me afterwards.'

'So?'

'He said — exact words, or near enough — "Is your new fella Sandy Johnson?"'

About to speak, Sandy caught himself and stared. 'And how is that any of his business?'

'It isn't. I said as much. But — oh God, Sand. I wasn't going to say anything. You see, it was the way he said it.'

'"The way he said it"?'

'Aye. Like he was implying something.'

Sandy watched her, looking mystified. Her face was burning now and she couldn't look at him.

'Did you ask him what he meant?'

'Sort of. To tell you the truth, I was so shocked, I just clammed up.'

She looked at him and winced at his pained expression, but it was too late to stop now.

'*Is* there something?' she pleaded, feeling emotion swell dangerously in her chest. 'Something from the past? I'm not bothered about your past — really, I'm not! But the idea of Graeme and Aidan *knowing* something they think they can hold against me. Against us. It's horrible. It's . . . Oh—'

The sob burst from her, making her hate herself. She clamped a hand over her mouth and turned from him.

'Come here!' he cried, taking her gently by the shoulders and turning her, then folding her in his arms, pulling her face into his T-shirt. She let him hold her. 'This is no good,' he said. 'No good at all. Look, there's nothing from my past. Nothing I can think of, anyway. And Graeme Izatt can go fuck himself. You know what he's like. He's all ambition and resentment. I've a mind to go see him.'

'No! Please don't do that.'

'But I hate seeing you like this, Lola. I *hate* it.'

She was calmer and wanted air. She pushed herself free, swiping at her cheeks with the back of her hand. 'I'm sorry,' she said. 'I'm still tired from being out all night.'

Sandy was calmer now too, his shoulders lower, the curl of anger gone from his upper lip.

'I feel like a mess,' Lola said.

117

'Have your shower,' he said. 'Then come down and we'll walk up to Pollokshaws Road. That Italian's nice. Maybe we can sit outside.'

'Okay,' she said, feeling a little better. 'Okay, let's do that.'

CHAPTER TWENTY-THREE

Friday 16 August

9.52 a.m.

The parcel had arrived at Portree Delivery Office that morning. Wendy Slater, who was doing the sorting, read the name and address — or what there was of it — with mild irritation. Then she turned it over and saw through the transparent wrapping what was inside.

'Aw, look at that,' she murmured to Sally Menzies, who was just back from her break.

'What is it?' Sally asked, uninterested.

'A kiddie's outfit. Looks nicely made. Looks like tweed, in fact! No address, though. Just a name. But look at the message on the back.'

'Let me see.'

'There: *Dear Postie. Please help this get to my darling niece. Silly me, I've lost the address. Thank you! Auntie C.*'

Wendy turned the parcel over and showed the address to Sally. '*Evie Mackinnon, care of Portree Delivery Office, Portree, Isle of Skye, IV51.* Any ideas?'

'There's plenty of Mackinnons here,' Sally said.

'I know. Could have been worse, I suppose. Could have been a Macleod. Oh, Angus!' she shouted to her colleague, who'd just come in from his smoke. 'The name Evie Mackinnon ring any bells?'

Angus Budge put his head back and frowned at the ceiling. 'No other clues?' he asked.

'She's got a young kiddie, so she's probably young too. There's a Frank Mackinnon over at Colbost, isn't there? He's got a daughter in her twenties.'

'Not her,' grunted Angus. 'She's Catriona and she's only in her teens. No kids either.'

'Well, who then?'

'What about Donny and Jessie?' Sally said, with sudden inspiration. 'Up above Glendale?'

'Don't know 'em,' Wendy said.

'Donny Mackinnon,' Angus said. 'He's got a girl living with him. His niece or whatnot. Her name's not Evie, though. It's Daisy or Denise or something. But, aye, she's got a boy. Can't be three yet!'

'Might be her,' Sally said to Wendy.

'That's Tom Clark's round,' Angus said. 'Ask him to drop by with it.'

'Good thinking.'

'That's teamwork for you,' Wendy said, looking at the clock. 'Took us no more than two minutes to crack that little mystery. Who needs Hercule Poirot?'

And the three of them laughed.

CHAPTER TWENTY-FOUR

10.08 a.m.

'Holy moly, it's like a mini Glamis!' Lola said, as the car emerged from the trees into the open parkland leading up to Clunie Castle.

The castle was a Hogwartsian baronial fantasy, painted pale pink, with multiple wings, steep roofs, circular towers and hundreds of tiny windows. A central clocktower was topped with crenellations and a flagpole. To one side of the castle, and presumably extending behind it, were numerous outbuildings: stables and storehouses.

'I don't know Glamis, so I can't judge,' Anna said.

'You've never lived,' Lola said. 'It's chock full of ghosts. Nice tea room, by all accounts.'

This was no visitor attraction, though. It was the home, or 'country seat' as his Wikipedia entry called it, of Duncan Gaunt, millionaire property magnate, owner of three newspapers and uncle of Carter Craig. It was here that Craig had learned to shoot and fish, and to inflict his personality on those he considered lesser than himself.

Lola wondered what his mother had made of Gaunt's influence on her son, and what her son had grown into. Thanks to Anna, they had an appointment to speak to Ms McQueen when they got back from Perthshire. Anna had spoken to the woman on the phone and said she'd sounded frank and open, volunteering that she wasn't proud of some of her son's behaviour. Normally Lola would have let Anna make the visit with one of the constables, but she was intrigued — especially by the possibility that she and Kathryn Main's friend could be one and the same person . . .

'The castle doesn't really fit the Carter Craig image, does it?' Anna said. 'Where's the bling?'

'Inside, I expect.'

'Are the family aristocrats?' Anna asked.

'Hardly. Duncan Gaunt made his money from newspapers — one of which he inherited from his own father, along with a few million to get him started.'

Anna parked in front of the castle, in the shadow of one of its looming wings, and they got out.

'*Not* there!' a high stentorian voice barked from above them.

A stern-looking thin woman with dark, greying hair tied in a bun was glowering down on them from the top of a flight of stone steps. She had on a black skirt and cardigan. Pearls gleamed against the black.

'Round the side, by the stable block,' she cried, 'as per my instructions, *please!*'

Lola and Anna exchanged glances.

'Better do as you're told,' Lola said quietly, 'unless you fancy being turned to stone.' To the woman, now descending the steps, she called, 'Ms Rossiter, is it?'

'*Miss* Rossiter,' the woman said, reaching the ground then stopping and peering properly at Lola. 'You're Miss Vaughan, are you?'

'*DI* Vaughan is moving the car,' Lola said nicely. 'I am Detective Chief Inspector Harris.'

Miss Rossiter wrinkled her nose in disgust. She had a sharp, narrow face and cross little eyes. She reminded Lola uncomfortably of a nun who'd terrorised her at school in her early teens. Perhaps it was the barely contained rage or the way she pressed her lips together.

Lola made reference to the beautiful view of the woods and the hills beyond, but Miss Rossiter was clearly not one for pleasantries. She huffed and puffed as they waited for Anna.

When Anna finally appeared, the woman tutted and said, 'This way.'

Anna raised her eyebrows and Lola had to crush a childish urge to giggle.

They traipsed up the steps after the housekeeper, then followed her through the doorway. She opened a second door, this of glass, and led them into a vast and impossibly high-ceilinged stone-flagged hallway. Lola craned her neck to look at the skylight. On two sides were gaping fireplaces, and before them a tartan-carpeted staircase leading up before splitting in two and rising to landings at either side.

A curvaceous young woman in a flame-red trouser suit was descending the stairs. She had clearly taken a lot of time over her appearance. Her chestnut hair was glossy and she wore full make-up. She stopped when she saw the guests, and peered down with some curiosity.

'For Duncan, Irene?' she called down, her voice echoing.

'Yes,' Miss Rossiter replied stiffly, a displeased Mother Superior.

The young woman nodded, then seemed to lose interest and continued to descend, her chin up and wearing a small, self-satisfied smile, not giving Lola or Anna another glance.

Miss Rossiter turned to Lola, who was watching after the young woman. 'Mr Gaunt is in the library,' she said. 'Let's not keep him waiting.'

Yes, Sister.

'Who was that on the stairs?' Lola asked Irene Rossiter as they made their way down a dark corridor.

Miss Rossiter stopped and turned, as if offended at Lola's temerity in asking the question.

'That was Mrs Gaunt,' she said.

'Mrs . . . ?'

'Juliana, his third wife.' She turned and walked on.

Lola raised her eyebrows at Anna, and Anna shrugged. Gaunt was over seventy. Juliana couldn't have been thirty-five.

At last they'd reached a high, oak-panelled door that stood ajar. The housekeeper pushed it open, announcing at the top of her voice, 'Mr Gaunt, your visitors!'

The library appeared at first to be empty. It was octagonal, and every wall was shelved. Arched windows sat high above the shelves and a tented ceiling rose to a point, its eight segments painted blue and dotted with gold stars. Gold lines linked some of the stars to depict constellations.

'Thank you, Irene,' a gruff male voice said, just behind Lola's left shoulder.

The housekeeper withdrew.

Lola turned to find a little man studying her. His dark eyes and hooked nose gave his freckled and pinched face a hawkish appearance. A mane of white hair, combed tightly back from his forehead, skimmed the collar of a baggy tweed jacket. Lola wondered if he had lost weight quite suddenly, as his red corduroy trousers also seemed too big for his small frame.

'Mr Gaunt,' Lola said, 'I'm DCI Lola Harris.' She extended a hand — which Gaunt ignored.

'Over here,' the man said, and shuffled past Lola and Anna. He turned once, twisting to check they were following, then threw out an arm towards a low gold-brocade settee that looked like something Marie Antoinette might have graced. 'You sit there,' he instructed.

They sat, and Gaunt lowered himself painfully into a wide armchair in the same overblown style. They were separated by some distance, a shining malachite coffee table filling the space between them.

'My time is limited,' he said, picking at the knees of his trousers as he made himself comfortable. 'So you will kindly tell me what you want to know. I shall then decide whether to provide answers.'

They'd already agreed Lola should lead while Anna would take notes, so it was Lola who explained to Duncan Gaunt that his nephew had been interviewed in relation to the death of Kathryn Main and that his solicitors had provided a detailed alibi. 'We're here to check whether Mr Craig had indeed spent part of the night here at Clunie Castle with his girlfriend.'

'He was here,' Gaunt said.

'He says he got here at three a.m.,' Lola said. 'Did you see him when he arrived?'

'No, our rooms are at the other side of the castle, over-looking the lake. But Irene saw them. She knew Carter was due and had set an alarm to meet them. Irene is very capable about these things — and so she should be, she's been here long enough. A visitor should be welcomed, whatever time of night he chooses to arrive.'

'And your wife, Juliana?' Lola said. 'Might she have seen the visitors arriving?'

'I have no idea. I haven't asked her. You can if you want to.'

He sat up suddenly and she saw he had a small black device in his hand, which he lifted to his mouth and whispered into. It was a walkie-talkie, Lola realised. A crackling reply followed and he dropped the device back into his jacket's inner pocket.

'Juliana will join us shortly.'

'Thank you,' Lola said. 'Now, the information we received from your nephew suggested that security staff here would have kept records of comings and goings as well. Would you say that was possible?'

'Yes,' Gaunt said. 'There are cameras on the gate. Carter said you'd be asking, so I've instructed our head of security to provide the footage. His office is in the mews beyond the south wing. Irene will take you to meet him.'

Lola glanced at Anna, who seemed surprised too at how helpful the man was being — or appeared to be.

'We'd also like to talk to the chauffeur who drove your nephew here from Glasgow in the early hours of last Monday morning.'

'That's Jack Courtney. He'll be here somewhere,' Gaunt said. 'He has a flat in the mews and uses the security office for his base when he's not driving.'

There was a brief rap at the door. It opened and Juliana, the curvaceous third Mrs Gaunt, came in, beaming away in her scarlet trouser suit.

'Hello, Mrs Gaunt,' Lola said, rising.

'No need to get up,' Juliana said. Lola got up anyway and crossed the floor to shake the woman's hand.

Juliana Gaunt allowed her hand to be taken, smiling and tilting her head so that her shiny chestnut hair bobbed and caught the daylight from the high windows.

'Sit here, sweetness,' the old man said, making very little room so that Juliana had to squeeze in beside him.

She draped her limbs over Gaunt's frame, like an octopus latching onto a treasure chest. She gazed down on his white head possessively, then turned her sparkling gaze on Lola and Anna.

'Mrs Gaunt,' Lola said, 'were you here overnight from last Sunday evening through to Monday morning?'

'She was,' Gaunt answered for her. Then, looking up into her beautiful vital face, he said, 'Tell them you heard nothing. You didn't, did you, chicken?'

She smiled broadly, revealing impossibly white teeth, then looked lovingly down into her husband's eyes. 'Not a thing, my love.'

'Is that so?' Lola checked.

'Quite so,' the woman said.

Lola gave Anna a wry look. 'I think that's us, don't you?'

Anna raised an eyebrow.

'Thank you for your time, both of you,' Lola said, rising.

The old man cleared his throat. 'You won't get him, you know,' he said, and his thin lips curled into a chilly smile as he eased himself up. The woman's possessive arms remained draped grotesquely round his skinny frame. 'You can't. He's free now and will remain so.'

Lola considered how to reply. 'This is merely a routine inquiry, Mr Gaunt.'

'Carter will continue to flourish,' Gaunt went on, ignoring her, while Juliana beamed away with flashing eyes.

Lola felt a prickle of unease across her shoulders but managed to suppress an actual shudder. She felt Anna stiffen beside her.

'In time he will take over my business interests. My media empire too. And he won't be touched. Not by you or anyone.' He was up now, one hand clutching the small of his back as if he was in pain. 'You may speak to Irene and to anyone else whose time you wish to waste. And then,' he added crisply, 'you will leave.'

* * *

10.42 a.m.

Irene Rossiter met them with a look of renewed distaste and led them to a tiny office tucked away near the main entrance hallway. It was chilly in there, to match the housekeeper's personality. A laptop computer sat open on a wide partner's desk. Miss Rossiter snapped it shut and sat, while Lola and Anna remained standing.

'What do you wish to know?' she enquired.

Lola explained.

'Yes, Carter was here,' the woman said. 'He arrived just after three a.m., with his friend. A young blonde woman. They come and go.'

'And you showed them to a room.'

'I didn't need to. Carter has a wing. I took fresh towels, that's all. Then I left them. I saw Carter at breakfast around nine the next morning. The young lady didn't come down.'

'I see.'

'I wish you would leave him alone,' Miss Rossiter said now, quietly. 'He's a good boy. He enjoys life, but he's *good*. The apple of Mr Gaunt's eye, and you'd do well to remember that.'

Lola had no response, so said they needed to speak to the security man, and had Gaunt's blessing to do so. She asked for directions.

'I'll take you to him,' Miss Rossiter said, rising. 'I wouldn't want you getting lost.'

Or poking around, Lola read into her words.

They passed down a wide corridor to reach the rear of the castle, and Lola spotted a large gold-framed portrait of the Gaunt family in gaudy oils. She stopped, much to Miss Rossiter's irritation, judging by her huffing.

Gaunt was at the centre of the family group, sitting in a high-backed chair. He wore a dark suit and looked bigger and more masculine than he did in real life, with his jawline emphasised and his eyes seeming to blaze with pride. Juliana stood close beside him, resplendent in a royal-blue dress with a tiara glinting in her hair, one beautifully manicured hand planted possessively on the old man's left shoulder. On Gaunt's other side stood Carter Craig, again suited and manly. While Gaunt appeared more masculine in the painting, Craig's masculinity had been softened somewhat. His neck and shoulders were less muscular, his features less sharp, his blue eyes kinder. He resembled the oldest go-getting son of many a US president: preppy and handsome, with a good military record, and probably a success in business. There was a fourth person in the family group, one Lola couldn't place. A woman with a strong-featured, square-jawed face under a bob of straw-coloured hair. She looked older than Craig and probably older than Juliana too. She wore a grey-and-black-checked dress and her gaze was as mild as the smile that barely curved her lips.

'Who's the woman?' she asked Miss Rossiter, pointing.

Miss Rossiter took her time clearing her throat, as if to signal her displeasure.

'That's Beth,' she said.

When she didn't elaborate, Lola raised her eyebrows and inclined her head.

'The daughter of Mr Gaunt's first wife, Louisa. She remained here after her mother's death and Mr Gaunt treated her as if she were his own flesh and blood. When Carter came along, the two were like brother and sister. Quite inseparable.' A fond smile had crept onto the housekeeper's lips.

'She's older than him,' Lola said.

'By ten or eleven years.'

'And where is she now?'

Irene Rossiter stared at the portrait, a pained expression on her face, and didn't answer.

'Miss Rossiter . . . ?'

'Edinburgh,' the housekeeper said sharply. 'Now, you'll be wanting to get on.' She turned and walked on down the corridor.

Lola caught Anna's glance.

'Miss Rossiter,' Anna said, 'we'd like to speak to her. Can you give us her contact details?'

The housekeeper spun round. 'Why?' she demanded. 'What can she *possibly* tell you?'

'That's for us to find out,' Anna said. 'Or we could go back and ask Mr Gaunt himself . . .'

Miss Rossiter closed her eyes for a moment, then opened them, blinking fast. 'Yes, all right. But I'll need to look them up. I'll bring them to you in a few minutes. Now please, do hurry up!'

The head of security was Eddie Young, an affable older man in a shirt and tie who had an office even smaller than the housekeeper's, in part of a mews.

He showed them digital footage, complete with time and date stamp, of Carter Craig and Lorelei West, arriving through the gates of Clunie Castle at 3.02 a.m. on the morning of

Monday 12 August. The car was a black Mercedes and chauffeur-driven. They watched it at the correct speed, then in slow motion. As the car passed through the gates, Craig's handsome face grinned out of the back window up at the camera — almost, Lola thought cynically, as if he knew police might be studying the image in days to come.

'I think we've seen enough,' Lola said.

'I can provide you with a copy of the footage,' Young said.

'That would be very useful.' Lola wondered silently what the catch was. 'The chauffeur. Where might we find him?'

'Lurking,' Young said, then craned his neck and shouted over his shoulder, 'Jack! Polis!'

A door behind Eddie Young stood slightly ajar, and through the gap they heard a rustling of newspaper, then the creak of a chair. So someone had been in there all this time, likely listening in.

The door was pushed fully open and a man looked out at them. He was dark and thin and wore a chauffeur's uniform.

'This is Jack Courtney,' the security man told them. 'A man of few words.' He eased himself out of his chair and reached for a packet of cigarettes that sat beside his keyboard. 'I'll clear out. Give you room to chat.'

'Have a seat, Mr Courtney,' Lola said.

The chauffeur slinked forward and folded his tall figure into Eddie Young's vacated seat. He sat very still, his palms pressed together as if he was praying, and stared fixedly into a corner of the room. Lola spent the next five minutes carefully prising information out of the man, including a confirmation that he had driven Craig and his girlfriend here in the early hours of Monday morning, having collected them around 1.30 a.m. from one of Craig's clubs, this one in Royal Exchange Square in the centre of Glasgow. Back at the castle, Courtney had gone to bed, slept solidly until eight, then driven Craig and the woman back to Glasgow around ten the next morning.

'You must have a number of different vehicles here,' Anna said, when Lola had finished with her questions and the man seemed more relaxed.

'A few,' he mumbled.

'Any of them red?'

'Red?' He looked up sharply.

'Yes.' Anna waited.

'No. Mr Gaunt favours black cars. Though one of the Mercedes is midnight blue. He talked about having it spray-painted, but I reckon he liked it when he saw it.'

'Any BMWs?'

'No.'

'Where are the cars kept?'

He sat up a bit, shifting in his seat, his eyes becoming anxious.

'Garaged out back.' He tilted his head towards the back wall of the office.

'Mind if we take a look?' Anna started to get up. 'Won't take us long.'

He was shifty as anything now. 'I don't know. Mr Gaunt, he . . . well, I'm not sure.'

'Mr Gaunt said you'd help us,' Lola said.

'Right, then.' He got up and pushed carefully past them, eyes down, heading for the door. Outside, they followed him round to the side of the stable block to a stone-built outbuilding that was the size of a barn. It had huge wooden doors like those of an aircraft hangar. The chauffeur undid a padlock and removed a chain, then slid one of the heavy doors forcibly aside, creating enough of a gap for them to step inside.

Inside it was gloomy, though light penetrated through dirty skylights. Six vehicles were ranged before them in a semi-circle, headlights pointing towards the doors. There was a dark-blue Mercedes, then another sportier Mercedes, a Range Rover, a Rolls Royce, a Bentley and a top-of-the-range Audi — all of them black.

But no BMW, and no red car either.

'Is this Mr Gaunt's entire fleet of cars?' Lola asked Jack Courtney.

'All present and correct,' the chauffeur muttered.

Heading back a couple of minutes later, they found Eddie Young in the courtyard, clearly onto his second cigarette and apparently deep in conversation with the glamorous Juliana Gaunt. The two of them started when they realised they were being observed. Juliana said something quietly to the security man, who nodded, then called to Lola and Anna, 'All finished, have we?'

Meanwhile, Juliana smiled broadly, showing off her big white teeth, then turned and stepped carefully away over the cobbles.

'Yes, that's us,' Lola told the security manager, but her eyes remained on Juliana.

Miss Rossiter's gloomy figure had emerged from a doorway at the back of the castle and she was coming their way, a folded piece of paper in her hand.

'Beth Grayling's address, telephone number and email address,' she said.

Lola took it and scanned the details. 'Thank you so much,' she said, but the housekeeper had already turned and was retreating back to her chilly dark lair.

'Come on,' Lola said quietly to Anna. 'This place is giving me the creeps.'

CHAPTER TWENTY-FIVE

1.25 p.m.

Number seventeen was a tall sandstone townhouse, one of a terrace on Hyndland Road, its front door reached by a wide flight of stone steps with iron balustrades. The bell gave a deep *ding-dong*, and Lola half expected a maid to open the door to them.

But Elizabeth McQueen had clearly been looking out and drew the door open.

'Do come in,' she said, with a polite if slightly chilly smile and a wary glance out into the street, as if to check they were unobserved.

It was a magnificent place, minimally decorated and full of light, and suited its resident well. She was a slender woman in her sixties, of medium height, dressed in white slacks and a white linen blouse. Her face was beautifully made up and her long blonde hair must have taken hours of work. Lola had been a hairdresser in her youth and knew a lot about hair. She estimated this cut and colour would have set Mrs McQueen back several hundred pounds.

'We'll go to the kitchen, if that's all right by you. There's a pot of coffee.'

The kitchen occupied the whole back of the house, all white cupboards and granite surfaces, with gleaming chrome. A back door led into a conservatory, and Lola glimpsed greenery and roses in a small garden beyond that.

'Mrs McQueen,' Lola began when they were sitting at a high breakfast bar, 'or may I call you Elizabeth?'

'Elizabeth is fine,' she said, inclining her golden head. 'I'm not entirely sure why you're here. I haven't seen Colin for so many years. My son, erm, he chose to cut me out of his life, I'm afraid.'

'I'm sorry,' Lola said, watching her carefully.

Could this elegant woman really be the Liz or Lucy who'd gone along to the court? Who'd befriended poor, lonely Kathryn Main, and given her a moonstone necklace, then somehow persuaded her to corrupt an entire jury?

And why? Because her son had cut her off? Would she really take revenge by seeing him jailed for life?

'Tell us about your son,' Anna said now.

'I'm sure you know everything salient already,' the woman said. 'Dates, his education, how he acquired his money.'

'Tell us how you and he came to be living with Duncan Gaunt,' Lola said.

'It was after my husband John died. Colin was six years old. I had very little money of my own. My sister Rebecca invited us to live with her and her husband at their place in Perthshire.

'Rebecca made us feel welcome, but Duncan was always so cool, so remote. We had our own apartment — a whole floor in one wing — and there were staff to clean it. We took meals with Rebecca and Duncan. Then, about five years later, Rebecca got ill and died within months. Duncan took it hard and he began to freeze me out. To separate me from Colin. He'd taken Colin under his wing, treating him as if he was his own son.

'They'd never had any children of their own, you see. Duncan has a stepdaughter — Beth, his first wife's daughter

134

from a previous marriage. He's very fond of her, I understand. But Colin has always been the apple of his eye and he treats him as his heir.' She said this bitterly. 'There was a terrible governess, Mrs Kennedy. She taught Colin at the castle until he was eleven, and they adored one another. She was like a second mother to him. Then, when Colin was eleven, he went to boarding school, not very far away, but far enough. Mrs Kennedy pined. Duncan found her other work. I took a job, administration in a primary school a mile or two away in the local village. I was feeling more and more like a spare part around the castle and yearned to live on my own somewhere. Duncan suggested I might find jobs around the place so I could "feel more useful". Blacking the grates, I expect he meant.' She laughed. 'I told him no. I said, "I want to leave and I'm taking Colin with me." Well, he didn't like that. Neither did Colin. He bawled me out one day. He pushed me into a wall and said I was ruining his chances of living the life he was entitled to. He was fifteen years old but already so violent. So I went to Duncan and asked what he would give me to leave. He offered me one million pounds. I left the day the money cleared into my account and I've never been back to Clunie Castle. I bought this place for a song and did it up. A cousin's husband helped me invest the rest.'

'It's a beautiful place,' Lola said. 'Did you hire someone to do the design, or . . .'

'Yes. A wonderful woman called Madeleine Wicks. She works out of Park Circus. Expensive, but such a professional — and her team are so skilled.'

Lola said nothing, and hoped her face hadn't betrayed her surprise. She shouldn't have been surprised at all: Maddie was based in the West End and people preferred to use locally recommended businesses.

'I tried to keep in touch with Colin,' Elizabeth said now. 'But he wasn't interested. He got in touch when Duncan gave him five million pounds for his twenty-first birthday. Also when he decided to change his name to that ridiculous one, like some sort of celebrity. Since then, I'm afraid I've spoken to Colin only twice. Both times were fraught and painful — for both of us, I expect.' She smiled sadly. 'He's Duncan's son now. And I believe he's still close with that old governess of his, Mrs Kennedy.'

'And Mrs Kennedy, what happened to her?'

'No idea.'

Lola signalled to Anna, who made a note.

'Elizabeth,' Anna began, 'we'd like to ask you some questions about your son's court case.'

She nodded. 'You want to know if I think he's really guilty, is that it?'

Lola said, 'We would be interested in your opinion.'

Elizabeth sat back, and stared briefly into the middle distance before refocusing on Lola's face and saying, with grim conviction, 'I think he did it. Something happened to Colin a long time ago. Duncan's influence, I've always thought, mixed with some of what he inherited from his father: a sort of toxic vanity. When I heard what he was accused of, my first thought was, *So he's finally committed murder. Why has it taken him this long?* She looked from Lola to Anna and back. 'I don't wish him any ill. I wish . . . I rather wish he'd see what he's become and regret it and try to change.' Her face twitched and Lola realised she was fighting back tears. She regained control, clearing her throat. 'I wish that one day he would come here and ask me to be his mother again. Of course, he would need to change before he could be my son.'

They sat for a moment in silence, then Anna asked gently, 'Did you go to the courthouse during the trial?'

'To the High Court? No.' The answer came easily, but then she frowned. 'Why would I?'

'You didn't ever go and perhaps sit in the public gallery?'

'No, absolutely not.' The frown deepened. 'Why, does someone say I was there?'

'Have you ever spoken to a woman called Kathryn Main?' Lola asked now.

'Who? Oh, isn't she the woman who caused the problems, that . . . ?'

'Did you ever meet her or speak to her?' Lola prompted.

'Of course not. What a question.'

She seemed irritated now, as well as confused. 'What is this about?' she demanded.

'A woman roughly matching your description is thought to have attended the court on at least one occasion and to have left with Kathryn Main. She might have given her a necklace,' Lola said calmly. 'And her name might have been Liz, or perhaps Lucy.'

'Well, I'm Elizabeth, but I'm never Liz. I've never been one for diminutives. Now,' she said, sounding strained, 'if that's everything . . . ?'

'It is,' Lola said. 'Thank you for your time.'

* * *

2.34 p.m.

'Duncan Gaunt's stepdaughter is called Beth,' Lola said when they were in the car.

'I noticed that too,' Anna said. She indicated to pull out into traffic.

'And she has blonde hair — or did when that picture was painted.'

'But, according to Miss Rossiter, she adores Craig. Why would she have tried to get him convicted?'

'Unless we've been looking at everything the wrong way round,' Lola said.

'Meaning what?'

'It's something that's bothered me from the start: the fact Kathryn Main was killed using a method Craig is suspected of using before — though he has a solid alibi *and* no motive.'

Anna was frowning as she drove.

'Kathryn Main was taken for a ride,' Lola went on. '"Liz" or "Lucy" befriended her and fed her a story about having evidence of Craig's guilt, saying she wanted Kathryn's help to make sure he was convicted. She even showed her photos of her daughter's injuries and gave her a necklace as a token of her friendship — one that has since been "retrieved". She was taken in, manipulated, exploited. Let's be careful not to fall for the same ploy.'

'Not with you, boss.'

'Look at the result of the meddling, as in the *long-term* impact. The conviction's no longer safe. Craig's free pending an appeal. What if that was the intention all along?'

'You mean . . .'

'I mean, what if "Liz" or "Lucy" was on Craig's side? She was working for his benefit, possibly with his knowledge, and playing a long game. What better way to ensure Craig got off than to undermine the entire conviction?'

They were approaching the Clyde Tunnel now, heading south.

'It would make more sense, wouldn't it?' Lola went on. 'A woman, acting in Craig's interests, befriended a lonely jury member, flattered her, bought her dinner and gave her a lovely present, and confided in her a terrible, upsetting story about Craig attacking her daughter. And Kathryn wanted to help. She did everything she could, even bringing other jurors in on it. Then, once the WhatsApp messages were made public and Craig released, Kathryn had to be got rid of. "Liz" or "Lucy" maybe told her she was in danger from the police and from Craig. She managed to track Kathryn to the place she was hiding and took her to — I don't know — "somewhere safer". And then she killed her.'

* * *

6.04 p.m.

The locksmith had done a good job at Aileen's flat. There were new stops in the window frame and a lockable bolt at the bottom. He'd also fitted internal locks on the doors of the spare room, the kitchen and living room, just in case. Aileen would have felt more grateful if it hadn't taken him nearly thirty-six hours to come round. What if she hadn't had somewhere else to stay? She would have been stuck in an unsecure house. But the man just shrugged her complaint off.

'Might want to think about getting bars for the windows at the back of the property,' he said now. 'Cost a pretty penny but worth it for the peace of mind.'

'I'll think about it,' she conceded, and he gave her the business card of an ironmonger friend.

Maddie was paying for the locks. Maybe she would pay for bars too. She probably would, given how guilty she felt — or claimed to feel.

When the chief inspector had come to Maddie's place two nights before and told them what had happened, Aileen had been consumed by panic, but in time another feeling crept in: a dark satisfaction that her aunt was now seeing so clearly the consequences of her betrayal.

Aileen paid the locksmith, accepted his receipt, then returned to the kitchen — her favourite room — and looked about.

It was her sanctuary again. Yes, someone had broken in, but now it was more secure than ever. She was happy to be here, and happy to be on her own.

I could come round this evening if you like, Maddie replied when Aileen texted to tell her how much the locksmith had charged. *Just say the word and I'll be there.*

No need.

She'd had enough of Maddie for a while. Enough of her nervous rabbiting, of her gushing apologies, of her wild ideas for protecting Evie and Hamish, including a suggestion they might move to one of the remoter islands and Maddie could rent them a house. She had a friend on Tiree, she said. Maybe Aileen and Hamish could stay with her. Tiree was meant to be lovely and sunny. Or what about Shetland? 'That's a long way away — practically Norway! Though I hear the weather's generally nicer in Orkney.'

DCI Harris had advised against acting rashly, but suggested perhaps alerting the police in Portree. She could help with that, and even offered to accompany Aileen to Skye. She could check the lay of the land, talk to the authorities there and offer advice about safety.

So you can meet Evie, you mean, Aileen had wanted to retort.

Well, it wasn't going to happen.

'The fewer people who know the better,' Aileen had said and the chief inspector had backed off.

But Uncle Donny needed to know. Aileen had phoned him from Maddie's the next morning and explained to the old man, as calmly as she could, that it was possible Craig knew where Evie was — not to worry him, but to alert him, in case he noticed anything out of the ordinary.

'Right you are,' he'd said, sounding as bluffly pragmatic as ever, though she was sure she detected a tremor in his voice.

He would be on the lookout now. Good.

Finally, others were beginning to understand the threat. To experience some of the burden Aileen had carried for so long.

She realised she was hungry. Starving, in fact. She had just set about boiling rice and chopping vegetables to make a Thai curry, when her phone started to ring.

She wiped her hands, and checked the name on the screen. It was Uncle Donny.

Hand trembling, she answered.

CHAPTER TWENTY-SIX

6.48 p.m.

Joe's brother Kev had texted again to say Joe was looking and sounding a lot brighter. The line on his Covid test was fading.

Sitting at her kitchen table, Lola stared at the words and wondered whether it would be wrong to not reply.

She was reading a new text — this one from Anna, saying she'd got them an appointment with Duncan Gaunt's step-daughter Beth Grayling the next morning — when her phone began to buzz.

She groaned aloud.

'Trouble?' Sandy asked, coming into the kitchen from the dining room, where he was finishing some paperwork.

'Maybe. I'll need to take it.'

'No problem.' He ducked back out of the kitchen.

She put the phone to her ear, said her name and was met with a barrage of sobbing.

'Slow down, Aileen,' Lola said. She eased herself onto one of the chairs at the kitchen table, while Sandy closed the door softly behind him. 'Take a deep breath and try to tell me what's happened.'

She could hear the young woman breathing in panicked gasps.

'It's happened,' Aileen Mackinnon said. 'It's Craig . . . He . . .'

'He what?' Lola said. 'Take your time.'

It took a minute or so before she got the crying under control.

'My Uncle Donny called five minutes ago. A parcel came for Evie. But it didn't make it to the house — *thank God!* It was baby clothes! Designer ones. *Now* do you see what you've done?'

It took several minutes, but Lola wearily pieced the story together, scrawling notes on a pad.

It seemed a parcel had arrived at Portree's mail sorting office, addressed merely to Evie Mackinnon, courtesy of the delivery office in Portree, with a winsome message written on the back pleading for a postal worker to help it find its destination.

Staff at the sorting office had wondered if the intended recipient might be the young woman who lived with Donny and Jessie Mackinnon at Skaravaig, though they didn't know her as Evie. They'd passed it to a postman called Tom Clark, who'd had every intention of delivering it in person — but he'd spotted Donny in Glendale, a few miles away. He'd collared the old man and shown him the parcel. Donny, already on the alert, took it from Tom and opened it there and then, finding inside it a toddler's fancy outfit — a tweedy suit for a boy of Hamish's age. There'd been a message inside, which read: *For the wee man, Love from Auntie C.*

Donny had driven up the hill to where he knew he'd have a signal and called Aileen. He'd read the message to her, and she'd confirmed she and Evie had no auntie whose name began with C.

'"C" — it's him!' Aileen cried to Lola. 'Don't you see?' She was getting angry now. 'He's mocking us. It's his way of telling us he *knows!*'

142

'Where is the outfit now?' Lola asked.

'In the bin in Glendale! I told Uncle Donny to get rid of it as soon as he could. I didn't want Evie seeing it.' She stopped. 'But now I'm thinking we should have kept it. You could get someone to find it and check it for evidence, couldn't you?'

Lola's heart was racing and her face burned. She'd helped cause this. If only she'd taken more care. If *only* she hadn't mentioned Skye to Elaine Walsh.

'Aileen, I want you to do something for me,' she said, determinedly calm. 'I want you to call your uncle and ask him to ring me on this number as soon as he can, from somewhere Evie won't overhear. Will you do that?'

'Okay,' Aileen said. 'I'll do it now.'

* * *

7.34 p.m.

Donny Mackinnon called Lola from the top of the field next to the croft. The breeze ruffled against the microphone. She made him recount what had happened and it matched Aileen's version.

'Now, I'd like you to go back to the bin where you put the parcel and retrieve it, wearing gloves.'

'I shouldn't have thrown the thing away — is that what you're saying?'

'It's all right, but we need to get hold of it and have the police take a proper look.'

'What type of gloves?'

'Any, it doesn't matter. Take something big enough to fit the parcel inside — a plastic or paper carrier bag will do — and fold it over. You can tape it up if you have any to hand.'

'Very well. I'll go now.' He sounded shaken and scared and she felt sorry for him.

'Good. Then I want you to stay put in Glendale and wait for a police officer to come and take the parcel from you.'

'A police officer?'

'I don't know who, but I'll contact the police office in Portree now and tell them to send someone out to meet you. Now, tell me exactly where you'll be once you've got the parcel.'

The officer on duty at Portree listened in silence as Lola calmly explained that a dangerous situation might be unfolding on the island, and that she needed urgent assistance.

'Bronagh Stewart stays out just beyond Glendale towards Milovaig,' the officer said. 'You promise me this is no' a wind-up?'

'I promise.'

He had Lola repeat her name and badge number and she heard him tapping at his keyboard.

'I thought I recognised the name,' he said. 'You're the one who caught the Clyde Pusher, aren't you?'

'That's me.'

'That was some case. Look, I've got your number. I'll give Bronagh a call, but she and her man have a smallholding, so there's every chance they'll be out in the fields — and the mobile signal out west is rotten.'

But Bronagh Stewart wasn't in the fields, and she called Lola back within three minutes, sounding wary but willing.

'Donny Mackinnon, up at Skaravaig?' she said. She had a lilting island accent, breathy on the vowels, and Lola wondered if she was a Gaelic speaker. 'Is he all right? Gerry over at Portree said there was some kind of situation brewing.'

'There could be, but it's a long story and we don't have a lot of time. I want you to meet Donny, and I'll tell you exactly where. He'll have an item for you. I'd like you to collect it and bring it to Portree — then call me from the police office.'

* * *

8.50 p.m.

Sandy went for carry-out pizzas from the Italian on Pollokshaws Road, while Lola rang Elaine to let her know what was afoot.

They ate in the garden — or, rather, Sandy did. Lola couldn't swallow a bite.

Try as she might to pay attention to Sandy talking about his cases, she just couldn't, and she knew it bothered him. He droned on about a suspicious fire law, until finally he stopped and frowned at her.

'It's eating at you, isn't it?' he asked. 'The girl and Carter Craig.'

'Oh, that. Aye, it is. I can't help feeling responsible. Either way, it's up to me to fix it, isn't it?'

She checked her phone again. The later it got the more anxious she felt.

Finally, it rang.

'That's me in Portree,' Bronagh Stewart said. 'I've got my gloves on and my colleague's here with me. Everything's laid out on the table in front of us: a toddler's tweed outfit and a wee card saying it's from an "Auntie C".'

'Right, I want you to look closely at the packaging and at the clothes,' Lola said. 'Every pocket, every seam.'

'What am I looking for?'

'An electronic tag,' Lola said. 'It would be small, made of plastic, probably, and a few centimetres across.'

The woman hummed softly as she checked, and Lola listened, eyes closed, muscles tight with tension.

'Aha,' Bronagh Stewart said with satisfaction.

'What have you found?'

'A plastic square. Not very big. There's a wee button on the back and a serial number. There's a hole in one corner. I guess that's so it could go on a keyring.'

'Can you text a photo to this number?' Lola said.

'Give me two secs.'

And moments later Lola was looking at a photograph of a tracking device. There was a second image with a close-up of the serial number. She could get someone in digital forensics to check that in the morning.

'So someone's trying to find Daisy and the boy?' the constable asked.

'We think so.'

'Wow. That's . . . nasty. Who is it? The boy's father, I suppose?'

Lola hesitated. 'What makes you ask that?'

'I just put two and two together. There's never been any talk of a dad, and they're out here in the wilds. I've also heard a whisper Daisy isn't her real name. I wondered if they were keeping out of someone's way.'

'It's along those lines,' Lola admitted, unwilling to say any more.

'Look, what do you want us to do about this?' Bronagh said. 'We're not tech experts here, but do you think we should try to disable it or something?'

'No,' Lola said. 'If whoever's tracking it realises it's at the cop shop, all the better. How did Donny seem?'

'Rattled, I'd say. Listen, if Daisy Mackinnon needs protection, then we can help. There's a DC on the island. Cara Phillips. She's good but she's the only detective and there's only a handful of us uniforms. You'll need to be straight with us about what's going on.'

Lola took a deep breath. 'I will,' she said. 'Soon.'

CHAPTER TWENTY-SEVEN

9.29 p.m.

Lola called Elaine Walsh and they spent ten minutes chewing over any steps that could be taken. The key question was how Craig might be monitored and contained. Elaine wondered about telling Izatt and seeing if there could be a way to arrest and detain Craig on a charge — any charge. But Lola recoiled from the idea. It would mean confiding in Izatt, and she didn't trust him to act with basic competence, let alone compassion. So they'd agreed Lola would talk to Maddie and Aileen and that Lola would then go to Skye herself to review the situation.

Maddie Wicks met her at the door of her townhouse with a grim expression.

'So, here we are again,' she said. 'Aileen's in the kitchen. She arrived five minutes ago.'

'I see,' Lola said.

She steeled herself and followed Maddie to the back of the house.

Aileen sat at the table, ramrod straight and glowering.

'Hello,' Lola said.

Aileen looked down at her hands.

'Coffee? Tea?' Maddie asked.

'Water would be fine,' said Lola. Maddie brought her a glass, then set about making herself herbal tea, chatting all the while.

Lola took the opportunity to examine Aileen, who seemed focused on her pale narrow hands, palm down on the table before her.

The young woman was a mystery to her. A talented interior designer, her aunt had called her, and yet Aileen was not in the least bright or colourful herself. Her clothes suited her slender frame but they were so plain. Lola had imagined all interior designers were vibrant and colourful and existed in the moment, but Aileen Mackinnon was such a stiff and silent creature. Lola wondered why.

'So,' Maddie said, bringing her tea to the table, 'you had Donny fishing in the litter bin.'

'Yes,' Lola said.

'And?' Aileen asked coolly.

'And it's now at the police office in Portree.'

'Was it from him?' Aileen asked, those pale eyes seeming to gleam with malice.

'We can't tell at this stage.'

'But you said you had something to tell us,' Maddie said, cradling her mug and frowning.

'Yes.' And there was no easy way to say it. 'It seems there was a tracking device folded into the seam of one the trouser legs on the outfit.'

Aileen let out a little choking gasp, then stared, eyes wide, lips parted, ready to speak. But no words came.

'*A tracking device?*' Maddie said, half laughing with bewilderment. 'To track the delivery, do you mean? But surely everything gets tracked these days. I get *constant* emails telling me where this parcel or that parcel is. Or— oh!' She stopped, hand to her mouth. 'You mean—'

'*It's Craig,*' Aileen spat. 'He wanted it to reach Evie so he'd know where she was. He knew she was on Skye — *thanks to you two* — and tried to get a tracker delivered right to Uncle

148

Donny's. And he nearly succeeded.' She turned her toxic jade gaze on Lola. 'That's right, isn't it?'

'Oh God!' Maddie cried. 'Lola, is this true?'

'We don't know for sure, but everything about it is suspicious: the timing, the note begging the post people for help, the note inside — not to mention the device itself.'

'But if it had got to the house . . .' Maddie said now, following the logic. 'God, but that's horrible!'

'It means he remembers Evie,' Aileen pointed out. 'And it means he wants to find her.' Her voice was like ice. 'The break-in at my place was just another attempt to find the exact location. Now do you understand what you've done?' she demanded of her aunt. 'He's coming for her. Coming for them both.'

'Oh darling, don't!' Maddie was weeping now, while Aileen was like stone.

Lola said gently, 'We will do everything in our power to protect Evie and her son.'

Aileen raised her eyebrows sceptically.

'They can go to my friend's on Tiree,' Maddie said decisively. 'They can go tomorrow. Get the ferry from Skye to North Uist, then travel down to Barra and get another ferry from there. That way they don't have to put a foot on the mainland. What time is it?' She craned her neck to look at the clock. 'I could try Nicole now.' She began to rise from her chair.

'And what's to stop him finding them there?' Aileen asked. 'Tiree's tiny compared to Skye. They'd be cornered.'

'But—' Maddie stopped, put both hands to her mouth in shock.

'Look, let's make a plan and act calmly,' Lola said.

'What sort of plan?' Aileen wanted to know.

'One that includes Evie in the decision-making,' Lola said.

Maddie nodded, sniffing. 'Yes, that's what we have to do. It's only right. I'll go to her. She needs to understand the danger she's in.'

'She won't though,' Aileen said. 'She never does.'

Lola eyed her with interest. 'Surely she will want to know that her son may be in danger.'

Aileen shrugged. 'She just thinks everything's fine and nothing bad will ever happen.'

And you resent that intensely, don't you?

The young woman scowled as if she'd read Lola's mind.

'I'll go up there first thing in the morning,' Maddie said. 'If I can talk to her, openly and honestly, then I'm sure she'll listen.' She turned to Lola. 'Oh, please tell me you'll come too.'

'Yes,' Lola said. 'I'm already making arrangements to travel to Skye. It'll give me a chance to meet the local police and also to talk to the post office people, in case it happens again. I've a meeting in Edinburgh in the morning but I'll drive up in the afternoon. I should get there some time in the evening.'

Aileen was watching the two of them with quiet rage.

'We could stay at the retreat,' Maddie said, brightening now she had something practical to think about. 'Jessie said they often have rooms, even in high season.'

'The retreat?' Lola asked.

'It's a spiritual centre, up behind the village. Lots of mindfulness and tai chi and yoga and craft. People go there if they're having a bit of a tough time. I had a lovely chat with the woman who runs it once.' She turned to Aileen. 'What's her name?'

Aileen blinked, clearly irritated. 'Zoe,' she said. 'I don't know her other name.'

'Zoe, that's right. I'll call her before I set off. Want me to see if there's room for you?'

'You could do,' Lola said.

Maddie wrote down the name of the village and also the postcode for Donny and Jessie's croft for Lola's GPS.

'And what about you, darling?' she asked her niece. 'Will I see if there's space for you too? We could always share a twin room. I could drive us.'

'I'll make my own way there,' Aileen said crisply. 'And I'll stay with Evie, like I always do.'

'Well, that's fine,' Maddie replied, but her own tone was brittle now. Cross, even, as though her patience with the young woman's hostility had reached its limit. 'But I want to be there when we talk to Evie about this. We'll do it together, *kindly*, and with her and Hamish's needs to the fore. Do you understand me?'

CHAPTER TWENTY-EIGHT

10.28 a.m.

Beth Grayling, Duncan Gaunt's stepdaughter, lived in a grand ground-floor apartment in Edinburgh's New Town with her husband and daughter. It was one of several homes, Anna found out, including a place in London and another in Devon.

She met them at the main door, the spitting image of the woman in the painting with her strong features and square jaw. Today she was in a white blouse and blue jeans, and her straw-coloured hair was held back by a blue Alice band.

'Thank you for seeing us, Ms Grayling,' Lola said once she'd led them inside a vast airy hallway with white walls and a dark-stained wood floor.

'It's all right,' the woman said, sniffing a little. 'I don't know why it couldn't have waited till Monday.'

'Time is of the essence,' Lola said.

'So you said.' She shook her head. 'You'd better come through. We're in here.'

Lola and Anna exchanged glances. *We?*

Beth Grayling led them into a long room with three sets of tall sash windows. The walls were wood-panelled and painted white, and hung about with fantastic abstract paintings. Lola suspected they came from Beth's gallery. Grayling's, in Edinburgh's Stockbridge, was exclusive, catering to its clientele by appointment only. Beth was married to an American businessman, who spent several months every year out of the country.

Lola spotted a man perched on a low settee at the far end of the room, papers in hand. He rose awkwardly as they approached. Lola recognised his white-blond curls.

'You've met Stephen Kitchener, I believe?' Beth said, in what Lola thought was an oddly guarded way.

'Oh, yes,' Lola said, nodding to the cherubic solicitor, who bowed and smiled an unpleasant smile.

Beth Grayling waved absently towards a long grey settee and Lola and Anna took a seat. She sat opposite them, beside the solicitor, who was busying himself with his papers while mopping his sweaty brow with a handkerchief.

'Well?' Beth said, with an air of someone too busy, or important, for this type of thing. 'I wish you'd explain why you're here.'

Anna began: 'Your stepbrother was on trial for murder earlier this year—'

'Carter isn't my stepbrother,' the woman said. 'He's a sort of step-cousin. We were thrown together by fate.'

'But you're close.'

The woman pressed her lips together and blinked rapidly before answering. 'I'm fond of him.'

'Do you approve of him?' Lola asked in a neutral tone.

'What's that supposed to mean?' came the snapped reply. 'I'm *fond* of him. Approval doesn't come into it.'

'Did you go to the court to watch his trial?' Anna asked.

'Did I *what*?' She seemed genuinely shocked by the question. Offended, even.

'Did you go to the High Court in Glasgow on any day of Carter's trial and sit in the public gallery?'

'No,' she said firmly, but her pale blue eyes were darting now. She was irritated. Or nervous. Possibly both.

'Did you go to the court but stay outside?' Anna asked.

'No. No, I didn't!' She turned to the solicitor, who peered up from his papers. 'Stephen, can they do this?'

The man pursed his lips and gave a theatrical shrug. 'Best simply to answer their questions,' he said mildly.

'I didn't go to the court. I didn't go to Glasgow at any time during that whole business.'

'Your name is Beth,' Lola said. 'I assume that's short for Elizabeth?'

'Yes,' she said, more quietly. Her eyes were now warier than ever. 'I've always been known as Beth. Always.'

'Never Liz?'

Beth Grayling screwed up her face and shook her head. 'Look, what is this about? These questions are . . . *bizarre*!'

The solicitor leaned in and murmured something, which only seemed to rile the woman more. She sat back, crossed her long legs and looked downright sulky.

Lola glanced at Anna. Anna gave a tiny nod in response. They'd got as far as they were likely to with that line of questioning.

Anna said, 'When did you last talk to Carter?'

'It's been months. I can't tell you exactly.'

'Since before his trial, then?'

'As I said: months! I said I was fond of him. I didn't say we were close. We're not . . . in contact, so to speak.'

The solicitor shifted in his seat, though he remained focused on his papers.

'And yet,' Anna said, 'Mr Kitchener here is one of Carter's personal legal team, isn't he? So you didn't speak to Carter to arrange for Mr Kitchener to be here?'

'Mr Kitchener is employed by my stepfather,' Beth said. 'My stepfather asked him to be here. I haven't talked to Carter.'

Anna looked briefly at Lola, who took over the questioning.

'You described his trial as a "farce". Do you believe he was innocent of the crimes he was tried for?'

A very slight pause, then: 'Of course he was. He wasn't even in the country.' She swallowed.

She's nervous, Lola decided. *Terribly nervous and barely able to conceal it.*

'And yet you didn't go to the court to support him?'

'No!' Then, more quietly: 'I preferred to stay away.'

Lola realised they weren't getting anywhere here. She felt instinctively Beth Grayling was telling the truth: she hadn't been to the court, and she wasn't Liz or Lucy. It would still make sense, though, to show her photograph, which appeared on her gallery's website, to both Susan McKenna and the male juror who'd seen Kathryn in another woman's company.

'What age are you, Ms Grayling?' Lola asked.

'Forty-four. Why?'

'So you're eleven years older than Carter?'

'Thereabouts.'

'When Carter and his mother came to live at Clunie Castle, he had a governess for a number of years. A woman named Mrs Kennedy.'

'Yes, I remember.' She said this neutrally, apparently without interest.

'Were you living there at the time?' Lola asked.

'I would have been, yes. Though I started university around then.'

'Do you know what happened to Mrs Kennedy?'

'What *happened* to her?'

'Do you know where she is?'

Her expression went blank, but Lola could tell she was thinking how to answer.

'I couldn't begin to tell you where she is right now,' she said at last.

'And do you remember her first name?'

'Her . . . her *first name*? I can't say I do.' She was becoming agitated. 'Why would I? Why are you asking about her?'

'What was Mrs Kennedy like?' Anna asked, ignoring the question.

'What was she *like*? I've no idea! She didn't teach me. She was Carter's governess.'

'What age was she when she was teaching Carter, would you say?'

A sigh. 'Not that old. In her thirties, perhaps.'

'And that was, what — twenty-something years ago?'

'Something like that.'

Lola and Anna exchanged glances. Neither had anything else to ask.

Beth Grayling took them back into the hallway. They went in silence, but at the door she surprised Lola by stepping outside after them and pulling the door almost closed behind her.

'I didn't ask for that man to come here,' she whispered. 'Stephen Kitchener, I mean. My stepfather insisted.'

'Then why did you allow him to?' Lola asked.

'Duncan is very insistent. Look' — she cast an anxious glance behind her, as if the cherubic face might be peering through the crack in the doorway — 'I haven't spoken to Carter for *years*. My choice, though I doubt he cares. He's toxic. But I can't say that, can I?'

'Can't you?' Lola asked gently.

The woman sighed and cast her eyes skyward. 'You wouldn't understand. This family — it's not *like* other families. It's Duncan. He controls everything. And he'd do *anything* to protect Carter.'

'But—'

'I'm sorry,' she said sharply, 'I have to go.' And she disappeared back inside, and pushed the door firmly closed.

* * *

11.32 a.m.

'She's frightened, isn't she?' Anna said. They reached the street corner and lingered there.

'Maybe,' Lola said. 'But not of Craig, if you ask me. More likely she's afraid of losing her stepfather's favour — and his money.'

'Discount her as a suspect, then?'

Lola thought about it. 'Not yet. Not entirely. But I don't believe she's Kathryn Main's friend. Do you?'

'No, boss.'

Anna headed off back to Glasgow and Lola took a minute to check her emails before hitting the road north. There was one from the detective on Skye, Cara Phillips. A fingerprint check of the child's outfit, including any labels, the notelet and the paper packaging, had produced nothing of significance. The good news was that a digital forensics expert in Inverness would be looking at the device and hoped to report within twenty-four hours. The DC was just waiting for a courier to collect it and take it to him. There was a chance coding on the device might indicate how it was being tracked, possibly even where from, and the serial number might even enable them to identify where it had been bought and by whom.

She typed a reply, confirming her estimated time of arrival in Portree and had just pressed send when her phone buzzed into life. It was Graeme Izatt calling. She groaned.

'Graeme. What a pleasant surprise.'

'You're going somewhere,' he began. 'Aidan got it out of one of your DCs — you're heading up north, "for a night or two". My question is, where?'

Lola silently swore.

'Graeme—'

'You're going to Skye, aren't you? You're going to see *her*. My golden goose. Well, you're not going without me.'

'All right. Yes, I'm going to see her with two of her relations, and I'm hoping to help her feel comfortable enough to make a statement. I'm going on my own and that's that.'

'Tell me where she is.' It was almost a hiss.

'Absolutely not.' She sighed and laughed grimly. 'Do you seriously think you'd help, Graeme? You're a bully. You threaten and shout. You use intimidation to get what you want. You haven't a grain of nuance or delicacy, or empathy, come to that. If you go and browbeat this young woman you will lose any hope of getting hold of the evidence. She's lived for long enough in fear of a different bully, so why would she cooperate with another one? If anyone can persuade her to come forward, it's me. *I'll* be the one to support her.'

'This is you all over,' he spat. Lola rolled her eyes. 'A sniff of the limelight, a chance to be the hero of the day, and you're in there like lightning. *And what about me?* he ranted now. 'I just get the shit.'

'Oh, give it a rest, Graeme,' she said. 'You're embarrassing yourself now.'

'Embarrassing myself?' he demanded. 'You don't think I'm embarrassed already? My reputation's in rags, and you—'

'And me, what?'

'You're not helping!'

'Why would I, Graeme? Why would I help a colleague who constantly berates me and — and *implies* things?'

'What "things"?'

'Snide remarks about the man I'm seeing.'

'What? Oh, that!' A dismissive laugh.

'First,' she said, 'my private life is my business. Second, if you've something to tell me, just come out and say it. What I will not stand for is insinuations. It's childish behaviour and it's beneath even you.'

'Look,' he said, now sounding caught off guard, 'I merely enquired if it was the same Sandy Johnson who used to work with us. If other people are talking, then that's not my fault.'

'"Other people"? Like who?'

'No, I'm not saying any more,' he said. 'You want to know, then you ask about. You've made it clear you don't want my help.'

'Goodbye, Graeme,' she said sharply and hung up.

CHAPTER TWENTY-NINE

3.24 p.m.

The drive was uneventful, but things slowed down when she turned off the A9 at Dalwhinnie and found herself sitting behind multiple caravans. Alone and engaged in a monotonous task, she couldn't help but stew about Izatt's words. Others were talking, he'd said. What others? And what were they saying? She knew cop shops were hotbeds of gossip and that the merest hint of something juicy had tongues wagging and texts flying. When she'd mentioned Izatt's insinuations to Sandy on Thursday evening, he hadn't seemed guilty, not even shifty, and her faith in him had been bolstered. She tried not to dwell, but her mind kept returning, and that in itself bothered her.

She stopped for petrol and something to eat north of Fort William and found a message from Anna asking her to call.

'Jonno found it,' Anna told her excitedly. 'Three seconds of colour footage from a camera outside a bar on the Saltmarket. A woman who's the spitting image of Kathryn Main, crossing the road, arm in arm with a blonde woman in a light-coloured jacket with a red scarf round her neck.

Third day of the trial, 4.17 in the afternoon. Looking at a street map, they could have come from the High Court and then were crossing the Saltmarket as if they were heading up to the Trongate.'

'So start looking for footage from businesses further up that side of the Saltmarket,' Lola said. 'Let's see if we can get a route. Who knows, they might have gone in somewhere together, or even got in a car.'

'I'll get Jonno right on to it, boss.'

'Before you go, Anna,' Lola said, her face burning, 'can I ask you something?'

'Yes, go on.'

'It's not to do with work.'

'Oh?' A more cautious tone now.

How to say it? How to ask the question lightly, without sounding utterly paranoid?

'I'd like to think you'd tell me if people were talking about me.'

Anna didn't speak for a moment. Then she said, 'Sorry, boss, but I don't understand.'

'About me. About my private life. Would you tell me if you heard gossip?' She felt horribly tense, as if her neck muscles might crack her spine. 'Are people at work saying things about Sandy?'

'About *Sandy*? Not that I've heard. Why? What's happened?'

'Oh, nothing.' She winced, wishing she hadn't asked. 'Listen, forget I said anything. And please, don't tell anyone, will you?'

'No, of course not. Boss—'

'It's okay. I'll talk to you later.' And she cut the call.

She saw a text from Maddie Wicks, saying she and Aileen were both now in Skaravaig, though Aileen had insisted on driving up to Skye separately. Maddie said she was settling into her room at the St Columba Centre and planning to walk down to Donny and Jessie's croft. She wished Lola a safe drive.

Going north, the traffic thinned, and Lola was at the Skye Bridge before she knew it. She'd been to Skye only once before, years ago with her sister Frankie. They'd stayed at a cottage near Elgol in the south, with a spectacular view across the turquoise sea right into the heart of the Cuillin mountains. They'd driven everywhere, walking in Glen Brittle and up to the Storr. Her strongest memory was of dining on some of the best seafood she'd ever tasted on the terrace of a tiny lochside inn, looking out over a serene sea loch. She was still thinking about it as she drove into Portree, and regretting the fact she would likely be too busy on this trip.

She parked up in the main square and took a few minutes to stretch her legs and breathe in lungfuls of cool, clean island air. She walked down to the pier and called Sandy, who was at home, 'making a miserable ready meal for one,' he joked. They talked about this and that, and then he asked her if she was all right — 'and you know what I'm talking about.'

'Aye, aye, I'm fine,' she lied. 'That's all forgotten.' She forced herself to smile so it would sound in her voice. 'I'll talk to you later.'

Feeling slightly refreshed, she climbed back up the hill and made for the town's main square and the police office.

The desk officer knew to expect her and dialled an extension.

'Cara'll be with you in a mo,' he said.

Lola recognised his voice from the phone call when she'd asked for help retrieving the parcel. He was PC Gerry March, according to the name on the desk. He'd been impressed that she was the detective who'd caught the Clyde Pusher. He was grinning at her now.

'Busy, are you?' she asked.

'Not really,' he said. 'Never am. You here to liven things up, are you?'

'Hopefully not too much,' Lola said.

'DCI Harris,' a voice said.

DC Cara Phillips, the island's only detective, introduced herself.

'We're in the back,' she said and led the way to a meeting room where two of her uniformed colleagues were waiting. They were Constable Bronagh Stewart, based out at Glendale, and who'd retrieved the suspicious package from the bin, and Constable Kris MacPherson, who worked out of Dunvegan, so Bronagh's closest colleague, geographically speaking. Bronagh was a tall, sturdy redhead in her thirties. Kris was a little older and darkly handsome. Cara herself was younger and boyish with short, sandy hair.

There was coffee in a pot and Tunnock's caramel wafers on a plate.

'We don't get these in Glasgow!' Lola joked, helping herself to a biscuit.

'Neither do we, normally,' Cara said drily. 'Bronagh got them from the Scotmid in your honour.'

Kris poured the coffee, all smiles. He seemed in awe of Lola, and her rank.

'We're all ears,' Cara said when they were settled. 'What's going on?'

'There's a young woman living out at Skaravaig,' Lola said. 'Evie Mackinnon — known here as Daisy. She has a wee boy, Hamish. His father might be trying to find him.'

'Oh, and that's not good, I take it?' Cara said.

'It's . . . a little more complicated than that.'

She'd wrestled on the way here with how much exactly to tell the local police, but decided in the end that the only way they could truly hope to protect Evie and her son was by being as open as possible with the right people.

She explained as succinctly as she could.

'My God,' Cara said when Lola had finished. 'And Carter Craig knows they're on the island?'

'Yes,' Lola said. 'And if the parcel is any indication, he means to find them.'

Her words were met with silence.

'We need to make a plan,' Lola said. 'And I believe it needs to include Evie and other members of her family.'

'We'll support you,' Cara said.

'Here's what I want to do,' Lola said. 'I'll go out to Skaravaig tonight, and then tomorrow morning Evie's aunt and I will explain the situation to her and we'll discuss options. One is to move the pair of them. Another is to put some sort of security in place here. Though, of course, neither of those options is sustainable.

'Realistically, the only way to truly keep Evie and her son safe in the long term is to persuade her to make a statement about what happened to her, and to allow us to take a sample of the child's DNA. It's not a happy thought, but realistically a new trial and a fresh conviction are probably the only way to guarantee their safety.'

* * *

7.46 p.m.

Lola was driving into Skaravaig when she spotted Maddie Wicks walking ahead of her in the company of another, older woman with long white hair braided down her back. She slowed and lowered her window, in case they wanted a lift.

'I will,' Maddie said, sounding delighted.

'Thank you, but I'm only round the corner,' the other woman said. She was red-faced and cheerful-looking.

'This is Theresa, who has the community shop and café,' Maddie said. 'She's Evie's — I mean Daisy's — boss.'

'Pleased to meet you. I'm a friend of Maddie's from Glasgow,' Lola said quickly, pre-empting Maddie blowing her cover.

Maddie got in and closed the door.

'Theresa's something of a local hero,' Maddie said when they were driving. She seemed breathless from the walk. 'If it weren't for her running the shop on a shoestring, the nearest place to get a coffee or box of teabags would be Glendale! She does charitable work too, linked to domestic violence.'

Lola drove on.

'I'm very glad to see you,' Maddie said now. 'Aileen isn't very pleased with me. I think she'd rather I'd stayed in Glasgow.'

'Were you with her just now?' Lola asked, setting off to drive the remaining half-mile or so to the St Columba Centre, which she could now see clearly on a slope behind the village.

'Yes, I was there for dinner. Have you eaten, by the way?'

'I had fish and chips in the car in Portree before I set off,' Lola said. 'That's what the smell is. I only managed to eat half of them. No doubt the seagulls will have had the remains out of the bin. How was Evie?'

'Oh, in her own world,' Maddie said a little wearily, 'though happy to see us. Aileen wanted to talk to her there and then — before we'd eaten — but I said, no, we have to wait until the chief inspector's here. That way Evie will understand that the authorities are aware and looking into it, and she'll feel reassured. I hope that was the right thing to do. I managed to persuade her, but, as I say, she isn't happy with me. She sat through dinner with a face like thunder and barely touched her food. And all the while, darling Evie is oblivious to anything. She's just delighted her big sister's here again, and so soon. It's rather sweet in a way, but I could see Aileen's frustration. I'm afraid she finds Evie's naivety very difficult to bear. Oh — it's not this turning. It's the one after.'

Lola drove on.

'Aileen bears a terrible weight of responsibility. She always has. It's not healthy and I wish she'd *talk* to someone about it.'

'Why is that?' Lola asked.

'Well, partly because of what happened to Evie. She blames herself.'

'Why?'

A groaning sigh. 'It's a long story. Yes — this turning, then follow the lane up and to the left.'

Lola did as she was told.

'I'll save the tale for another time,' Maddie said. She began to speak again, then hesitated. 'I know you must be exhausted from your drive, but do you — would you consider coming to the croft with me this evening? I do think we should talk to Evie tonight, if we can. It can't be *ethical* to hold back information like this. Another thing I'm very concerned about is that Aileen might just take it upon herself to break the news, and I'm worried she won't do it in a sensitive way. I think she might choose to terrify Evie into understanding the threat. My niece can be a *very* wilful and controlling young woman.'

Lola bit her lip as she negotiated a series of ruts in the track. She'd hoped to leave talking to Evie until the morning, partly because by then she might have the report on the tracking device, but Maddie was talking sense: the ethical thing to do was to tell Evie tonight. It was what Lola would want if she and her child were in the sights of a psychopath.

She parked the car and turned to her passenger. 'Let me check in here, then we'll go to the croft together.'

'Oh, I'm so pleased!'

They got out of the car and Maddie led Lola inside the modern building, which was one storey high and appeared to be circular in design, with wings emerging at odd angles. The staff had left for the day, but Zoe the manager had entrusted Maddie to show Lola her room.

'It's built in the shape of a Celtic cross,' Maddie said, leading her into a cool, circular area that looked to be a kind of day room. There were easy chairs set about, next to floor-to-ceiling windows giving expansive views across the peninsula. A couple of the chairs were occupied, one by an older woman with a frizz of yellowish hair. She appeared to be sleeping. In another chair a younger woman sat reading intently. She didn't look up as they passed.

'The bedrooms are in the shaft of the cross,' Maddie said, pushing open a door. 'Yours should have a good view of the sea.'

They passed along a corridor with doors on both sides. 'I'm in here on the right,' Maddie said, her hand on the handle of a door marked seven. 'You're number one, right down at the far end. Zoe said the key's in the lock on the inside. I'll give you a chance to freshen up, then I'll drive us to the croft. Meantime, I'll phone Donny and say we're coming back. I'll ask him to mention it gently to Aileen. Oh, I do hope there won't be any drama.'

CHAPTER THIRTY

8.21 p.m.

'And this is Evie!' Maddie said brightly, when Evie emerged from the house onto the wide patio where they were standing.

'What's going on?' the young woman asked, eyeing Lola warily then turning her questioning gaze on her sister and aunt. She was as thin as her older sister, but shorter, and looked much younger. Her wild curly fair hair fell about her shoulders and, in her close-fitting red-and-black tartan dress, she could have been a schoolgirl about to take part in country dancing.

'Lola is a detective chief inspector,' Maddie said, maintaining her bright tone. 'She's here because there are things we need to talk to you about, Evie. Now, why don't we all go inside for a wee chat?'

Donny and Jessie remained outside, taking 'a tour of the garden,' as Donny had put it.

Lola had liked the elderly pair. They were typical island types, based on her limited experience: rugged and windswept in appearance, but comfortable in their skin, and polite though reserved. 'Both in their seventies,' Maddie had told her on the short drive from the Centre, 'though he's older. Nearly eighty, I'd say.'

'What does she want?' she heard Evie asking her sister as she came into the kitchen. 'I'm not letting her anywhere near Hamish.'

Aileen didn't reply, but stood calmly by the sink, her face blank, though Lola saw accusation in her eyes.

It was cool in the kitchen, with its small windows and stone-flagged floor. Evie stood in the corner where the counters met, as if backed there by malignant forces, alarm in her eyes.

'We want to talk about Carter Craig,' Lola began, 'and how to make sure you and Hamish are safe. You need to be part of that conversation.'

Evie looked at Aileen, then at Maddie, then back at Lola. 'We are safe,' she said, and gave a little laugh. 'We *are*! Has something happened?'

'Evie, darling. Why don't we sit—'

'No, tell me what's going on! I want to know.'

'He knows where you are,' Aileen said in a loud, clear voice. 'Craig knows, and he's trying to find you. He's trying to find Hamish.'

For a moment it was as if all the air had been sucked from the room.

Then Evie gave that girlish laugh again. 'What are you talking about?'

'I think we should sit down,' Lola said firmly, and directed Evie towards the kitchen table and a chair.

Stunned, Evie allowed herself to be guided. Lola sat beside her and waited while Maddie and Aileen sat too.

'Now, there's something you need to understand,' Lola said. 'Carter Craig knows that you had a child and that the child is probably his.'

'Hamish *is* his,' Evie said, frowning. 'But . . . how? How did he find out?'

'We can come to that.' She was conscious of Aileen shifting her chair, and could feel her judgemental gaze. 'At the moment, the important thing is that he knows you're on Skye.'

'No. No, he can't. That's . . . It's not *possible*.' She looked at her sister, then at her aunt. 'It's not, is it?' she demanded of Aileen.

'I'm sorry, but it is,' Aileen said coldly, with a note of near satisfaction in her voice.

Lola leaned forward to gaze into Evie's wide, scared eyes. 'We believe Craig might have sent a parcel here with your name on it, containing a child's outfit.'

'What?' she said, mystified. '*When?*'

'It arrived at Portree Delivery Office on Friday, with your name and a request for the postal workers to find you.'

'There was a note inside it,' Aileen chipped in, 'saying the outfit was from someone called "Auntie C". We don't have an Auntie C.'

Evie stared at her sister, blinking as if she couldn't understand what was being said.

'I still don't understand,' she said, turning back to Lola. 'If he sent it to Portree, then he can't know where I live, can he?'

'There was a device in the parcel,' Lola said, 'tucked into the hem of the pair of trousers.'

Evie laughed in incomprehension. 'What do you mean? What sort of device?'

'A cellular GPS tracker.'

Evie's lip trembled. 'So you mean — it would be delivered here and then he'd . . . he'd know where it was? He could come here? Oh my God.' She clamped a hand over her mouth as if to contain a scream.

'That's exactly what it means,' Aileen said, eyes blazing.

'But it didn't get here,' Lola said firmly. 'The postman met your uncle in Glendale and your uncle realised it was suspicious, so he threw it away.'

'Uncle Donny called me and I told the chief inspector here,' Aileen said. 'She had it recovered from the bin and taken back to Portree.'

'That's right,' Lola said, eager to take back control of the conversation. 'It's been examined for fingerprints and the device is now in Inverness for examination by an expert.'

'Glendale,' Evie murmured, eyes away in a corner of the kitchen as she thought it through. 'That's not far from here. So he might know I'm nearby.'

'It's still a good distance away,' Maddie said. 'Ten miles at least.'

'Seven,' Aileen corrected. 'It's seven miles away.'

'Oh God, Aileen,' Evie sobbed, and threw her arms round her sister's neck. 'Don't leave us. You've got to stay here. Don't leave us, please!'

'Of course I'll stay here as long as you need me,' Aileen said, reaching to embrace her sister, her voice dripping with pity. All the time she glared daggers at Lola over Evie's juddering shoulder.

Lola met her gaze. She disliked this sanctimonious young woman intensely. Aileen seemed almost to be enjoying her sister's misery.

'Evie, darling, we'll do everything we can to protect you,' her aunt said. 'Meanwhile, the chief inspector has already been to see the island police.'

'That's right,' Lola said. 'And they would like to meet you to help plan to keep you and Hamish safe.'

'But what can they do?' Aileen demanded. 'I mean, really! They're a bunch of rustics. How can they stop a sociopath like Craig?'

'I'm not sure this kind of talk is really helping,' Lola said stiffly, eyes boring into the young woman's. Changing her tone, she said, 'Evie, I'd like to talk to you alone for a few minutes. Would that be okay with you?'

'Yes, I think that's an excellent idea,' Maddie said, rising from her seat. 'Why don't you have a chat with the chief inspector, just the two of you. Aileen, you come outside with me.'

'I'm not going anywhere,' Aileen said, arms possessively encircling her sister's shoulders.

'Come on, Evie,' Lola said brightly, standing herself now. 'Aileen will give us some time to talk. I'm sure she understands why it's so important.'

Aileen's shocked expression turned to one of teeth-baring anger. 'It's thanks to you she's in such terrible danger.'

Oh God. Here we go . . .

'What do you mean?' Evie asked, lifting her teary face and studying her sister. 'What do you mean, it's thanks to her?' She peered round at Lola, and her eyes were red and fearful.

'And not just her,' Aileen went on, still pinioning Evie in her arms. 'Ask Maddie what she did too.'

'Darling, no!' Maddie cried.

'Ask them, Evie,' Aileen ordered. 'Ask them to explain themselves.'

Evie looked around in confusion, first at Lola, then at Maddie.

'Aileen, please.' Lola made a hand signal to Maddie not to engage.

'Not my fault,' Aileen said. 'I'm not the one who's done anything wrong.'

'I was only trying to help,' Maddie began, to Lola's dismay. 'I'm the one who asked for advice.'

'Advice about *what*?' Evie demanded.

'Whether Hamish's DNA could prove Craig was in Glasgow at the time of the nightclub murders. I'm sorry, but those grieving families are in *pieces*. I thought perhaps it was time to come forward, to try to help.'

'And so Maddie told DCI Harris here,' Aileen said, picking up the narrative with acidic glee. 'And DCI Harris told some of her colleagues — who told Craig.'

'Now hold on a minute—' Lola began.

'Told him, in fact,' Aileen went on in a sing-song superior tone, 'not only that you'd had a baby, *but that you were here on Skye.*'

'Oh, Aileen,' Maddie said, then bit her lip and looked appealingly to Lola.

171

Lola knew the damage was done and said nothing. There'd be time to explain things later.

Evie didn't seem to know where to look. She pulled away from Aileen and looked anxiously at the door and windows as if expecting to see Craig at any moment, her breathing coming in shallow gasps. Aileen glared at the other two women with a dead-eyed satisfaction that frankly sickened Lola.

'I need to check on Hamish,' Evie said now, rising from her chair and knocking it so it nearly fell.

'Darling, Hamish is fine. He's safe,' Maddie cried after her as she darted from the kitchen.

'He isn't though, is he?' Aileen asked her as Evie's feet thumped up the stairs. 'Neither is Evie. Not now.'

'Oh, be quiet!' her aunt snapped, turning on her. 'For once, just keep your holier-than-thou opinions to yourself and *be quiet.*'

Aileen said no more but stood and pushed her chair neatly back under the table. Without a glance at either Lola or her aunt, she left the room, and they heard her light tread on the stairs.

Maddie put a hand to her forehead and let out a deep sigh. She reached for a chair and sat, then put her face in both her hands. Lola waited.

'It couldn't have gone worse, could it?' Maddie said at last. Her big blue eyes were shot with red and she looked exhausted. 'Whatever can we do?'

'Wait a while,' Lola said gently.

'You don't think I should I go up and try to talk to Evie?'

Lola took a deep breath. 'I wouldn't,' she said. 'Not while Aileen's there. Let's come again tomorrow, and we'll try to talk to Evie on her own.'

'Yes,' Maddie said. She took out a tissue and blew her nose. 'Yes, let's do that. Sleep will help, won't it?'

* * *

Maddie drove the two of them back to the St Columba Centre in near silence. They said goodnight in the corridor, and Lola went into her room, showered, then called Sandy. The signal wasn't great, but they managed a short chat. She felt better for hearing his voice. She didn't tell him about Izatt's further insinuations. Instead, she told him she hoped to be back by the next evening.

Joe's brother Kev had texted. She'd taken to expecting the messages, which were bland updates, to which she responded with yet blander, shorter replies. Tonight's said, *Joe's back on his feet. The surgeon hopes to have him in again next week. Looking like Tuesday, but I'll let you know.*

She sighed and shook her head. In the end, she just wrote, *Thanks for that. L.* and pressed send.

She checked her emails, and found one from Anna sent just after six with an update. Neither Jonno nor Marcus, the two constables, had had any success going through CCTV footage from businesses on the Saltmarket looking for images of Kathryn Main and her mystery friend. More promisingly, though, another juror from Craig's trial had come forward, not one who'd been part of Kathryn Main's WhatsApp group, but another.

Her name's Sharon Trent, Anna wrote, *and she says she was approached on the second evening of the trial by a 'blonde lady in a red scarf', as she was walking towards Central Station, and that this woman said she'd been watching the trial. She asked the juror to go for a coffee. The juror said no thanks. She didn't think anything of it, just that the woman was lonely. Only she remembered her name — it was Liz. I'm meeting her in the morning. I'll be in touch after that.*

Liz, who'd befriended Kathryn and taken her for dinner; who'd likely given her a moonstone necklace, one that had since been 'retrieved' from Kathryn's flat; who'd then seemingly vanished off the face of the earth, leaving Kathryn dead and a psychopath free to stalk a mother and child.

Lola wrote in reply, *I'm sure you've already thought of this, but get a photo of Elizabeth McQueen and show it to the juror.*

An email reply came quickly, so Anna was clearly still working. *Already onto it. Emailed Elizabeth McQ and asked for a photo 'for elimination purposes'. Will chase her in the morning if not received by then. I'll show her one of Beth Grayling too.*

CHAPTER THIRTY-ONE

11.09 p.m.

Lola was too wired to sleep.

She lay in the dark room, the blind up and the window open, listening to the shushing of the sea less than half a mile away, and the call of night creatures in the fields surrounding the centre. Her body was tired but her brain was too busy worrying about Evie Mackinnon and her son, and Evie's controlling, punitive sister, who seemed determined to take such enjoyment in others' mistakes. Ideally, Lola and perhaps Maddie would have time to talk to Evie alone in the morning. Then, if Evie was willing, Lola would invite DC Cara Phillips and her uniformed colleagues here to meet Evie, to make sure she knew how to call for help, and to check Donny and Jessie's croft was secure. They might advise on better door locks or motion sensor lighting, perhaps even recommend a domestic personal alarm linked to the Area Control Room. But she doubted she'd get any time with Evie without Aileen sitting there, all the time gazing at Lola with eyes that brimmed with blame. Or perhaps . . . A plan began to form in her mind. Yes, that might work. She'd talk to Cara first thing.

Her mind still wouldn't settle. And now her thoughts returned to Graeme Izatt. She groaned and sat up again.

Oh God . . .

It was infuriating. She turned on the light beside her bed and looked about the nicely if minimally decorated little room, wishing she was back in Glasgow.

She picked up her phone and read her most recent text conversations with Sandy. His replies had come quickly and cheerfully.

Are you still awake? she typed, then hesitated. How could she receive assurance through text messages? They'd only end up talking, and with a frustratingly bad signal.

She deleted the message. Anxiety had dried her mouth and she reached for her glass of water and drank half of it, then lay back on her pillows, feeling wretched.

This was ridiculous. She was torturing herself. Rather, she was allowing Izatt to torture her. It was his petty revenge because she hadn't handed Evie Mackinnon and her son over to him like the human sacrifice he wanted.

She racked her brain for a way to find out what Izatt meant. He'd worked for the MIT for several months now. If he had indeed heard people discussing her and Sandy, then it was likely there, in that office. Who else did she know there?

A thought: hadn't her old pal DI Mairi Marshall moved to the MIT a month or two back? Mairi was a good sort, honest, and not the kind who played games. She wouldn't engage in gossip, but she might reveal something she'd heard others saying, if pushed. Lola scrolled through her contacts and found Mairi's personal number. Yes, if there was something to tell, Mairi would reveal it. She might sugar-coat it a bit, but Lola would see through that.

Hi Mairi. It's Lola H — not sure if you've got my number stored in your phone. Hope you and the wee one are doing well. I'd quite like a chat at some point. Let me know when suits.

She read it over a couple of times, doubt chewing at her, then pressed send.

Mairi began to reply straight away, as if she'd had her phone in her hand.

All good with us! A photo appeared: a selfie of her and her eighteen-month-old child. *Sidney's got a cold and isn't sleeping, so I'm going to be up for a good while yet. Tell me what you're after.*

Lola thought for a moment. *Might be easier to chat*, she typed. *Don't suppose you'd be able to talk just now . . . ?*

Sure thing. Let me hand Sid over to Danny and I'll give you a buzz.

Lola sat in a state of miserable apprehension, her heart thumping away, wondering how long it could take to pass a baby to your husband, but after three or four minutes Mairi was ringing her.

'Hi, Mairi. Thanks for agreeing to talk so late.'

'That's all right. Is everything okay?' There was buzzing on the line.

'Hmm, not really. Listen, I'm on Skye and the signal's crap. If it drops I'll go outside and ring you back.'

'No worries.'

'The thing is,' she began, feeling foolish already, 'something's got me worried. It's probably nothing, but you know how things play on your mind.'

'Aye, go —' Mairi's voice dropped out — 'is it — in case you —'

Lola cursed.

'Mairi, you're breaking up. I'll call you in a minute.'

Mairi heard that and said that was fine.

Lola hung up and scrabbled for her trainers.

The signal outside wasn't much better, even at the far end of the car park. She looked around in frustration. Behind the St Columba Centre steep crags rose black against the indigo night-time sky, hardly good for reception. She'd had more bars in the village and beyond, she remembered.

She hurried back inside for her car keys, then jumped in the Audi and drove down the bumpy track into Skaravaig, keeping an eye on her signal, which remained poor. She drove out of the village, towards Donny and Jessie's place, and picked up a second bar. Another half-mile and the road rose, close to the cliffs before beginning its long descent into Glendale. At the brow of the hill she had three bars, so pulled into a passing place and turned off the engine.

'Hello, Mairi, can you hear me?'

'Oh, that's loads better!'

'I drove up the hill. Anyway, I can hear you now.' She took a deep breath. 'Where to begin, eh?'

She told Mairi what Izatt had said, and how she'd challenged him earlier today.

'So I just wondered if you'd heard anything — and, well, whether you feel you could tell me what it was.'

Mairi hummed and clicked her tongue. 'Sandy Johnson?' she said. 'I can't say I've heard the name. Honestly, Lola, that's the truth.'

'Is it?'

'I'd tell you, I swear.'

Lola believed her, and felt mildly reassured. If Mairi hadn't heard 'others talking' then maybe Izatt was simply lying.

'I'm sorry,' Mairi said now. 'He's a rotten bastard, isn't he? Graeme, I mean.'

'Aye, he can be. It's because he's unhappy. Not an excuse, but it makes sense.'

They talked about trivial stuff for a few minutes. Lola asked about baby Sidney. Then Mairi said, 'Look, I hate to think of you worrying. Why don't I ask about? I can be subtle about it. I could drop your name into conversation in the canteen, even mention Sandy. See what folk say.'

She thought about it. The idea made her feel shivery, but if it helped put her mind to rest . . .

'Aye, go on then. If you wouldn't mind. Thanks, Mairi.'

She sat in the quiet car for several minutes, toying with her phone and wondering whether it was sensible to let Mairi dig on her behalf. Didn't digging only ever turn up dirt? And what if Mairi's digging led to more talk? What if word reached Sandy's ears? What if he concluded that she didn't trust him?

Oh God, stop it!

She got out of the car and stood in the cool stillness of the evening. The sky was blue and purple, but lighter in the west, where it was still peachy and yellow. It was darker directly above, and stars glittered like chips of ice. There was no breeze at all, just the sound of waves on shingle below, and the occasional call of a bird. It was as if the whole ocean — the whole world — lay before her, but concealed in shadow. To her left, hidden by hills, was Glendale. The sinister parcel had reached that far, stopped only because of Donny's quick thinking. Was Craig on his way to the island yet, or was he already here? Of course, he might steer well clear and send some lethal minion instead, perhaps the same person who, on his behalf, had murdered Kathryn Main and the drug dealer Mack McBurney. In which case, who was the killer? How might they be recognised, singled out — and stopped? Lola's skin crawled to think the predator could already be on the island, perhaps disguised as just another tourist, or perhaps passing as a local.

Two miles to the north she could make out the lights of Skaravaig, strung out like a necklace on the dark plateau. Above the village, the St Columba Centre was distinct on the hill, and a little to the east was a lone house, with what looked like a single lamp shining at its door. Further to the east was Donny and Jessie's place, somewhere in the darkness.

A noise shook her from her reverie: the buzz of a motorbike. She heard it before she saw it, then it rounded a bend and came over the brow of the hill from the direction of Glendale, its headlamp's beam momentarily blinding her before it flashed past and the bike buzzed off down the hill. It was a small thing, more a scooter or moped than a motorbike. She'd barely glimpsed the driver, but it was someone slim and not very tall. A young woman perhaps. On her way home from work in Portree? She imagined a scooter would be worth its weight in gold to a young person on the islands: such freedom. She watched the bike wend its way north, following the road almost as far as Skaravaig — but then it stopped, just at the entrance to Donny and Jessie's driveway.

Lola's heart skipped.

She was back in her car in a flash and turning, then belting down the hill, counting the seconds.

If the rider meant ill, the noise of Lola's engine and the blaze of her headlights might scare them off.

She stopped the car a few hundred yards before the entrance to the croft's driveway and killed the lights, then got out and peered hard through the darkness. She could see a torch moving near the gate, could see its beam scanning the gate and wall.

She got back in the car and was at the driveway in seconds, her lights on full beam, so that they seemed to pin the rider, who froze, but only for a second. Lola saw wide, startled eyes inside a helmet, then the visor was snapped down and the rider was scrabbling for the bike, righting it and climbing on, then revving the engine so that the light blazed back at her. The road was narrow here, with wire fences on both sides. Lola turned her car, making a wedge that blocked the road. The bike came at her, then seemed to skew and wobble. She heard it connect with the Audi's back bumper, then there was a horrible scraping as the rider wrenched the bike past the back of the car and free — and it was off, flying away from the village, the buzz of its engine like a retreating mosquito, back in the direction of Glendale and into the night.

* * *

11.50 p.m.

'I heard the stramash,' Uncle Donny said, peering into the darkness over Lola's shoulder. 'Won't you come in?'

Jessie came into the kitchen as Donny was bolting the door behind Lola. The old woman's face was a grimace of concern. 'What's on earth's happened?'

'There was a motorcyclist at your gate with a torch just now,' Lola said. 'I disturbed him. Whatever he was doing, he bolted like the wind, damaging my car in the process.'

'Oh, Donny,' Jessie said, a hand to forehead. Her white hair was loose and she seemed suddenly frail and confused.

'He seemed to be interested in the sign on your gate. I'm afraid I levered it off with a stone and it's now in the boot of my car. Best if this address is unmarked from the roadside. I'm going to call Portree and ask them to send a uniformed officer to keep watch overnight.'

'What's going on?' a steely, unwelcome voice asked from the staircase. Aileen.

'A man on a motorbike was messing about at the gate,' Jessie told Aileen.

'A *man*?' Aileen stared wide-eyed at Lola.

'A boy. Maybe even a woman. I didn't get a proper look. A slight figure, not very tall.'

Aileen blinked several times and seemed genuinely shocked. 'Oh God,' she said. 'Oh God, no. I have to tell Evie.'

'Aileen—' Donny called.

'Leave her be,' Jessie said.

It was too late anyway, she was gone.

'I'm sorry to alarm you like this,' Lola said to Donny. 'I'll stay till an officer arrives who can keep watch. You'll be fine if you make sure the place is locked and bolted front and back, including any windows. I'll come by first thing in the morning. And I'll ask the detective constable who's based on the island to come and join us. It's time to take action.'

CHAPTER THIRTY-TWO

8.58 a.m.

'Like an intruder, you mean?' Maddie said, visibly paling when Lola told her about the mystery biker.

'Hardly an intruder, more like someone making a reconnaissance.'

'"Checking the lay of the land", so to speak. How awful. You should have woken me.'

'There was nothing you could have done.'

Maddie looked unconvinced.

They were down for breakfast — for Lola, a single slice of toast and an apple — at a corner table in the Centre's little dining room. The place was fairly busy, with maybe a dozen guests milling for cereal, or taking coffee in the easy seats by a floor-to-ceiling window with a view of clifftops and a partial glimpse of the sea. She couldn't help studying the people, wondering if any of them might be an agent of Craig's in disguise. The thin young man in round glasses, perhaps? The middle-aged woman who'd brought her knitting to breakfast? No, the idea was laughable.

The Centre's manager, Zoe, a cheerful island woman in her thirties, appeared at their table.

'I hope you slept well,' she said.

'Oh, yes,' Lola lied with a smile.

She hadn't got back from the croft till gone two, after a very young-looking constable from Portree had turned up to keep watch on the croft from the driveway. Jessie had fussed around him, even making him a flask of hot coffee, which he'd been grateful for. Aileen had returned to the kitchen when he arrived, peering anxiously at the PC as if he was wholly inadequate.

'The meeting room's all ready for you,' Zoe said. 'It's the door to the right of the reception. It's yours all day if you want it.'

'That's very kind.'

'I hope it won't all be meetings for you, though. We have so much to offer. I'm sure Maddie will have told you about some of our activities,' Zoe said now, 'but there's tai chi this morning in the east field, and our popular crag ramble this afternoon followed by fireside meditation tonight. There isn't a fire, in case you were wondering. We just put on an orange light. More eco-friendly.'

Lola smiled and nodded until Zoe went away.

'It seems as if he knows, then, doesn't it?' Maddie said. 'He must. The parcel found its way to Glendale, and now one of his minions has tracked down the croft. People like Craig have followers everywhere, thanks to the internet.' She bit her lip and gazed towards the big window. 'We have to get the two of them away from here. I could take them today. There's a ferry to North Uist from Uig.'

'There may be no need,' Lola said quietly. 'But if we do decide it's best for Evie to go away — which *she* would need to agree to — then I think it would make more sense to take her back to the Central Belt. An island community is small and vulnerable. Better for them to be somewhere where there are hundreds of thousands of people, not to mention plenty of police.'

'Yes, I see what you mean,' Maddie said and replaced her coffee cup in its saucer. 'But then there's the Aileen problem.'

'Yes,' Lola agreed, and watched the conflict in Maddie's expressive face. 'You were going to tell me why Aileen blames herself for what happened to Evie. Why she feels such responsibility.'

'I was, wasn't I? Well, it's not such a long story after all. Aileen is older than Evie and she cared for her when their mother, my sister, died six years ago. Aileen was nineteen, Evie fourteen. She became Evie's "kinship carer". I helped and there was a social worker too, though she and Aileen often locked horns. I was the one often tasked to *unlock* them.' She smiled ruefully. 'Evie got older and insisted on leaving school at sixteen. She said she didn't want to study anymore. She wanted to become a "fashion influencer" — a concept that was new to me. She said, "You can't train for it. You just have to know people and put yourself out there on social media and then you become famous." Anyway, she started going to parties, drinking — yes, underage, I know! My goodness, she's such a different girl nowadays. Aileen told me she sometimes even took drugs, so I had a word with her. Cue the tears and tantrums. Then Aileen found out that Evie was getting close to Carter Craig and his set. She was going to parties at his nightclubs, and for those you needed a personal invitation from Craig himself. Then she was going to his house — it's just outside Milngavie, one of these sprawling modern places made of white boxes, with artificial lawns and a heated swimming pool. She thought she was in love with him.'

'That must have been worrying,' Lola said quietly.

'Oh, you're telling me!' She sighed. 'Aileen attempted to enforce a new regime. She grounded Evie, relieving her of her phone and access to money. Evie said she was being abusive. She fought Aileen and even threatened to call the police, to say Aileen was keeping her under a kind of house arrest. She had a friend come and break her out. She called Aileen horrible names and told her she was a psychopath. Aileen said that if Evie left she would never take her back, and that they would be strangers to one another.' Maddie registered Lola's expression. 'Awful, isn't it? Manipulative bullying, or just plain controlling? Anyway, thanks to Aileen's threats Evie didn't go with her friend that night. She retreated to her room. I called round a few days later, as I did from time to time. I asked Aileen where Evie was, and she said, "I've locked her in her room." I said, "You've done *what*?" And she said if she didn't protect her, she'd end up dead. I said, "*No* — this cannot happen! You cannot do this." Aileen became very upset, and I unbolted Evie's door myself. I took her with me that night, to my place in Strathbungo. I told Aileen to stay away for a week.'

Maddie stopped. She seemed exhausted by the telling.

'Anyone for more coffee?' a cheery waitress asked.

They both accepted.

'What did you do?' Lola pressed.

'I found a family therapist. She saw the three of us together, then she saw Aileen and Evie together, without me. Things calmed down. A new way forward was agreed: Evie would have freedom, her phone, her friends, but she would respect Aileen's need for reassurance given she was *in loco parentis*. But before long Evie was pushing at the boundaries again, and Aileen was tightening the rules. She even set a curfew, which was tricky because by then Evie had a job, waitressing at a restaurant in Glasgow, and some of the shifts ended late. And then things came to a head. Evie said she was moving out. Another girl at the restaurant had a spare room in her flat. Evie got her things together and she and the colleague moved her into the flat. Aileen was devastated. She *pined*. It was horrible to see.'

Maddie paused, seeming to wrestle with uncomfortable emotions.

'Weeks passed,' she said at last, 'and Aileen was still in a bad way, but then Evie called late one evening and asked to come home. She'd argued with the girl who owned the flat. She hated her job and wanted to go back to college. Only, Aileen said no.'

Maddie sipped her coffee and took her time before continuing.

'She said Evie had made her choice and must live with it. She couldn't help her anymore. That was in the August three years ago. Two nights later, Craig had Evie collected from work. That was the night he raped her. As I said, Aileen has carried the burden a long time. She's never, ever forgiven herself and I don't think she ever will. And now her compulsion to protect her sister has become . . . "pathological", wouldn't you say?'

'I can't say, no,' Lola replied. 'I'm not a psychologist. But I hear your concern.'

Maddie seemed satisfied with that. She nodded, then looked at the clock on the breakfast room wall. 'What time is your DC joining us?'

'Anytime now,' Lola said. She checked her phone. 'In fact, she's just texted to say she's outside.'

* * *

9.20 a.m.

Cara Phillips was standing by her car squinting up at the St Columba Centre, a vape in hand. She tucked it guiltily away when she saw Lola emerge. Maddie had scooted back to her room for her phone and bag. It was misty outside and cooler than Lola had felt it for weeks.

'This where you're staying?' Cara asked. 'I've never been inside.'

'Aye. It's not bad. Clean and comfortable. I got you a meeting room — it's the door to the right of the reception. Any problems, ask to speak to Zoe — she's the manager. And this is Madeleine Wicks,' Lola said, as Maddie came down the steps to join them.

'Call me Maddie. Pleased to meet you.' She put out a hand. 'Though I must just say that I feel dreadful about this. It feels horribly like an ambush.'

'It's necessary,' Lola said. 'And it's the right thing to do. Donny and Jessie both agree.'

Lola had spoken to the pair first thing. She'd also chatted to the officer who'd taken over from the lad who'd spent the night watching the house. He seemed excited that activity might be imminent.

'And will Aileen ever speak to me again?' Maddie said. 'I wouldn't.'

Lola noted the strain in the woman's face and sympathised, but remained confident of the plan.

She and Cara spoke for a couple of minutes, then Cara got in her car and drove off. Lola and Maddie got into Lola's car and followed on behind, but turned off in the village and parked in one of the three spaces at the side of the community store and café.

They waited there for a tense few minutes, then Lola's phone buzzed. A text from Cara.

'Is that her?' Maddie asked.

'Yes, Aileen's agreed,' Lola said. 'So now we wait till we see the car pass.'

Less than five minutes later, Cara's Ford passed the store, heading through the village in the direction of the St Columba Centre. Aileen was in the passenger seat.

'That's us,' she said, climbing back in the car and reversing quickly. 'Now, we might not have long. Let's make every minute count.'

* * *

9.44 a.m.

'What's going on?' Evie wanted to know. She stood in the doorway between the kitchen and living room, Hamish balanced on her hip.

'We just wanted a chat,' Lola said. Donny and Jessie lingered shiftily behind her.

'But Aileen's not here. She's gone to make some kind of "statement".'

'Which makes this a good time,' Maddie said. 'We want to talk to you alone.'

'If it's about what happened last night then I already know. Aileen told me about it. He knows we're here and it's because of what you did — both of you.'

Lola took a breath and managed to hold her tongue. This wasn't the time to explain that this mess was no one person's fault.

'We need to talk about how to keep you safe,' Lola said.

'But Aileen should be here. She's taken care of me so far.'

'Evie, this is important,' Maddie said.

Lola could see from Evie's body language — the way her shoulders had dropped a little, the way she could now meet Lola's eye — that she was already relenting.

'Come on through to the living room,' Maddie said. 'We can talk in there.' With a hand, she steered Evie gently back through the doorway, cooing, 'And look at this handsome boy in his lovely green T-shirt!'

'Thank you,' Lola said quietly to Donny and Jessie. 'I know this is very difficult for you.'

Donny nodded and grunted.

'I'll put the kettle on and make some coffee, then,' Jessie said. 'It sounds like you're going to need it.'

CHAPTER THIRTY-THREE

9.56 a.m.

Evie sat awkwardly in an armchair, legs pulled up and arms round her knees. Maddie knelt on the rug with Hamish, while he showed her his wooden train.

Lola settled in an armchair beside Evie's. 'I wanted to chat to you about something personal. We can do it alone, just the two of us, or Maddie could be here, if that's what you want. It's about what Carter Craig did to you.'

Evie considered her for a few moments. 'Maddie can stay,' she said. 'But' — she looked towards the kitchen door — 'maybe Jessie could take Hamish. I know he wouldn't understand, but it feels wrong to talk about it in front of him.'

'Yes, of course,' Lola said.

Jessie came in a minute later with a tray bearing a cafetière and three mugs along with some shortbread. She took Hamish back into the kitchen with her, and then it was just Lola, Maddie and Evie. Maddie moved to the end of the settee, while Lola poured the coffee slowly, purposefully lowering the pressure in the room.

'Was it him last night?' Evie asked quietly.

'I don't think so,' Lola said. 'I disturbed whoever it was. It was someone with a small build. And the bike was just a scooter. I think it was probably someone local.'

'One of his followers, then?'

'Possibly.'

'He'll be back, though, won't he? Or someone else will.' She spoke very quietly and with weary acceptance. 'We can't stay here. Not anymore.'

'There could be another way,' Lola said carefully, eyes on Evie's face. 'A way to make Craig go away forever.'

'What do you mean?' She looked sceptical. 'Aileen said nothing can stop him now. He killed one of the jurors from his trial, she says. Strangled her like he strangled Alex Sanderson before he shot him. He's killed a witness too. The one who said he sold him drugs. Now he knows about Hamish, he won't stop till he's got hold of him and—' She stopped and screwed up her face. 'Aileen says . . . Aileen says I should go away. Far away, where nobody knows me. She said she'd come with me. Or she said she could take Hamish back to Glasgow. Look after him there while I live somewhere else.'

'She said that, did she?' Lola could feel Maddie's shocked eyes on her. 'When was this?'

'Last night. But she's said it before. She said she could take Hamish and tell people she'd adopted him.'

'I see.'

Lola glanced at Maddie, who'd sat back in her seat, a hand over her mouth.

'And how did you feel about that?' This wasn't going in the direction she'd expected, but it felt important. Dark too.

'Aileen really loves Hamish,' Evie said with a sad smile, but still hugging her knees defensively. 'She's so anxious for him. For both of us. And I . . . I want the best for him, but really I just want him to be *safe*. Maybe he can never be safe with me.'

Lola thanked Heaven she'd got Evie away from her sister's pernicious influence, even for this short period.

Lola could see Maddie itching to speak and quieted her with a hand gesture.

She said, 'Evie, are you aware that your testimony could send Craig to prison for several years?'

'What?' Evie looked at her as if she was mad.

'I believe you have evidence that could convict him — not necessarily of what he did to you, but of murdering those people at his nightclub.'

She stared at Lola, uncomprehending, then turned to Maddie. 'What's she talking about?'

'It's true,' Maddie said.

The air in the room suddenly felt electric.

'The night he attacked you is the same night he's alleged to have killed those two people at the nightclub,' Lola said. 'His whole defence was that he was in Jersey for the month of August. But he couldn't have been if he attacked you — and made you pregnant with Hamish.'

Evie frowned. 'But they proved he could have come back to Glasgow and killed the people. It was part of the trial!'

'I don't think they proved it, darling,' Maddie said, looking to Lola for confirmation. 'I think at most they persuaded the jury he *could* have come back to Glasgow. It was about throwing doubt on his claim.'

'That's exactly right,' Lola said.

'And now you want me to say he was in Glasgow to throw some more doubt?' Evie asked, incredulous. 'What if they don't believe me?'

'They will. Because it's not just your story. There are the antenatal scans. They took some at seven weeks. They can narrow down the date. Those, together with your testimony and . . .'

'And what?'

'*And Hamish's DNA*,' Maddie said, almost in a whisper. 'DCI Harris has already checked with the Crown Office — they're the ones who decide if the evidence is strong enough to take to a trial. And, darling, *they think it would be.*'

Evie stared at her aunt in complete amazement.

'It's true,' Lola said. 'But nobody will make you give evidence, or release your medical records, or take a swab from you or Hamish — not without your agreement. But if you wanted to do it, there is a very good chance a jury would be persuaded Craig was in Glasgow that night and that his alibi was worthless. Which means there is a strong possibility a jury would convict him of those murders.'

'And then you and Hamish would be safe,' Maddie said. 'There'd be no more hiding. No more running away.'

A noise from outside. A car engine, then a door slamming and a high-pitched shout. Next, raised voices in the kitchen, and Aileen burst through the living room door and threw herself on Evie.

'Don't listen to them!' she cried. 'You'll be in danger but they don't care about that. They'll take Hamish from us.'

'Aileen, no!' Maddie cried.

Donny was in the room now.

'Please, Aileen,' Lola said, pulling at one of Aileen's arms. 'Stop this now.'

'Get your hands off me and get out of this house. You too!' she screamed at Maddie. Then she lowered her voice and cooed to Evie, 'They only want to use you. You're safe with me. Tell them to leave.'

Cara was in the doorway now, pushing gently past Donny, looking flushed. *Sorry*, she mouthed to Lola.

Lola went to her. Together they retreated outside. Lola took a big breath of air.

'I'm sorry,' Cara said. 'I couldn't keep her there. We got to the Centre and she started to get panicky. She wanted to know where you and Maddie were. I think she realised we'd laid a trap. She said she wanted me to drive her right back here. I did my best to keep her there, but what could I do? She was screaming, so I put her in the car and brought her back — as slowly as I could. I don't think I went above second gear!'

'It's okay,' Lola said.

'Did you get what you needed to?' Cara asked, wincing.
'No. Sadly.'

Cara's phone was ringing. 'Inverness,' she said, looking at the number. 'Might be the digital forensics guy about the tracker. I'd better answer it.'

Cara took the call, one finger in her ear. Lola tried to follow the gist of the conversation but struggled.

The sun was high and warm, but during the past hour morning mist had thickened over the peninsula. The village and the cliff edge were invisible. The crags above the St Columba Centre were like a black wall emerging from the cloud.

Cara came off the call. 'It's a legit tracker,' she said, 'and it had a live battery in it, but the forensics guy says it wasn't set. It was effectively a dud.'

'A "dud"?'

'He suggests whoever sent it didn't really know what they were doing.'

'So whoever was tracking it wouldn't have registered any signal at all?'

'None, whether it was in Glasgow or Portree or out at Glendale. That's good news, isn't it?'

'Yes, I suppose,' Lola said, earning a frown from the DC. 'But it doesn't explain the person on the bike, does it?'

Her thoughts were interrupted by her own phone ringing. It was Anna Vaughan.

'I'll need to take this,' she told Cara. 'You go inside and try to keep the peace.'

CHAPTER THIRTY-FOUR

10.35 a.m.

Lola spoke to Anna from her car, still parked in Donny and Jessie's driveway with a view over the clouded peninsula. The signal held.

'How are things?' Anna asked.

'Tricky,' Lola said. 'But you rang me. What's up?'

'Hmm. Bad news first. Graeme Izatt and Aidan Pierce are travelling to Skye today. Word is, Aidan has somehow managed to charm some guy on the desk at Portree into telling him what he knows about the situation there. Sorry, boss . . .'

Lola closed her eyes. Anna had to mean Gerry March, the grinning desk officer. So happy to help! The idiot . . .

'Pierce is a devious shit,' Lola said. 'I've a mind to ring Graeme. Tell him if he crosses the bridge from the mainland, he'll be meeting with trouble he could never have imagined.'

'There's some better news too,' Anna said.

'Oh?'

'I met Sharon Trent at nine this morning. She was the juror who was approached by the woman from the public gallery in the court — "Liz".'

'Oh, yes. What's she like?'

'Mousy, and I don't mean just in appearance, though she is. She's a nervy woman. Early thirties, thick glasses. Looks lonely, if you know what I mean.'

'Lonely like Kathryn Main.'

'Exactly. She told me about Liz. Gave a pretty good description, and yes, it could be Elizabeth McQueen: a middle-aged woman with ash-blonde hair. Average height, quite slim. But I showed her a photo of Elizabeth and Sharon said it wasn't her. She was adamant. And it wasn't Beth Grayling either.'

'And that's the better news, is it?'

'Not quite. After I'd left her, I got to thinking about who else it might have been. Remember we said that Liz was either someone who wanted to get Craig put away for a long time, or someone who wanted to get him liberated by playing a longer game? Well, I thought about who else might do that, and it seemed possible it was his uncle. What if Duncan Gaunt paid a woman to play the part of Liz? I wondered if it might even be his wife. I googled her, and there she was, a load of photos from various magazines, press nights, gala dinners, that kind of thing. I realised pretty quickly that Juliana Gaunt couldn't possibly be a woman in her late forties or early fifties, wig or no wig. I don't know what I was thinking. But then I saw it. In one of the photos, Juliana was at a charity ball, and she was wearing *a moonstone necklace*. There it was, round Juliana's throat, the stone sitting in her cleavage.'

'My God.'

'I checked the image against the photo we've got on file: the one Kathryn had sent to her sister. I'm not completely sure, but it could be the same necklace.'

'Ask Juliana Gaunt about it. If she says she has it, go to the castle and retrieve it. If she hasn't got it, or says she hasn't, then come back to me. We might want to get a warrant.'

'Right, boss. Oh, and Sharon took me to the place where Liz approached her. There's a bookies and a café and a pub with a CCTV camera outside. I've got Jonno down there now, asking for any footage. Worth a try.'

'Thanks, Anna. Talk soon.'

Next she rang Elaine Walsh, her heart hammering.

'I know about Graeme,' Elaine admitted. 'Apparently he got the go-ahead from his superintendent. There's not a lot we can do to stop him.'

'But Pierce has made a pal on the island who's feeding him info. How long before he's here, banging down the door to get at the kid? We're talking lifelong trauma for the child and his mother — not to mention attracting even more attention to the croft.'

Elaine went quiet for a moment. 'What do you propose to do?'

'I think we need to move them. We can use the Protected Persons scheme. They must have places in the Highlands.'

'We could . . .' Elaine said and Lola heard her clicking her tongue as she thought. 'I might have a better idea. Have you got a good signal where you are?'

'It's okay just now,' Lola said, frowning at the question.

'Then don't move. I'll call you back in a few minutes.'

A text had arrived from Mairi, her old colleague who'd promised to dig for gossip about Sandy.

Oh God, not now . . .

But, too late. She'd pressed READ.

Some news re what we discussed. Call me when you can. M.

Lola writhed in her seat and finally got out of the car to pace the lawn. She stood by the fence at the bottom of the garden, looking out at the thickening mist. The crags were almost completely shrouded now. So much for Zoe's afternoon 'crag ramble' or whatever she'd called it. Maybe they could do some fog-bound tai chi instead.

Her phone was ringing.

'Hi, Elaine.'

'Right, listen. My husband's sister Deborah has a house at Staffin. It's north of Portree. Deborah's there just now, but there's an annexe, a couple of rooms for visitors. It's free and Evie and the boy can stay for up to three weeks if need be. Deborah's terribly discreet. As, of course,' she added meaningfully, 'are both you and I — do we understand each other?'

'Of course, boss. We haven't even spoken.'

'Now, got a pen?'

* * *

Lola was still obsessing about Mairi Marshall's text when Maddie Wicks emerged from the croft. She stood on the steps outside the front door, looking shattered. Then she spotted Lola, now back in her car, and made her way over.

Lola got out.

'We need to move Evie and Hamish,' Lola said quietly. 'Temporarily, at least. I have access to a house in Staffin.'

'Like a safe house, you mean?'

'Not an official one. But they will be safe there.'

Cara Phillips came out of the house, phone pinned to her ear. She acknowledged Lola with a distracted nod, then walked down the drive. Lola heard her speaking but not what she said.

A minute or two later Cara came back to the house, looking as if the weight of the world was on her shoulders. She stopped and eyed Lola.

'I'll come into the house in a minute,' Lola said to Maddie. 'See you inside.'

'Okay,' Maddie said, taking the hint.

'That was my sergeant in Fort William,' Cara said. 'There's a posse of MIT detectives on their way from Glasgow.'

'Ah, yes . . .'

'Apparently Gerry at the station has been "overly helpful", shall we say? Anyway, the DCI who's coming is demanding to know Evie's whereabouts.'

'Evie's whereabouts are about to change,' Lola said. 'I've found another place on the island.'

She explained, then Cara's phone rang again and she answered it.

'Go on, Kris . . . Oh, what?' Cara's face changed while she listened to the caller. She put an anxious hand to her forehead. 'Yes. Okay. Dear oh dear.' She sighed and closed her eyes. 'And where is he now?'

Another minute of questions, then Cara came off the call, looking sick.

'One of the constables — Kris, the guy you met last night in Portree — thinks his sixteen-year-old son overheard him talking to his wife about Evie.' She took a deep breath. 'The kid's a big fan of Carter Craig's. He's got a moped.'

Lola's skin prickled. 'And where is he now?'

'Missing,' Cara said and winced. 'Kris is in shock. I think I'd better go over there. Do you want to come?'

Lola reeled for a few seconds, then pulled herself together. 'Where does he live?'

'Dunvegan. Twenty, twenty-five minutes from here.'

Lola thought fast. 'I can't,' she said. 'You go. Ring me when you know anything.'

* * *

11.02 a.m.

Lola explained to Evie about the proposed move without disclosing the location. Aileen sat glowering beside her sister the whole time, her breathing becoming shallow and fast as though she was working up to an outburst.

'Is the place on Skye?' Evie asked.

'Yes,' Lola said. 'But another part of the island.'

'Will we be safe there?'

'It's wiser than staying here, given what happened last night,' Lola said. 'And it might only be for a few days.'

'If you go, I'll come with you,' Aileen said. 'We'll stay there together.'

'I'm not sure there'll be room for you,' Lola said.

Aileen turned sharply. 'You know that for a fact, do you?' To her sister she said, 'You want me there, don't you, Evie?'

Evie nodded, but it looked half-hearted to Lola.

Maddie came into the room.

'We're going to move Evie to a safe house,' Aileen told her, with a defiant glance in Lola's direction. 'I'm going with her.'

Maddie looked at Lola. 'Really?'

'Yes. It's best that the three of us are together. Isn't it, Evie?'

Evie looked at her sister, then uncertainly at Lola. 'I don't know. I think . . . I think we might be best just me and Hamish. After all, you've got your work. You—'

'Nonsense!' Aileen said sharply.

'It's my choice, isn't it?' Evie said, chin up and angry.

Aileen stared at her. 'After everything — *everything* I've done for you both! You want to—'

'It's not about *you*!' Evie cried. 'Stop making it your business.'

Aileen recoiled as if her sister had slapped her. Then she rose and ran, sobbing, from the room. Lola heard the front door open and slam shut, then caught a glimpse of her tearing down the garden.

'Should I go after her?' Maddie asked.

Lola shook her head.

'She always has to take over,' Evie said. 'To try and control everything.'

Maddie was about to speak, then appeared to decide against it.

'Can we go see the house before I decide?' Evie asked. 'Maybe we could take Hamish and look around. I'd feel happier that way.' She added, quietly, 'And I'd rather Aileen didn't come.'

'I'll drive us there,' Lola said. 'We can go as soon as you like.'

'I've been thinking about what you said,' the young woman said. 'About the evidence. About the scans and the dates and the DNA — and what it all means.'

'Oh?' Lola tried to sound calm, though her heart had picked up.

'Would we get witness protection? I mean, for as long as we needed it?'

'There are ways to protect people, yes.'

Evie nodded and looked down at her hands. 'Then I think we should do it, whatever my sister says.'

CHAPTER THIRTY-FIVE

11.41 a.m.

'It was the youngest lad who told the wife,' Kris MacPherson said to Cara. He looked sheepish as hell and his eyes were red.

Cara's heart ached for him. For Morag, his wife, too. The pair of them looked ruined with stress. Cara sat with Kris at the kitchen table of the new-build house they'd only just moved into. Morag couldn't settle and bustled around the kitchen, tidying, wiping.

'Come and sit down,' Kris said to her now.

'I can't,' she said in a thin voice. 'I can't.' She looked over at Cara. 'Don't you think I should go get Ferg? Bring him home?'

'No,' Kris told her.

The younger child, Fergus, aged ten, was at school. It was their older boy, Gordon — or Gordie — who was missing. Cara, though she had no kids of her own, could empathise with Morag MacPherson's wish to go fetch the younger boy. To protect him.

This was a horrible situation for everyone. The island was a close-knit community, the network of police tight. It would be disastrous for Kris's career, whatever the outcome.

'Am I gonnae be disciplined over this?' Kris asked Cara now.

'Don't think about that now,' Cara said. 'The most important thing is to find Gordie. Now, when did you last see him?'

Morag answered: 'Just after eight this morning. Ferg just came out with it,' she said. 'He said Gordie had been talking to people about Carter Craig. He'd heard him chatting to someone in the night, saying his dad was a copper and he'd overheard him and me discussing Craig and the young woman. Gordie told Ferg he'd "found where the woman was hiding". Oh God . . .' She paused, sniffing, then snatched for a piece of kitchen roll and blew her nose. 'I got Kris and Kris went into Gordie's room and Gordie kicked off. Swore at him, then he pushed past me as I was coming up the stairs. Shot out of the house and rode away on his bike.'

Cara asked about Gordie's friends, the places he might go, but Morag said they'd tried all the families they could think of.

'Craig's poison,' she said. 'And now Ferg is telling us Gordie is one of his disciples. A policeman's son! I've noticed changes in him lately, haven't you, Kris? The answering back, the swearing, the . . . the way he talks about women.'

She was crying again.

'You can have his laptop,' Kris said to Cara. 'Do what you have to do, though I don't know the password. Everything's secret with Gordie. Or has been lately, like Morag says.'

Cara took a description of the moped and what Gordie was wearing, then went outside to ask for a lookout broadcast to go out on the radio.

That done, she rang Lola Harris.

CHAPTER THIRTY-SIX

12.17 p.m.

The mist — or 'haar', as Donny called it — had begun to disperse as they left the croft, tearing here and there so that the landscape came back together like a ragged jigsaw. The crags stood clear of the cloud like dark sentinels. Most of the village was visible again, as well as the ragged line of the cliff edge. From the road Lola got a glimpse of a dull teal sea, but she started when she saw a black shape sitting in the bay: a huge yacht, large and streamlined and grey-black like a raven's wing.

Maddie was in the passenger seat of Lola's car, while Evie sat in the back, next to Hamish in a baby seat they'd transferred from Donny's jeep.

Maddie talked away, recounting the story of the Edinburgh hotel that her company was designing, and how the owners were on at her day and night, and appeared to be 'simply livid' that she was currently ignoring them.

'"Family matters," I told them. It's been constant and it's coming to a head! Frankly I've had enough.'

Lola wondered whether she talked like this because she couldn't bear a silence, especially an awkward one, or if that

203

was how she processed her ideas and anxieties. She wondered who Maddie talked to when there was no one else there. Herself?

The fifty-mile drive would take an hour and a half, whichever route they took. The road through Portree was probably better, but her instinct was to stick to the back roads. So she planned to cross the island on the north side, then turn off towards Uig and go over the high pass down into Staffin.

They were curving round the bay at Edinbane when her phone rang. It was Cara. She pulled into a layby and jumped out of the car to answer, listening to Cara's concise update.

'I'll need to go to Portree to try to sort this business out,' the DC said. 'I've got swab kits there, so I'll pick some up and bring them over to Skaravaig later on. You know, we're not geared up for all this activity here. I'm minded to request a couple of CID officers from Fort William.'

'I think that might be very sensible,' Lola said. 'We're on our way to Staffin just now. Let's keep in touch.'

Graeme Izatt tried to call her as she was getting back into the car but she declined the call. He could leave her a message if he wished.

Maddie was quiet as they headed north towards Uig. In the back, Evie gazed from the window and hummed lightly to herself like a sleepy child.

* * *

1.20 p.m.

Deborah's cottage was a little north of Staffin and reached up a short driveway from the road. Lola pulled up beside a Land Rover and got out. The L-shaped bungalow was called Two Pines, though the cottage was in fact sheltered by a sizeable copse of firs, which Lola was pleased to note. Yes, the trees made a solid screen. From the road no one would be able to see her, even though it was only a hundred metres or so away.

'Is it Lola?' a voice called, and Lola turned to find a smart woman with neat blonde hair in her fifties coming down a path from the house. She had on a mustard blouse, blue jeans and sandals. 'I'm Deborah Lewis.'

They went inside the house, which was open-plan and modern in a minimalist but comfortable way, then through a door into the annexe, allowing Hamish to take the lead.

'He already seems at home, doesn't he?' Deborah laughed. 'This part of the house has its own entrance, so you can come and go. The woods and the fields on both sides and behind are ours too. And in time I can show you how to get down to the beach and the slipway. There are dinosaur footprints on the rocks, though they're easy to miss.'

'I love it,' Evie said, eyes wide as she took in the bright living room and corner kitchen. The huge picture window looked directly down the driveway to the road and the meadows beyond. And there, not half a mile away, was the sparkling sea, and a green and gold island in the middle of the bay.

'It's only one bedroom, I'm afraid,' Deborah said.

'Oh, but that's all right, isn't it, Evie?' Maddie chimed in. 'You and Hamish are used to sharing.'

'Are you happy to move in today?' Lola asked. 'If so, we should head back to Skaravaig so you can pack and say your goodbyes to your aunt and uncle. And to Aileen.'

Evie smiled to herself, then turned to Lola and nodded. 'Yes, okay. And thank you.'

Lola said, 'I'll leave you all to it while I make a phone call or two.'

'That's fine,' Deborah said, beaming. 'If you go up the garden towards the far corner you should get a better signal.'

Standing by a fence in the shade of a pine tree, Lola steeled herself and called Graeme Izatt. He answered on the second ring. She could hear he had her on loudspeaker and that he was in a moving car.

'It's fine,' he barked when she asked if he was safe to talk. 'Aidan's driving.'

'Driving . . . to Skye, would that be?' she enquired pleasantly.

'Just turned off the A82, so not long now. Where are you, and, more importantly, where's the kid?'

'The kid's with me,' she said, trying to sound relaxed. 'The good news is, the mum's agreed to make a statement that Craig attacked her, and to provide a sample of her own and the child's DNA — and she's given permission for us to access any and all medical records. The bad news, for you, is that you've made a wasted trip. I'll be taking the samples later today and heading back to Glasgow, where you'll have full access to them.'

'Right.' He hesitated, momentarily wrong-footed. 'That's good. I still want to talk to her. Actually, I want to bring her and the kid back to the city where I can keep a close eye on them.'

'No chance, Graeme.' She rolled her eyes. 'She's safer here and everything's in order. As I said, you're wasting your time and taxpayers' money for petrol. Turn round now.'

There was a shocked silence, then he shouted, 'Just who do you think you are? This is my case! And anyway, we know where we're headed. It's past Glendale, isn't it?'

'Is it?'

'I know it is. So give me the address.'

'Didn't DS Pierce's pal in Portree tell him that? Oh, and by the way, the leak hasn't gone down *at all* well here, let me tell the pair of you.'

'This isn't a game, Lola,' came Izatt's response.

'No, it isn't,' she said. 'I suggest you stop treating it like one and go home.'

She hung up and dialled DC Cara Phillips.

'An update on my colleagues who are about to gatecrash,' she said when Cara answered. 'They'll be on the island in an hour or so and his sergeant's had word Evie and Hamish are "somewhere beyond Glendale", so I expect they'll head straight out west.'

'Want to do the test away from the croft, then? I've got the swab kits here with me in the car so I can come anywhere.'

206

'No. I'll meet you in Skaravaig as planned. Evie needs to pack her and Hamish's stuff. Just keep your eyes peeled for an angry man in a crumpled suit with a smooth sidekick.' She checked the time. 'Right. We'll be back from here about three thirty. Be there, with your kit. We'll take the sample, then I'll get Evie to start packing. I want her here by the middle of the evening, tonight.'

'That's all fine.'

'Any sign of Gordie MacPherson and his moped?'

'Not yet. I'll let you know.'

She was about to ring off when she spotted a fishing boat parked up behind Deborah's house, a small thing with tarpaulin clipped over it, and it jogged her memory. 'Before you go, Cara,' she said quickly. 'There was a boat moored off the cliffs this morning. A big dark yacht. Any way to find out who it belongs to?'

'I didn't notice one. I'll ask about.'

'It's probably nothing, but if it's there could you maybe check the registration number or name, if it's got one. See who it is? Stuff like that makes me nervous.'

* * *

2.48 p.m.

Evie and Hamish were in the back field with Deborah. Lola could see them through the pines, Hamish running in circles round Deborah, and Deborah clapping and laughing while Evie stood by. Evie looked happy enough.

Lola considered her phone and wondered if it was really sensible to call Mairi. The news might upset her; but she'd never been someone who shrank from knowing the worst, so she bit her lip and dialled.

'Two mins,' Mairi Marshall said, then the line was muffled. A toddler screamed. The wait seemed interminable, but at last Mairi was back on the line. 'Right. Sorry about that. How are you doing?'

'Aye, I'm okay. Please just tell me. And don't sugar-coat anything.'

A slight pause. 'Okay . . .' A warier tone now. 'Well, it seems a couple of folk remember Sandy from when he worked here, *and* it seems to be common knowledge that you and he are, well, in a relationship.'

She swallowed. 'So?'

'It seems Sandy was known as a player.'

'"A player"? Meaning what?'

'He played around. Played the field, so to speak. But then that was eleven years ago, or however long it was.'

'Twelve. It was twelve years ago.'

'Some of his relationships may have . . . *overlapped.*'

'Right . . .'

Mairi hesitated, then sighed. 'And there's something else too.'

Lola closed her eyes.

'You sure you're okay to hear it?'

'Aye, like I said. So, out with it.'

'There's a rumour going about that one of the boys here saw Sandy with a blonde woman in a café in the West End three or four weeks ago. Looked like they were having some kind of deep and meaningful.'

Lola said nothing. She couldn't. It was as though her throat had closed over.

'It might be nothing, but . . . that's not what people are saying. But then folk just love to gossip, don't they?'

'What café and what day?'

'The big Italian one on Hyndland Road before you get to Clarence Drive. Il Vicolo, I think it's called. It would have been a Saturday or a Sunday. They were in a booth at the back.'

'Is that all?' Lola asked dismally.

'Pretty much. I'm sorry.'

'Don't be,' Lola said. 'I'm fine. And thanks, Mairi. You're a good friend.'

She stood reeling for a minute, trying to centre herself and failing.

Sandy? With a blonde?

The sound of voices broke the trance.

Deborah had brought the visitors back to the house, and everything seemed settled. They'd agreed that Evie and Hamish would move in tonight. Maddie offered Deborah money, but she wouldn't take it, conceding only that they could review the arrangement 'if it becomes longer-term'.

'I think that's us,' Maddie said, turning to Lola, all smiles.

But Lola's phone was ringing. It was Cara's number.

She hurried back up the sloping garden.

'Hi, Cara.'

'We've just had word of a serious road traffic collision at Struan, a few miles south of Dunvegan.' She sounded strained, as if she was holding something back. 'I'm going to have to go pitch in. And I'll have to bring in the constable who's keeping an eye on Donny's place.'

'That's okay. I'll be with Evie when we go back.'

'There's something I should tell you,' Cara said, quieter now. 'The RTC involved a moped. Rider's a young lad.' She took a breath. 'He's dead, I'm afraid. And the officer who was first on the scene says something doesn't add up.'

CHAPTER THIRTY-SEVEN

4.27 p.m.

Lola was exhausted by the time they got back to Skaravaig.
She'd driven faster than she should have, part-propelled by tension. She was worried about Izatt's imminent arrival, and about
the road traffic collision too. The news that a teenager had lost
his life sat like a stone in her gut, but it also meant Cara would
be delayed bringing the swab kits, and there was no constable
keeping watch at the croft. And through all these worries, there
was still Sandy. She'd told Mairi she was fine. She wasn't.

Mairi's news had thrown her, and that in itself was alarming. She'd spent so long in an affair with a married man, she
thought she'd got used to the slings and arrows of relationships. She'd thought her skin was thick, but this had cut her
to the quick. Her heart raced with anxiety. *I really love Sandy*,
she thought to herself. *The stakes have never been this high.*

One positive: there was no sign of the sinister yacht as
they traversed the cliff road between Glendale and Skaravaig.

Donny came out of the house as she climbed stiffly from
the car.

'The constable had to go,' he told her, looking anxious.

'I know,' Lola said. 'Don't worry. I'm here. We won't stay long. Evie's going to pack some things and then we'll be off again. I'm so sorry about all this.'

He nodded miserably, then ducked back into the house. Lola's attention was caught by movement at one of the upstairs windows. Aileen was there, her face a perfect pale oval. She stared down at Lola with hate-filled eyes, then drew back into the room and out of view.

Lola texted Sandy from the garden, having composed a message during the drive: *Any chance we could chat? It's about what Izatt said. I really need to talk to you.*

Before she could change her mind, she pressed SEND, then felt a cold shiver of dread.

She took a breath and looked about. Maddie was leading Evie and Hamish into the house, so Lola took herself across the lawn and rang Cara.

Cara answered and Lola told her they were back at the croft.

'I'm not going to get away from here any time soon.' The DC sounded under severe stress. 'I've got the swab kits in the car if you want to come and get them.'

'I don't really want to leave them here without protection if I can help it,' Lola said. 'Is it Kris MacPherson's lad?'

'It is.' A sigh. 'And something's not right at all. The position of the body, the position of the bike. The condition of the bike too. It looks like it skidded ten metres or so, but there are barely any scratches. I reckon it's been staged.'

'I see . . .'

'A car came along not long after it must have happened, didn't see Gordie or the bike in time and spun out of control. Then a van went into the side of the car. This whole side of the island is impassable.'

Lola put a hand to her head and tried to think. 'Is there no way someone can get the swab kits to me and be here while we take the sample? I don't want to wait. My colleagues are about to stage an ambush. I want to do the sample and go.'

Silence at the other end of the line. Breeze ruffled the microphone. 'Bronagh Stewart's not on duty,' the DC said after a moment. 'She's out Milovaig way. I'll ring her. See if she can come here for the swab kits then head out to you.'

'Thanks so much, Cara. And I'm sorry I'm not there to help you. I would come if I could. One good thing: that yacht's disappeared.'

'Oh, that, yes. I did call the coastguard in Stornoway, just to see if they knew who it might be. The guy said he'd have a look and phone me back. Not heard anything yet.'

'Don't worry. You've got enough on your plate.'

It was ten minutes later when Cara called back.

'Bronagh's up for it,' she said. 'She's out in the fields, so just heading back home for her truck. She'll be with you as quick as she can. I gave her your moby number in case she has any problems.'

'Thank you so much.' The relief was enormous.

'And . . . you're not going to like this,' she said. 'The coast-guard just called. He thinks he recognises the boat — it's a six-ty-five-metre motor yacht called the *Black Swan*, usually moored at Crinan. He's checked with the marina and it's registered to Gaunt Property Holdings in the Cayman Islands. One of the directors is Duncan Gaunt. That's Carter Craig's uncle, isn't it?'

* * *

5.10 p.m.

The news was like being doused with iced water. Cara said the Stornoway coastguard had a chopper out on training and would fly around the west side of the island to look for the yacht and report back. She heard it now, the distant ominous roar of blades cutting the air.

For several moments Lola felt shaken — a sensation that was highly unusual for her, and therefore alarming. It was partly the magnitude of the threat but also her lack of familiarity with what resources were at her disposal here on Skye, and with the geography of the island too.

She took a moment to stand and calm herself. To try to order her thoughts. She gazed out over this idyllic place: the little village, the sloping emerald fields, the towering crags and the sparkling sea. And yet there was terrible danger here — at sea as well as on land.

She still hadn't heard back from Sandy, though she could tell he'd seen the message, and she couldn't bring herself to call him. Anxiety was like a blockage in her throat and she began to feel faint, but then remembered she hadn't eaten since breakfast. She went into the house and asked Donny if she could make a sandwich.

Sitting at the kitchen table, she forced down a cheese and pickle roll and a mug of hot black coffee. She distracted herself by going into Google Maps and calculating the journey times from Milovaig to Struan, then back to Skaravaig. The whole journey might take an hour or just over. so Lola hoped she might expect Bronagh Stewart by 5.45 p.m.

But just then Bronagh called to say she had a problem. A big one.

* * *

5.24 p.m.

'I was just about to jump in the car and head down to Struan,' the PC said, 'but one of your colleagues has just turned up *at my home*. A DCI Izatt. He's angry and he won't leave till I take him and his DS to Evie Mackinnon. He doesn't know I'm phoning you. I said I needed to get my stuff together.'

Lola was momentarily lost for words. She rose from the table and hurried outside, then said, 'How did he know where you stay?'

'Seems one of my colleagues has been free and easy with my personal information! DCI Izatt's blocked the drive with

213

his car. Said he'll move it but intends to follow me wherever I go. I'll be making one stinker of a complaint about this.'

'And I'll help you write it.'

'He's got no signal, he says, so he wants use of my phone too. I said, "On your flaming bike."'

'I'm so sorry about this, Bronagh.'

Her thoughts raced. What to do? Leave Bronagh to distract Izatt and Pierce and wait for Cara to come so they could do the swab? Or get Evie and the boy out of here now, safe, and take the swab tonight or tomorrow? The boat preyed on her mind. No, the swab was everything. She had to get it today, then get the boy and his mum to Staffin and safety and leave them there in peace. That way Craig and Izatt would be thwarted and there could be no comeback.

An idea was forming. A reckless plan that might just work . . .

'You're in Milovaig, aren't you?' she asked Bronagh. 'You have to pass through Glendale.'

'Aye. It's ten minutes from here.'

'There's a community centre with a car park in Glendale, isn't there? I'm sure I've driven past it.'

'Yes.'

'With one entrance?'

A moment's pause, then, 'Aye, that's right.'

'Okay,' Lola said. 'Listen carefully.'

CHAPTER THIRTY-EIGHT

5.31 p.m.

'We'll be fine,' Maddie said. 'You go. I'll be here.'

'I won't be too long, but I really need to sort this.'

'I understand. Jessie said her friend from the village is planning to pop by, so that'll be a distraction for Evie.'

'What friend?' Lola asked sharply.

'Theresa, the lady you met. She runs the store and café.'

'Yes. Yes, okay, that's fine. Sorry to be so jumpy.'

'It's quite all right. Now, you go and don't worry about us.'

Lola tore along the cliff road and reached Glendale in thirteen minutes flat. There was no sign of that sinister boat, which was reassuring. She parked the Audi where Bronagh had suggested, in the little car park next to a café, and then hot-footed it back along the lane to the edge of the village. The community centre sat in a dip and had its own car park, reached through an open gateway with a cattle grid.

The centre was closed but there were a couple of cars parked at the side.

She texted Bronagh, then found a bench in the shade. It was evening but the sun was still warm. The air was very still, the leaves in the trees and the grasses and flowers in the fields unmoving. From over the hill, she could hear the sound of the helicopter.

Her phone buzzed with a text reply from Bronagh. *I'll tell him where you are. Should be with you in ten or fifteen minutes. Fingers crossed this works.*

A text appeared from Cara: *Word from the coastguard. The yacht's turned round and is headed back to Skye. Looks like it's coming in at Loch Bracadale. Coastie's tried to make contact with the captain but no response.*

Lola went into her maps app and found Loch Bracadale, which was less of a loch than a vast bay, dotted with islands, and plenty of places for a boat to anchor or dock. As the crow flew it was ten miles south of here, though much further by road.

What's the hell's he doing?

With time to kill, she called Anna.

'Everything all right?' Anna asked.

'Mostly. What happened about the necklace?'

'I got the image of Juliana wearing it and showed it to Kathryn Main's colleague and sister. Both said it looked like the same one. I did a reverse image search of the necklace online and it could be a piece by a designer in London, worth about a thousand pounds. So I contacted Juliana Gaunt. It took a lot of persuading to get past the security guy we met, but Juliana called me back and let me text her the image. She went to check while I was on the phone. Said the necklace wasn't where it should be, but then she found it in another drawer, one that's lockable. I asked if she'd missed it recently and she said she hadn't. Imagine having so much jewellery you can't keep track of it! I've asked to collect it tomorrow. She wasn't sure about that — said she'd have to ask her husband, so I'm expecting a call from Gaunt's lawyers at any moment.'

'You said the drawer was lockable. Who has keys?'

'She does, and the head of security has a spare set.'

'Interview both Juliana Gaunt and Eddie Young tomorrow. If it's the same necklace, we need to know who could have taken it. Did you get information about Mrs Kennedy, Craig's old governess?'

'Miss Rossiter, the housekeeper, replied to that one — she said Mrs Kennedy's long gone and no forwarding address. She remembers her but says she was only there two or three years. Can't even recall her first name.'

'We've got to find her. Any luck with CCTV of so-called "Liz" approaching Sharon Trent in the street?'

'Jonno got a promise from the manager of the bookies to let him have some footage. We'll keep on it. Oh, and Marcus has found something very curious.'

'Go on.'

'It was his idea to seek some CCTV from the main road near Clunie Castle. He's got a few seconds' footage showing one of Gaunt's cars being driven away from the castle at four twenty on Monday morning — a few hours before Kathryn Main's body was found in the river.'

'Any glimpse of the driver?'

'A man, by the looks of it. Big hands on the steering wheel. Looks like he's wearing gloves.'

'Craig?'

'I don't think so, boss. More likely Jack Courtney or possibly Eddie Young.'

'Good work. Go back to them and ask who the hell was out at that time of the morning. And a big well done to Marcus.'

She came off the call and saw Sandy had replied to her text. It gave her a jolt of adrenaline mixed with fear. *Free now*, he'd written.

She checked the time. Izatt would be here in a few minutes, but she couldn't hold off any longer.

'It's me,' she said, sounding breathless to her own ears. 'Where are you?'

'Retail park at Darnley. Just arrived. Come to buy a drill. Thought I'd get you a wee CCTV camera to go under your eaves — what with Craig making threats an' all. Maybe one of those doorbell cameras too. I got your message, by the way. What's up?'

She took a deep breath and shut her eyes.

'Sandy, I need to ask you something. I'm sorry, but I have to. Were you in a café in the West End a few weeks ago, sitting in a booth with a blonde?'

'Wha—' He made a sound that was a mix of astonishment and mystification. 'A blonde?' A moment's silence. 'Lola—'

'*Just tell me*,' she demanded. 'I'll know if you're lying.'

'If I'm . . . You think I'd *lie* to you?'

'It was an Italian place on Hyndland Road.'

'Hyndland . . . But that was Sam. I met her for lunch. Sam Forrest. I told you that. I'm sure I did.'

'Did you?'

'Used to be called Sam Maxwell. She was a DI in Lanarkshire. Set up her own PI business with a colleague, only the colleague's wanting to retire, so she wondered if we might work together. Don't you remember?'

She did. It came back in a rush. An old colleague had wanted to talk about merging their businesses. Sandy hadn't been interested, but had planned to meet her to talk about partnering on bigger investigations when the need arose. Shame burned in her cheeks.

'Oh God, Sandy, I—'

'We had lunch, that's all. She's your mystery blonde.'

Lola took her phone from her ear and went into her phone calendar, then scrolled back a few weekends.

And there it was, in their shared appointments calendar: *Sandy meeting Sam F lunch, W End? tbc.*

'I'm so sorry,' she said quietly.

'Is this what Graeme Izatt has been talking about?' he said, sounding very annoyed now.

'Seems that way. Sounds like we're the talk of the steamie.'

She heard him muttering curses.

'And you believed him?' he said now. 'You really thought I'd do that?' He muttered something she didn't catch.

'I didn't, no! I mean . . . Oh, Sandy, I'm so sorry. I—'

'Forget about it,' he said. But she could hear he was angry, and with her.

She heard the sound of a car being driven fast.

'Oh God,' she said, turning to scan the valley, 'I need to go. Are we all right, Sandy?'

'Aye, I guess.' But he didn't sound convinced. 'I'll talk to you later.'

'Aye, okay.'

He cut the call.

Lola could have screamed at herself.

* * *

The car was approaching from the west, so there was every chance it was Izatt and Pierce. The noise grew louder, then it appeared, coming too fast through the village, almost bouncing along the bumpy lane. A Vauxhall pool car, and yes, there was Izatt hunched over the wheel. He slowed and turned, rattled over the cattle grid as he came into the car park, then drove at her. He jammed on the brakes with only a couple of metres to spare, and jumped out.

'Hello, Graeme,' she said, trying hard to put Sandy out of her mind. 'Fancy meeting you here.'

'What in God's name are you playing at?' he snarled.

Aidan Pierce slid quietly from the car and stood holding the open door, gazing at her with contempt.

'Aidan! Quite a reunion.' She felt panicked but was hiding it, or so she hoped.

A big blue Toyota truck was trundling through the village now, at a much steadier pace. She caught a glimpse of a woman with red hair at the wheel and felt a rush of adrenaline.

'Well, where is she?' Izatt demanded.

'"She"?'

'The girl! The bloody girl who's got the bloody kid.'

219

'Oh, you're not going anywhere near her,' Lola said. 'Not a chance in hell.'

He gaped at her.

'You'll get your DNA evidence, and your statement, and access to the antenatal records, don't worry about that. But I will not let you within half a mile of that young woman or her child just now. It would be unethical, unprofessional and negligent of me. Life's tough, Graeme, though I'm sure you'll get over it.'

Out on the road the Toyota had slowed.

Izatt exchanged glances with Pierce, then turned, smirking, back to Lola.

'Think you're going to follow me, don't you?' she said. 'Tail me in hot pursuit over the hills, till I lead you to her?'

The smirk only intensified.

'Well, I'm going, but you're staying here,' she said.

She heard the jangle of his car keys as he reached for them, ready to follow.

'Oh, I'm not parked here,' she said with a big smile, starting to leave. 'No, I'm over there by the wee café.'

And then Izatt saw the Toyota, parked at an angle across the cattle grid, blocking the car park's only way in and out. The red-haired woman was outside the truck now. She returned Lola's cheery wave with one of her own.

'Engine just cut out,' she yelled across to them. 'Can't seem to get it going again.'

'I believe you've already met PC Stewart of the island constabulary,' Lola said brightly. 'Oh, and by the way, she's mightily pissed off that you got her personal details and went to her house. As am I! Bye, Graeme.'

CHAPTER THIRTY-NINE

6.26 p.m.

Lola's phone buzzed as she climbed back into the Audi — a text from Cara saying she was leaving the RTC and heading over to Skaravaig with the swab kits herself.

See you there, she typed back, and drove out of the village. Bronagh's Toyota was still wedged into the gateway of the community centre car park. Bronagh had the bonnet up and was making a performance of examining the engine. Izatt was remonstrating and waving his arms, while Pierce stood crossly by, watching Lola as she flew up and out of Glendale. She lifted a hand in a wave and allowed herself a secret smirk of triumph.

Over the brow of the last hill before Skaravaig, her worries about Sandy pushed to one side, she allowed herself to enjoy a moment of relief. Within minutes she would be at the croft, then Cara would arrive and they'd administer the swabs. Maddie would then take Evie and Hamish to Staffin, and Lola would call there either late tonight or first thing in the morning to take Evie's statement. And then they'd be home and dry. The evidence would be obtained and Craig would be going back to court.

But anxiety still ate at her. Somewhere, only a few miles behind her, was Craig's uncle's yacht, and a young lad lay dead in suspicious circumstances — which suggested someone was already on the island.

She floored the accelerator and swooped down the hillside towards the cliffs and the isolated village.

She found Maddie at the kitchen table drinking coffee and chattering away to Jessie while Donny chopped vegetables beside a stew pot.

'That was no time at all,' Maddie cried as Lola came in. 'Everything go to plan?'

'I think so,' Lola said.

'There's coffee if you'd like some,' Jessie said, rising, 'or tea?'

'Coffee's fine. Black, please. Cara will be here any time. Where are Evie and Hamish?'

'Theresa's showing them the late orchids,' Donny explained. 'Wild orchids are her speciality.'

'Where?'

'Out in the back field,' Maddie said.

Lola went to the window at the back of the kitchen and peered up into the field. She could see figures in the far distance. There were three adults.

'Is that Aileen with them?' Lola asked. But it didn't look like Aileen, even from this distance.

'Theresa's friend,' Maddie said. 'Remember, she provides respite holidays for women leaving a violent partner. What was the poor woman's name, Jessie?'

'Paula,' Jessie said.

'Frightened wee thing,' Maddie went on. 'Very nervy. She only got to the island yesterday.'

A prickle ran up Lola's spine.

'They need to come back,' she said. 'I'll go call for them.'

Outside, she climbed the sloping garden behind the house to a gate in the fence. The field was soft underfoot, with tussocks that did their best to trip her. The retreating group was further away now, into the next field. She tried to shout, but the wind whipped her words away. She could make out Evie, and another figure, Theresa's friend Paula, who was holding hands with Hamish and pulling — no, *dragging* — him along while Evie frantically tried to keep up. There was no sign of Theresa.

Lola scrambled up the field, then cried out when she almost tripped over Theresa's prone figure lying in the grass. She stopped and knelt, panting.

The woman was on her side, eyes closed, and there was blood from a cut on her cheek. Lola found a pulse just as the old woman's eyes opened. 'My leg,' she gasped. 'I think it's broken.'

Lola rose and looked back to the house. A car was coming up the track. It looked like Cara's.

Trying to contain her panic, she hurried down to meet her.

'Theresa Macleod's been hurt,' she shouted, 'and a strange woman has got hold of Hamish. She's up there in the field. You'll need to call for backup.'

Jessie had come out of the house. Lola called to her to phone for an ambulance.

Just then, Aileen appeared from inside.

'Where's Hamish?' she screamed.

'We'll get him back,' Lola said. 'You go inside.'

But Aileen was already tearing away up the garden and into the field.

Maddie was there now as well, Donny behind her. 'Go up into the field and look after Theresa,' Lola told Maddie. 'Take water and blankets.'

Maddie darted back into the house.

'Backup's on the way,' Cara told Lola now. She nodded towards the fields. 'Looks like she's headed for the crags. We can try to cut them off.'

Lola's phone was buzzing. It was Anna. She rejected it.

'We need help ASAP,' she told Cara and put her phone to her ear.

'It's Lola Harris,' she said when Bronagh answered. 'You'll need to let them go. Bring them here immediately. A woman's been hurt and the child's been taken.'

* * *

6.22 p.m.

Anna rang again and this time Lola answered.

'Two things, boss.' She sounded excited. 'The flat on Otago Street, where we think Kathryn was held — it belongs to a property company called Rusholme Holdings, which is registered in Juliana Gaunt's name.'

'My God.'

'Kirstie found the records. And better than that,' she said in a rush, 'I've found Craig's governess. It was simple in the end. I asked Eddie Young, the security chap at Clunie Castle.'

'What did he say?'

'She *was* called Mrs Kennedy, and her first name was *Irene*. Then she got divorced.'

'She's Irene Rossiter?' Lola asked in disbelief.

'The very same. Gaunt told us she'd had a number of roles, didn't he? Eddie says Miss Rossiter has "gone away for a few days". It seems everyone's away: Gaunt and the chauffeur, Jack Courtney, are too. It's her, isn't it, boss? Irene Rossiter is Liz. She manipulated Kathryn Main to ensure her favourite pupil got set free. She knew there was no hope of corrupting a jury to get him off — but she could drive an unsafe conviction that could be overturned at a later date. The question is, where is she now?'

'She's on the island,' Lola said. She felt sick. 'And she's got the boy.'

* * *

224

Donny wasn't going to take orders from anyone when a child's life was at risk. He told Lola so while adjusting the butt of his shotgun in his armpit.

'You could hit the wrong person. You could kill Hamish! *Just wait.*'

But he wasn't having it, and began powering up the garden. Lola scanned the fields, but she couldn't see the group now, only Aileen tearing across the brow of the hill.

'What can we do?' Maddie called to Lola.

'Stay here in case Evie comes back,' Lola told her.

'I'll drive to the St Columba Centre,' said Cara. 'It's the closest a car can get to the crags. I'll try to cut the woman off there.'

She got in her car as two vehicles came tearing over the brow of the cliff road — Bronagh's Toyota followed by Izatt's Vauxhall.

Lola steeled herself.

Izatt was out of the car in a flash, eyes ablaze and teeth bared. 'Happy with yourself?' he screamed.

'No,' she said. 'A woman calling herself Paula has got the child. It's possible she's Irene Rossiter, the housekeeper at Clunie Castle.'

'*Irene?*' Izatt said. 'I've met her. You're telling me she—'

'They're crossing the fields. She's attacked the woman she was lodging with. I suggest you two follow the old man,' she said, pointing to where Donny was struggling up the field. 'Try and get the shotgun off him. I'll go to the village. We're going to try to cut them off at the crags.'

Izatt was away towards the field, Pierce behind him.

'Bronagh,' she said, 'follow me down the drive and block the road with your car. Then I'll drive us down to the village.'

She jumped into the Audi and flew down the drive, Bronagh's Toyota following. Bronagh wedged her vehicle diagonally across the single-track road, then dashed over to Lola's car. Lola sped off.

Bronagh answered a call.

'It's Cara,' she told Lola, then turned to speakerphone.

'I'm at the St Columba Centre,' she said. 'I just saw a woman with a child heading down from the moors towards the woods. There are derelict farm buildings in there. She might have a vehicle there.'

'Thanks, Cara,' Lola said and accelerated, heading for the woods less than a mile ahead.

Approaching, she spotted Evie barrelling towards the side of the road and stopped hard. Evie was over the fence and running towards the car.

'Where are they?' Lola said as the young woman approached. Her clothes were torn and she had blood on her face.

'*There!*' Evie screamed, pointing further along the road, to the woods.

'Are you hurt?'

'Just scratches. Please — just save my boy!'

As they approached the trees, a huge black Land Rover with tinted windows thundered out of the undergrowth and turned into the lane facing them. It tore towards them, mounting the verge to get past. Lola tried to turn the Audi but the bigger vehicle clipped it and sent it jolting back across the road.

'We need a roadblock this side of Glendale,' Lola told Bronagh breathlessly as she righted the car, 'or before Dunvegan. I think she's heading for Loch Bracadale and the yacht.'

The Land Rover was approaching the place where Bronagh's own Toyota Rover was wedged across the road. The vehicle slowed for a moment, then effortlessly bulldozed the Toyota out of the way.

CHAPTER FORTY

7.02 p.m.

Irene Rossiter was an excellent driver, and clearly used to the Land Rover. She was away in the distance, while Lola tried to close the gap. She lost sight of the Land Rover as it cleared the brow of the highest hill, and, by the time Lola herself was on the other side, it was well away.

No way would officers have chance to block the road before the Land Rover reached Glendale, which meant it then had access to a number of routes.

'Call Cara,' she said to Bronagh. 'Ask if the coastguard chopper can track the Land Rover.'

Bronagh did as she asked and put Cara on speakerphone.

'Already on it,' Cara's voice said.

And there was the helicopter, a giant red-and-white insect hovering in the sky two or three miles ahead of them. Lola plunged down the single-track road towards Glendale.

Cara's voice came over the speaker. 'Word from the chopper relayed through the coastguard,' she said. 'They've got sight of the car. It's turned *west* out of Glendale. And the yacht's moving up out of Loch Bracadale. Reckon they're planning a meet-up at Neist Point.'

'There's a lighthouse, isn't there?'

'Aye, and a hundred-plus steps down the headland to sea level. Would make a good landing point if they have a dinghy.'

It would take Rossiter some time to descend, especially with a small, and probably traumatised, child in tow, but Rossiter had a good head start.

'Any chance the chopper can put down in Glendale and pick me up?'

'I'll suggest it. Meanwhile, I'll get officers sent to Neist Point.'

A minute later Cara was calling again.

'Chopper's on its way,' she announced. 'I suggested the field beside the community centre.'

'Understood. And thanks. Now wish us luck.'

* * *

7.10 p.m.

The chopper was landing as they came into Glendale, filling the bowl of the valley with noise. Lola could feel vibrations through the car. She pulled onto a verge beside the field and got out, then gave Bronagh her car key and said to drive to Neist Point to meet them. Then she climbed over a gate as the chopper settled, though its blades continued to spin.

A door slid open as Lola jogged across the field. A man in an orange jumpsuit and helmet stepped down and put up both palms to stall her. He indicated he would come to her. She waited.

'Put this on,' he mouthed and handed her a headset. Immediately the racket was cancelled.

The man turned and waved to the cockpit. A hand behind the glass waved back. 'That's us,' he said to Lola, and led her, keeping low, under the disc of the turning blades. Lola could feel warm air from the engine outlets and smell the aviation fuel. The man stepped up into the aircraft and put out a hand to help haul her in.

'Have you been in one of these things before?'

She shook her head and hoped her sudden nerves didn't show.

'Nothing to worry about,' he told her through the headset. 'Thing's as safe as houses. I'm David, by the way.'

The inside of the craft was largely empty but for a bed, complete with straps, and baskets of brightly coloured floats, life jackets and blankets. Down one side of the cabin were jump seats.

'You sit here,' David told her through the headset. 'Strap yourself in — like this.'

He showed her how to work the buckle, then said, 'Good to go, over,' into his mic.

One of the pilots replied and immediately the engine roared and the cabin began to vibrate.

David slid the side door shut, unhooked himself from his harness and returned to Lola's side.

'You okay?' he asked her, smiling.

'Not really,' she said.

She hated heights but was fine on planes. This was an unknown quantity. A light jerk, then the helicopter tilted and rose into the sky. Lola closed her eyes.

Seconds later they were flying level. Then, moments after that, a swooping sensation and they were tilted to one side and speeding up. Through the small windows across the cabin she saw blue sky and a green hilltop.

Then they were flying level again.

One of the pilots spoke over the headset: 'We've got sight of the vehicle,' he told her. 'It's passing by Loch Mor. We can land in a field by the car park or go down onto the headland and wait for them there. Your call.'

'Car park, please,' Lola said.

A minute later, they were coming down. The windows filled with green slopes, then, gentle as a feather, they were on the ground.

David helped Lola unbuckle her harness, then helped her climb down from the side door.

'Faster than Ryanair,' she said as they moved away from the aircraft. 'Can you stay close by?' she asked him over the racket of the blades.

'No problem. We'll hover and track you.'

'Excellent. Thanks so much.'

Headset handed over, she was away across the field towards the busy car park. There were people staring and some taking photos of the helicopter. She called Bronagh once she was away from the noise of the aircraft.

'Passing Loch Mor,' Bronagh told her. 'Where's the Land Rover?'

'Arriving now,' Lola said, heart jumping. 'It'll be in the car park in one minute. I'm going to have to do what I can. Get here as fast as you can and be prepared for trouble.'

'Will do.'

The helicopter was in the air again. It swooped over the cliff edge and flew over the headland.

Lola made her way between cars towards the top of the steps and looked over the long headland to the lighthouse. And there it was: the sinister yacht, the *Black Swan*, moored only metres from a beach on the eastern side of the peninsula. A small vessel floated beside it. A speedboat or another kind of launch. Ready to collect the child from the shore, no doubt.

'You devil,' she muttered, then drew her eyes away and turned to find the black Land Rover coming to a halt nearby.

Two people climbed out: a woman and a man. She recognised them both. Irene Rossiter, formerly Mrs Kennedy, had been in the passenger seat. Jack Courtney, Duncan Gaunt's chauffeur, had been driving.

The pair hurried together to the vehicle's left side. Irene opened the door and reached inside, while Courtney peered about. Lola pretended to look at the view and hoped he wouldn't see her.

She heard the door bang shut, then heard a child's cry and a woman's raised voice.

Lola's heart hammered and her mouth was bone dry. She could have stopped Irene Rossiter on her own, but not her and the man.

Where are you, Bronagh?

She craned her neck to try to see over the tops of the cars. And there was Lola's Audi, flying this way.

Courtney was coming, the boy in his arms. The child was wriggling but Courtney had him pinned. Rossiter followed, nodding and smiling reassuringly to a couple of tourists who were eyeing them with concern.

Lola saw Bronagh leap from the car. She waved and Bronagh spotted her.

Courtney was near the head of the steps now. Lola stepped forward to block his path. At first he didn't seem to see her and was about to go round her.

'Jack Courtney!' she yelled in his face. 'Stop and put the child down.'

He froze and stared in fright. Rossiter appeared at his shoulder.

'Go past!' she screamed and shoved at the small of his back with both hands.

Courtney tried to pass, but Lola blocked him.

Bronagh was there now, face flushed, eyes on Lola for a signal.

'Get the woman,' Lola yelled.

Irene Rossiter turned, teeth bared, arms flying as Bronagh Stewart tried to wrestle her.

Courtney barged into Lola's shoulder, making for the steps. He plunged downward.

Lola went after him, then stopped. There was a railing down the side of the steps but a sheer drop beyond it. It would be too dangerous to tackle him here.

The helicopter was close again, its racket shaking the ground. She waved her arms, pointing down at the bottom of the steps and mouthing, *Land down there!*

The helicopter tilted, then spiralled neatly down to the headland below.

As its noise retreated, Lola could hear a woman screaming. She turned to find Irene Rossiter in full cat-fight with
Bronagh and Bronagh doing her best to restrain her.

Lola yelled, '*Stop!*' at Rossiter. It worked and the woman
was distracted long enough for Bronagh to get her on the
floor.

'No cuffs,' she said to Lola, wincing. 'Sorry.'

'Sit on her,' Lola said. 'I'm going after the man.'

Ignoring the gathered tourists who watched on in alarm,
she threw herself towards the steps and down, taking them
two at a time, screaming, 'Out of my way!'

Below, Courtney had reached the foot of the steps.

The helicopter was down now and David, the crew member who'd helped her, ran to confront Courtney.

She saw Courtney stop and there was a stand-off as two
more crew from the helicopter came forward.

Lola was down now and breathing hard from the exertion.

She took a lungful of air and forced out the words: 'Put
him down, Jack!'

Courtney whirled round, face twisted with anger and
fear. She saw there were tears in his eyes.

'Put him down,' Lola said, coming close to him. 'It's over.'

She saw his lip tremble, then the crew members were
grabbing Courtney's shoulders and David was extracting the
child from his arms.

Courtney howled with a kind of defeated despair and
crumpled to his knees.

David came to Lola with Hamish in his arms.

She took him, cooing gently to soothe him.

'You're okay, Hamish,' Lola said to him. 'You're safe with
me.'

CHAPTER FORTY-ONE

7.43 p.m.

Bronagh arrived down the steps with uniformed officers behind her. The officers ran straight for Courtney, while Bronagh came to Lola, eyes on the child.

'Is he all right?' she asked.

'Seems to be. Did they arrest the woman?'

'Yep. On suspicion of kidnap. Cuffed and in the back of a car right now, ready to go to Portree. She's cold as ice! But — something interesting. I said to her that her plan hadn't worked and that she'd even messed up the tracker — and she said she didn't know anything about a tracker. Denied all knowledge.'

Lola stared. 'That is interesting, isn't it?'

'She could be lying . . .'

'Here,' Lola said, repositioning the child. 'Take this wee man and keep a hold of him.'

Bronagh took the boy in her arms. He went willingly.

'Could you see the yacht as you came down the steps just now?'

'It's on the move,' Bronagh said. 'Already out past the lighthouse.'

Lola nodded. There was probably nothing that could be done to stop the vessel right now, though tracking it would be important.

She turned to see the two officers in the process of cuffing Jack Courtney.

'DCI Lola Harris,' she introduced herself. 'Arrest is on suspicion of abduction of a minor.'

She spotted David away to one side and went to him. She was aware there were dozens of people observing them: tourists everywhere, forming a circle around the unfolding scene.

'What now?' David asked. 'Get the boy home?'

'That's the plan. I'd like him back with his mum as quickly as possible. Can you help?'

'Ach, I guess so. Skaravaig's kind of on our way, I suppose.' He winked.

Lola went across to Bronagh.

'Would you go in the helicopter with Hamish?' she asked.

'Sure thing,' Bronagh said, grinning and stroking the boy's golden hair.

'I'll be happier when I know he's back with his mum. Good work today, Bronagh. I owe you one. A couple, probably.'

* * *

8.49 p.m.

Bronagh came out of the croft as Lola drove up the track.

She parked and jumped out. 'How are things?'

'The boy's fine, Evie's fine. But your colleagues are giving her a hard time.'

'Right . . . What about Theresa?'

'Away in an ambulance to Portree.'

'Good. That's good.'

'Cara suggested to the helicopter crew that they might keep an eye on the yacht. They're going to do a couple of circles. Try to gauge which way it's headed.'

'Thanks so much, Bronagh.'

Cara was out of the cottage now. She looked shattered and wired at the same time. From inside, Lola heard a man's voice raised in anger. Izatt.

'Sorry,' Cara said, 'but you need to come in and referee this lot.'

'No problem at all,' Lola said, and readied herself for the next bout.

Donny and Jessie were in the kitchen, sitting hunched and miserable at the table. They eyed her wearily. Jessie looked quite defeated and Lola's heart went out to her.

'I mean it,' Izatt's angry voice came through the wall.

She went into the living room, Cara behind her. Bronagh stayed with the old couple.

Evie was curled up in an armchair with an exhausted Hamish over her shoulder. Maddie sat beside her. Graeme Izatt stood over them, teeth bared. Pierce stood by a wall, staring blankly into space.

Izatt whirled round. 'Finally!'

'What's happening?' Lola asked mildly.

'*She*'s refusing to talk to us.' Izatt jabbed a finger towards Evie.

'Aye, well, I'm not surprised,' Lola said.

He drew close to her. 'Aidan's got the swab kits ready but she won't have it. You said—!'

Lola ignored him and said brightly to Evie, 'I'm so happy to see the two of you back together.'

Evie peered up at her and smiled weakly.

'We'll need to have a doctor check Hamish over in a wee bit,' Lola said.

The young woman nodded.

'Now, will you *tell* her to damn well *cooperate*?' Izatt half shouted.

'No,' Lola said, turning to him. 'I won't. I want you to leave her alone. Now.'

Izatt gave a sneering laugh. 'Who do you think you are?' he said. 'After what you did to us. You've no authority—'

235

'Enough.' She met his gaze, and a feeling of utter calm came over her. She pitied the man, really she did. So much rage. So little self-esteem.

She turned back to Evie and knelt, though her thighs ached from all the tense activity. 'Evie, why don't I do the swabs on you and Hamish? Bronagh or Cara can be with us to corroborate the evidence. These two men will leave the house.'

Evie eyed Izatt, then looked back at Lola. She nodded.

Lola got to her feet. 'There,' she said to Izatt. 'You'll get your swabs, you'll get your statements, but right now you need to go.'

'But—'

'Just *go*, Graeme! It's a beautiful evening — go look at the flowers!'

* * *

9.15 p.m.

In the end it was Cara who took the mouth swabs from the mother and son: three swabs from each. Once they were bagged and the bags labelled, Lola said, 'That's us!'

Cara headed outside to hand over the bags to Izatt, as Lola had instructed. Bronagh stayed behind.

'That wasn't so bad, was it?' Maddie asked Evie.

Evie smiled and shook her head.

Hamish was sleepy, his head lolling.

'I need to feed him,' Evie said. 'Will we still go to the other place?'

'I think you should, for a few nights,' Lola said. 'But how about waiting till tomorrow morning?'

Evie nodded and looked relieved.

'And someone will visit you there — probably Cara here — to take a statement about what Craig did to you three years ago.'

A sound behind her caught Lola's attention. Aileen was standing in the doorway, looking even thinner and paler than ever.

'Can I hold him?' she asked plaintively, cowering by the doorframe.

Evie considered, then said, 'If you like. But only for a minute. I want to feed him and put him to bed.' She began to get up. Maddie put out a hand to help her.

Aileen came slowly into the room, head down. There were scratches on her arms and face and Lola wondered if she'd got them when she went tearing into the field in a panic earlier. Aileen put out her hands, took Hamish from her sister and pulled him to her, lowering her face and smelling his hair. She began to weep, softly at first, then more loudly, with great gasping sobs. Lola caught Maddie's concerned glance.

'Why don't you sit down here, Aileen?' Lola said, stepping forward.

But Aileen didn't move. She stood, clutching the child and sobbing her heart out.

'Don't take him from me!' she cried. She swayed, pushing her face into the boy's soft neck.

'Give him back, Aileen,' Evie said. 'Give me my boy!'

'Let Evie take Hamish from you,' Lola said firmly. 'Come on. Hand him over.'

But Aileen turned her back on Evie, sobbing more violently.

Lola stepped close and reached for the boy, but then Aileen turned sharply away. 'You can't take him. You can't have him. I don't want him to go.'

The boy began to cry.

Bronagh was on her feet and round the other side, a hand on Aileen's shoulder. She eyed Lola, waiting for the nod. Lola gave it.

'That's us,' Bronagh said gently, and pulled Aileen's arm back to loosen her grip on the boy, while Lola stepped in and levered him free of the woman's grasp.

'Get her out of here,' Lola said quietly to Bronagh, who gripped Aileen's upper arms and steered her from the room.

Lola passed Hamish to Evie and went to the door and closed it.

'That girl,' Maddie said, hands to her mouth. 'She's so unwell.'

Evie held Hamish tight and wept.

'Look after them,' Lola said to Maddie. 'I'll go after Aileen.'

* * *

There was no one in the kitchen because they were all outside.

At the far end of the garden, Izatt and Pierce skulked like a pair of sulky teenagers. Izatt was smoking. He saw her looking and turned away in disgust.

Donny was remonstrating with Aileen as she tried to get past him to her car. He spotted Lola. 'She's trying to drive!' he cried.

'Aileen,' Lola called, running over. 'Wait!'

But Aileen had got round the old man and was in the driver's seat. She started the little car and was soon bumping down the track towards the road.

'She'll hurt herself,' Jessie cried to Lola. 'You have to stop her.'

'When Hamish was taken, she said she wanted to die,' said Donny. 'I took her car keys off her but I gave them back when we heard Hamish was coming home.'

'I'll go after her,' she told the pair. 'Try not to worry.'

Aileen's car was on the road now, headed for Skaravaig. Lola drove after her, leaning on her horn and flashing her lights, but Aileen only sped up, turning at last into the driveway of the St Columba Centre.

With a sinking dread Lola recalled how close the Centre was to the cliffs.

Aileen was out of the car and running for a stile into a neighbouring field.

Yes, she was heading towards the crags — and a sheer drop to the rocks and the foaming sea.

Lola went after her but Aileen was already ahead by some distance, tearing up the sloping moor towards the foot of the crags, but veering left, towards the highest point of the cliff.

'Aileen!' Lola cried, but the young woman didn't appear to hear.

Lola sprinted. Aileen began to slow, her body bent against the steepening slope.

Lola closed in. 'Aileen, *stop*!' she yelled, breathless herself.

Then Aileen was upright again and staggering towards the cliff edge. It couldn't be a hundred metres away.

Lola willed herself on and began to gain. She clamped a hand on the young woman's left shoulder, though Aileen struggled to get away.

'Aileen,' Lola panted. 'Think of your family.'

'Let me go!' the young woman cried.

'No. This isn't the way.' Lola had a hand on her upper arm now. It was so thin, nothing but bone.

'I want to die!' She fought to free herself.

'It's not worth it.' Lola positioned herself so she now had a firm grip on both shoulders.

'You don't understand.'

'But I think I do,' Lola said. 'I think I know what you did.'

Aileen's eyes widened with fear.

'I know about the parcel,' Lola said. 'That's what this is about, isn't it?'

Aileen stared in horror, then seemed to give up. She sank to the ground and Lola knew she was right.

'You sent the parcel to Evie,' Lola said, but gently. 'The one with the tracker.'

Aileen said nothing, just gazed at the sky before closing her eyes. She swallowed hard and whispered, 'Yes.'

'Why did you do it?'

'So she'd understand the danger she was in,' Aileen said softly. 'She didn't seem to care, not after she moved here. When I came to see her after Craig got out of prison, she didn't seem bothered at all.'

'And that was tough for you?'

Silence for several seconds. Lola sat on the ground beside her.

'Yes.' She opened her eyes. 'I also wanted to show you and Maddie the danger you'd put Hamish in. It was because of you two that Craig knew Evie and Hamish were on Skye.'

'It was very clever,' Lola said. 'It took everyone in.'

'I know.'

'But then things took a serious turn, didn't they?' Lola said. 'Because of the fuss caused by the parcel, a young man who followed Carter Craig got wind and decided to help his idol. You panicked.'

'I realised then what I'd done. I only meant to scare Evie. I didn't mean to put them in real danger, her or Hamish . . .'

Neither spoke. They listened to the waves and the bird calls.

'Am I in trouble?' Aileen asked miserably. 'I mean, have I broken the law?'

'You've wasted police time,' Lola said.

Aileen nodded.

Minutes passed and the two women's breathing slowed.

They sat, their backs to the crags, looking south over the peninsula, the sea a sparkling blue shield stretching away to their right. The waves smashed against the cliffs below while birds circled noisily over them.

'Did you buy the outfit the day you drove back from here to Glasgow?'

Aileen nodded. 'From a craft place in the West End. I got the tracker from the computer store at Braehead.'

'The handwriting on the envelope and on the message — that wasn't yours, though, was it?'

She shook her head. 'I went to a café on Clarence Drive with a sling on my arm. I had one from when I sprained my wrist. I asked a woman sitting in the next booth to write it for me. She was so pleased to help. She even taped up the parcel for me.'

'It was some act,' Lola said now. 'The way you tore into me and your aunt. Saying we were to blame for the parcel, that we'd endangered Evie and Hamish.'

'It felt like a release.' There was a light breeze. It lifted Aileen's hair. She smiled softly to herself, but then the smile disappeared. 'But then I was so frightened. It was all because of me. That night you came to the croft to say you'd seen someone on a bike . . . I thought about killing myself right then, but how could I leave Evie and Hamish?' She looked at Lola, fear in her eyes now. 'You're going to tell them, aren't you?'

Lola sat quietly for a few moments. The young woman beside her had been carrying so much for so long.

'I don't think so,' she said. 'I think you might choose to do that at some point.'

Aileen looked relieved, then bit her lip. 'I don't think I ever could.'

'Then so be it,' Lola said, and smiled kindly. 'Let's get back to the croft, shall we?'

Lola pushed herself to her feet, then put out a hand to help the young woman up. Together, she and Aileen Mackinnon made their way down to the slope towards the car park.

Back at the croft, Cara told Lola she'd had an update from the coastguard. The helicopter had tracked Gaunt's yacht some miles out into the Atlantic — headed, they thought, for Irish waters.

'It looks like we're safe for tonight,' Cara said, and Lola felt the tension leave her body.

CHAPTER FORTY-TWO

Monday 19 August

11.23 a.m.

Irene Rossiter was a statue. She sat in the stuffy interview room, unmoving, staring blankly ahead, her solicitor looking somewhat uncomfortable at her side. Lola and Anna took turns reading aloud the various pieces of evidence that pointed to her and Jack Courtney's guilt in relation to the kidnap of Hamish Mackinnon — and also in relation to the murder of Kathryn Main.

'It was you who befriended Kathryn, wasn't it, Irene?' Lola said. 'Called yourself Liz. You'd tried to befriend another juror before that, but she wasn't having it. Her name is Sharon Trent, by the way. She's picked your photograph out of a selection of photos we showed her. Another piece of evidence for the file. Oh, and she's happy to stand up in court.'

No response.

'Why did you settle on Kathryn, out of interest? What was it about her that seemed so vulnerable to manipulation?'

Irene Rossiter's lips quivered at one side: the hint of a smirk.

'She seem lonely to you, was that it? In need of a friend?'

Still the woman wouldn't speak.

After an hour, Lola announced she needed a break from Irene Rossiter.

'Back to Jack Courtney?' she suggested to Anna in the corridor.

The man had been a wreck when they'd interviewed him earlier, weakly denying evidence, including the fact he was on camera driving out of the gates of Clunie Castle in the early hours of the morning Kathryn Main's body was found, and didn't return until 7 a.m. He wept away while his solicitor looked on in concern and tried to intervene, continually reminding him he could answer 'no comment'.

When Lola and Anna went back into the room now, though, Courtney was sitting upright and seemed calmer. The solicitor said, 'My client would like to make a statement,' and Lola restarted the recorder.

Courtney spoke for the next forty-five minutes. He confessed that, under the guidance of Irene Rossiter, he had murdered Kathryn Main and also Martin 'Mack' McBurney. He took responsibility, he said, but claimed the housekeeper had made him do it.

'You're saying she had power over you?' Lola asked him.

He nodded, his bottom lip trembling. 'She knew what I'd done . . . years ago, I mean.'

'And what was that, Jack?' Lola asked, leaning in.

Tears were in his eyes. He sniffed and bit his lip. He said, very quietly, 'I hurt a kiddie.'

'Did you?' Lola steeled herself for where this was going.

The solicitor said, 'Jack, we need to—'

'No,' he said sharply. 'It's okay. I want it to come out.'

'Tell us what you mean, Jack,' Lola said to the trembling man.

'I hurt a child.' He swallowed and Lola heard the click. 'A little girl — not like that,' he said quickly. 'I mean, I was driving after I'd had a drink. I hit her. Knocked her off her bike. She didn't die, but she nearly did.'

'Did you go to court?'

A miserable shake of the head. 'I drove off, you see?' He swallowed.

'Ah.'

'Then I got the job driving for one of Mr Gaunt's newspaper editors. I drove Mr Gaunt himself a couple of times. He said . . . he said he liked the way I handled the car. Did I ever drive classic cars? I said yes. He gave me the job. I've been with Mr Gaunt all these years.'

'And Miss Rossiter knew what you'd done?'

He said in a whisper, 'She found out.' He screwed up his face. 'I couldn't believe it. But she'd spoken to an old flame of mine. That's how she operates, see?'

'And she held it over you.'

A small nod. 'She said she would tell Mr Gaunt what I'd done and that he would fire me. That I'd never get another job. I'd never drive again.'

'And all for Carter Craig?'

'She loves him, you see?' Courtney said. 'She had a boy of her own, but he died very young. An accident. A stupid thing. He fell from a tree and even though it wasn't far, the way he landed, he twisted his neck and broke it. She said Carter was her son now. That he'd come along and made her life complete.'

They asked questions, pinning down locations, timings and methods. Courtney explained how he and Rossiter had travelled to Skye in a Land Rover they'd rented in Stirling. How Rossiter had found Theresa's room advertised on a charity's noticeboard, giving its general location; and how she'd called, giving a false name and a story about living with a violent spouse, and been stunned to hear just how close Evie lived to Theresa. And Theresa had welcomed her with open arms. She stayed there while Courtney slept in the truck. The chauffeur explained that he had made contact with Gordie MacPherson, who'd passed on information about Evie's whereabouts through Craig's website, meeting him at a remote layby near Struan. The boy had taken off his helmet

244

and shown an interest in Courtney's vehicle. Courtney had offered to show him the engine, then struck Gordie on the side of the head with a hammer before staging an apparent road accident.

'Why did you kill him?' Lola asked.

'Irene said to,' Courtney answered simply. 'She'd spoken to him on the phone. He'd told her his dad was a copper. She got worried.'

Another hour passed, and the statement was complete.

'We'll take a break,' Lola said, and she and Anna went in search of food.

* * *

12.32 p.m.

Lola was exhausted. She'd driven from Skye through the night, setting off at midnight and arriving at six this morning. She'd texted Sandy, saying she was on her way back. She got a short reply saying he was going to be busy for the next day or so. She read the words with resignation. She'd hurt him. Possibly destroyed everything. But she was too tired to process it.

She'd had two hours of sleep before coming into work. Unlike Skye, Glasgow was still experiencing a heatwave, which didn't help. Coffee, however, did. She and Anna sat over empty plates going through emails, reading out snippets of information to make sure they were both fully clued in.

Cara had taken Evie and Hamish to the cottage in Staffin first thing that morning, and reported that they seemed to be settling in well. She would return there later in the day to take a statement about the rape. Evie's Aunt Maddie would attend. Aileen was staying at the croft in Skaravaig for a few days and seemed — in Cara's words — to have 'flaked out, but in a good way'. She seemed more cheerful, less distressed, and was talking about going back to Glasgow, with the intention of visiting again soon.

The *Black Swan* was still unaccounted for. Irish coast-guards reported it, having left Irish waters, heading west into the high seas.

Carter Craig was in London. Had been since Saturday afternoon, according to the finely detailed alibi his solicitors had submitted. Local officers had gone to Clunie Castle the night before and found Juliana Gaunt in residence, along with Eddie Young, the head of security. Both claimed to have no knowledge of Gaunt's whereabouts. Told that the castle's housekeeper and chauffeur were under arrest, Eddie Young had apparently guffawed, while Juliana had become very quiet and watchful, claiming a headache and asking to be excused.

'Of course Craig's got an alibi,' Lola said. 'Which is suspicious in itself, not that he probably cares about that. But he's got a shock coming.'

DC Kirstie Campbell had gone first thing to the Princess Royal Maternity Hospital to meet an obstetrician and the lead sonographer in the early pregnancy unit. There she'd been shown scan images of Evie Mackinnon's seven-week-old foetus, along with measurements that narrowed the date of conception to within five days. She was returning to HQ with printed copies.

Lola checked the time and drained her coffee. 'Shall we?' she asked Anna.

* * *

1.42 p.m.

'Your colleague, Mr Courtney,' Lola began, 'has volunteered a detailed statement in which he admits to murdering Kathryn Main and Martin McBurney. He says he committed these acts under your instruction. What do you have to say to that?'

The woman stared straight ahead, barely blinking.

'He says that, following your orders, he broke into Aileen Mackinnon's flat, looking for an address for her sister and nephew. And that he went into Kathryn Main's flat using a key you'd given him to retrieve a certain moonstone necklace.'

Still nothing.

So Lola read Courtney's statement, taking her time, pausing to eye Irene Rossiter occasionally, but still seeing no response.

When she was done she laid down the pages and looked at the solicitor, eyebrows raised.

The solicitor cleared his throat. 'My client has no comment.'

Lola sat for a minute or two, thinking, wondering how to get through to the woman. She recalled Courtney's words: *She had a boy of her own once, but he died very young.*

Lola wasn't going to use that. It was the kind of stunt Izatt might pull. Instead, choosing her words very carefully, she said, 'Carter Craig — maybe you call him by his real name, Colin — he's going to prison for a long, long time.'

She blinked twice in quick succession. But that was all.

'Such a waste, really. He has so much charisma, and he's so handsome.'

The twitch of an eyelid.

'We've got the child's DNA,' Lola went on. 'It won't be long before we confirm the boy is his. Today the mother is making a statement that will accuse Craig of raping her on the night of the twenty-first of August 2021. One of my DCs has obtained the pregnancy scans, taken at seven weeks, from the hospital this morning. Together, the evidence is enough to persuade the Crown Office to go to a new trial — they've confirmed as much. I believe a jury will convict him of the nightclub murders. There'll be no jury-tampering this time. He's looking at life, with a minimum tariff of thirty years. He'll be in his sixties when he's released — if he's released. You're fifty-one, Irene. You'll be in your eighties. Chances are he'll be somewhere very secure. Very tough. Colin's tough, isn't he? Your Colin. Is he tough enough for that?' She saw the eyelid twitch again and leaned forward, studying the woman's face. 'Are *you* tough enough for that, Irene?'

And suddenly Irene's entire body seemed to flinch. Her shoulders lifted and came together and her head came down as she brought her hands, balled into fists, up to her face. She was trembling all over and a groaning, almost creaking sound emanated from her throat.

The solicitor rose in alarm and put out a tentative hand as if to comfort, or perhaps restrain, his client.

'You did your best to protect him, didn't you?' Lola asked, keeping her voice level. 'You did everything in your power.'

She looked at Lola now, her face crumpled. 'That bloody child,' she whispered. 'That *worm*.'

'What would you have done with him once you got him on the boat, Irene?'

'What do you think?' the woman said, teeth bared.

'I don't know,' Lola said. 'I suppose you meant to harm him. To kill him, perhaps.'

'Into the sea,' Rossiter said quietly. 'Like a kitten in a sack.'

The solicitor looked horrified.

'Irene,' he said. 'Please, you don't have to answer their questions.'

But she turned on him, savage as anything. 'Oh, why don't you just *shut up*?'

And he sat back down.

'You'd like to tell us all about it, wouldn't you?' Lola asked. 'Get it all off your chest.'

'Would I? I'm not so sure.'

'You could tell us how clever you were.'

'Psychological games, eh?' Rossiter said.

The solicitor looked wary.

'Not at all,' Lola said. 'I hoped you might tell us when you first had the idea of corrupting the jury, for instance. I mean, that was your idea, wasn't it? Not Colin's?'

'He had nothing to do with it,' Rossiter said. 'He *didn't*.'

She took a deep breath, laid her hands flat on the table and closed her eyes for several seconds. Eventually she opened them again.

'I'd realised,' she said in a low, flat voice, 'there was every chance a jury would find Colin guilty of the nightclub murders. Especially once they found that drug dealer to make a statement.'

'Did you know he'd done the murders?' Anna asked.

Irene Rossiter bridled. 'He was innocent! *He was!*'

Lola and Anna exchanged glances.

'I thought at first there might be a way of persuading members of the jury that he wasn't guilty, but I quickly realised that would be a lost cause. How much easier, I thought, to get them to convict him. And then I knew I had my plan. I would corrupt the jury and usher them towards a guilty verdict, but then expose the corruption. It would mean his freedom.'

She smiled as she remembered her cleverness.

'I knew I needed a woman, a pathetic one who would perhaps enjoy another woman's company, who would be flattered that someone was taking an interest. One, as well, who might be vulnerable to a sob story or two. I chose my target and followed her from the court one afternoon, but she didn't bite. Next day I picked another: Kathryn Main. And she took the bait.

'I took her for dinner. I said I was lonely and that the court case had upset me and I needed another woman's company. I told her I'd had a daughter, one Colin had attacked. She lapped it up. Very quickly — within hours — we became fast friends, swapping phone numbers and addresses and making plans. We met again the next night. She was so excited. I wore a moonstone necklace that second evening, one I took from Juliana's jewellery collection. Kathryn liked it. I gave it to her. That was a mistake.'

The woman's face darkened as she remembered.

'I realised as soon as I'd done it. I couldn't think how to get it back from her without arousing her suspicion. I asked her about it and where she kept it. Then Jack went to get it back after she was dead.'

'Jack Courtney,' Lola said. 'Your personal assistant.'

'If you want to put it that way.'

'And the screenshots of the WhatsApp conversations,' Lola prompted now. 'Was it you who sent them to the judge?'

'Yes. I found it very hard to be patient, as I'm sure you can imagine. I hated the idea of Colin in that prison, but I didn't want to act too soon.'

'How did you get hold of the screenshots?'

'From Kathryn. It was very easy. I asked her to share them with me to give me "hope" that people were truly on my and my daughter's side — and Kathryn complied. I have to say, I enjoyed watching the outrage in the press once the WhatsApp conversations were made public.'

'But then Kathryn had to die,' Lola said.

'Yes, but at the right time.' She said this without a hint of remorse. 'I contacted her just before I sent in the screenshots, saying I'd heard a rumour their behaviour had been found out. I said I didn't want her — my dear friend — to get into trouble. I told her Colin — Carter, I mean — was likely to be released in the next few weeks and that he would come after her. I suggested she find somewhere to hide and to give me the address. That way I could keep in touch with her. Then, when Colin was released, I told her I wanted to move her somewhere safer and that my brother would collect her from the place she was staying.'

'And that was Jack Courtney?'

'He borrowed a car from a neighbour in Perthshire and changed the plates. The neighbour's an old man with several cars and poor security. He never knew a thing.'

'The red BMW,' Lola murmured.

'Yes.'

'And Jack Courtney took her to Otago Street in Glasgow?'

'Correct. To a property owned by one of Duncan's many companies. I knew two of the flats in the block were being renovated. I'd been there with Colin once, you see. Colin was going to take over that company, but in the end he didn't. I knew the backyard extended to the river. Courtney took Kathryn there on the Friday night and drugged her, gagged her and tied her up. He collected Colin and his . . . lady friend that Sunday evening and brought them back to the castle, then he returned to Otago Street, strangled Kathryn and tipped her body into the river. I'd told him to leave the wire round her throat.'

'But why the wire?' Lola asked. 'Wouldn't that just draw attention to the method used in the nightclub murders?'

'Yes,' Irene said simply. 'Courtney used a wire on McBurney too. That was part of a bigger strategy altogether.'

'Oh?'

'To suggest that it might be the same perpetrator as the nightclub murders, when in fact the chief suspect had an unimpeachable alibi this time.'

'Thus suggesting . . .'

'That it was never Colin who committed the nightclub murders, but someone who was keen to implicate him. Not, of course, that it was likely ever to come to trial again.'

'Especially if one of the witnesses who claimed he'd seen him in Glasgow was now dead too.'

'Indeed.' She smiled, pleased with herself — but then her face fell, as if she'd just remembered what Lola had told her about the new evidence.

'You have no pity, do you?' Lola asked her. 'Not for Kathryn, not for McBurney, not for their loved ones, not for the people killed in the nightclub murders.'

She frowned, seeming genuinely puzzled at the suggestion.

'I have one goal,' she said.

'Colin.'

She nodded, smiling again. 'Colin.'

She confirmed that she'd ordered Courtney to break into Aileen Mackinnon's flat to try to find an address for her sister on Skye, but that he'd found nothing. He'd fixed a window so he could get in again quietly if need be.

'How could you possibly have known to target Aileen Mackinnon?' Lola asked.

'I've been looking out for Colin for a long time,' she said. 'When I first knew he was in serious trouble three years ago and might be arrested for the murders, I said to him, "Is there anyone who poses a threat?" He told me the name of this girl. I tried to find her. I found her sister, but I never found her. But then everything went quiet.' She became very still. 'When I heard this past week that there was a child . . . I knew it was time to act — and fast.'

'How did you find the croft?'

'Colin has a number of loyal friends,' she said. 'One sent him a private message. Colin trusts me to filter his fans' messages. He lets me reply to some of them. I knew what this one meant. I got onto the internet and looked at accommodation. Then I saw an advert for respite holidays. I called the woman and she took the bait. If she hadn't I'd have come anyway, but it would have been a good deal less convenient.'

'You attacked Theresa.'

'She was getting in the way, silly old woman.'

'She's going to be perfectly fine, in case you were interested.'

Irene snorted impatiently.

'The yacht,' Lola said. 'Duncan Gaunt was on it, wasn't he?'

She shrugged. 'You'll need to ask him.'

'We will,' Lola said. 'And did Colin know what you were doing, Irene? Did he know you were going to find and kill his child?'

'No comment.' Her eyes narrowed.

'He did, then?'

'No comment.'

'His *own child*?'

But then Lola remembered one of the darker stories about Craig, and how he'd boasted on TV about threatening a former girlfriend so that she would abort her pregnancy.

She sat back, exhaustion weighing heavily on her now, so that her bones ached as well as her muscles.

They took a break. Anna would continue and would take a statement.

'I'll send Kirstie along to join you in a minute,' said Lola. 'As for me, I'm away home to bed.'

Except she wasn't, not yet. She had a message on her phone calling her to a meeting.

CHAPTER FORTY-THREE

3.10 p.m.

'I shouldn't have done it, I agree,' Lola said wearily. 'But you know what? If I was in that situation again, I reckon I'd do the same thing.'

Elaine gave her a dark look.

'You're a bad woman,' the superintendent said.

'I'm not that bad. I'm just a bit wild sometimes.'

'No, well . . . Graeme isn't going to take out a grievance — against you or against the island police officer who blocked the entrance to the car park.'

'Oh. Well, that's good,' Lola said sheepishly.

'But it took all my powers to persuade him.'

'Thanks, boss.'

'In return you need to cooperate with him on the Craig stuff going forward.'

'I will. The evidence is Graeme's — that is, if he ever manages to find out where Craig has disappeared to. But Graeme can't bully his witnesses, boss. If I get one sniff that he is, I'll come after him.'

'I'm sure you will,' Elaine said drily. 'The other thing you need to do,' she went on, 'is to persuade our colleagues on

Skye *not* to take action against the officer who gave Bronagh Stewart's address to DS Pierce.'

Lola bridled at that. 'That's not my call.'

'Yes, it is,' Elaine said. 'You pride yourself on your ability to cut a deal. Cut this one.'

'But that officer was out of line. So was Pierce, as it happens.'

'I know! But do you really want to be facing a grievance?'

She slumped back down and mumbled, 'Not really.'

'Go home, Lola,' Elaine said.

She was at the door when Elaine added, 'You're not a bad woman. You're a very good one. You're just . . .'

'Just what, boss?'

'A pain in the backside sometimes.'

CHAPTER FORTY-FOUR

9.37 p.m.

Lola slept for an hour on the couch, then woke, disorientated and hungry. In the kitchen, while a mushroom stroganoff meal-for-one rotated in the microwave, she checked her phone, hoping against hope for a text from Sandy, but not finding one.

They had spoken when she'd got home from work, and he'd been friendly enough, if muted. He said they could meet later in the week, but part of her was convinced she'd ruined things between them.

Joe's brother Kev texted while her dinner was still heating. She'd heard from him twice today already. Joe was at the Golden Jubilee, ready for his operation tomorrow. This latest message assured Lola that Joe was comfortable and in a positive frame of mind.

Glad to hear it, she texted back — then immediately saw the three dots as Kev began to reply.

You will come and see him, won't you? Tomorrow night, maybe?

The microwave pinged.

I'll come if I can, she typed. Then, to stem the conversation: *Off to bed just now.*

Kev sent an enthusiastic reply, then added, *Joe says hi.*
She didn't respond.

* * *

10.04 p.m.

The stroganoff wasn't nice, and she was scraping the remains of it into the bin when her mobile phone went.

'Lola, where are you?' Elaine Walsh asked.

'At home, why?'

'Are you on your own?'

'Yes,' she said, feeling awkward. 'What's the matter?'

A pause. 'Graeme Izatt's flat's been set on fire.'

'Oh God.' She went cold and the kitchen seemed suddenly too bright. 'Is he all right?'

'He was out, luckily. It happened this evening. Someone put petrol through the letter box and set it alight. The whole block's just about destroyed.'

'Craig?' Lola said. She hurried to the door that led out into the garden and checked it was locked.

'We don't know,' Elaine said. 'But it could be him or one of his followers.'

'I'll need to get out of here.' Her thoughts flew immediately to Sandy, except—

Oh God . . .

'You can come here,' Elaine said, 'if you don't have anywhere else, that is.'

'I'll go to my sister's,' she said. 'Could you send someone to keep an eye on the house?'

'A car's on its way, but it could be another ten minutes. Just collect your stuff, Lola, and get out of there.'

She rang Frankie as she climbed the stairs.

Frankie was beside herself. 'Just leave!' she ordered. 'You can wear my clothes. We'll get you a toothbrush at the all-night garage.'

'I'll just put a bag together. See you in a bit. Thanks, Frankie.'

She hung up and her phone began to buzz again. Sandy this time. She bit her lip but chose not to answer. She could ring him once she got to Frankie's. Maybe he'd join her there. Right now she just had to clear out.

She was packed in minutes and hurried back downstairs and into the kitchen to retrieve her car keys — and yelled in shock.

Carter Craig, dressed all in black, was sitting at her kitchen table, legs wide, a gleaming grin on his handsome, evil face. At his feet was a blue holdall.

'Hello, Lola,' he said, then sprang up and was in her face. 'On your way out, are you?'

'Officers are on their way, Craig,' she told him.

'Is that right?' His grin seemed to widen. He towered over her, moving into her space so that she was backed now against the kitchen counter.

'You torched Graeme Izatt's place, didn't you?' she asked. 'Did I?'

He was so close to her now. She could feel the breath from his nostrils.

'I think you did,' she said, managing — somehow — to sound calm. 'You know the game's up, don't you? The boy's DNA's at the lab right now.'

He made a puzzled face and shrugged, lifting his hands as if to take her shoulders and making her flinch. In her pocket, her phone buzzed into life again. If only she could reach it and activate it and get a message to whoever it was. She thought about the counter behind her, and what was on it. Her knives were in a block at the far end. Just to her right, against the tiles, were three glass jars for pasta and rice. Heavy things.

'No one can touch me,' Craig said. 'You must know that by now. You can't link me to *anything* that's happened. And do you really think a jury would believe a man like me — someone who believes in traditional values — would *ever* harm his own son? No. I can't account for what Irene or anyone else was planning. And I can't be held responsible for it. People love me. People help me. *I wasn't even there.*'

'Weren't you? Weren't you on the boat with your uncle?'

He shrugged. 'What boat?'

'Why are you here?' she asked him, moving slightly to her right, closer to the glass jars.

He narrowed those beautiful blue eyes, so they became slits. 'Why do you think I'm here?'

'I think you want to hurt me. Possibly to kill me. To take me down with you.'

A wicked smile.

'I think I'm right.' She took another tiny step. 'It would be typical of you, being a narcissist and all that.'

He made a hurt face.

'You're a cruel man,' she said. 'A hateful man. Ultimately, I think you're very unhappy.'

'Oh, is that so?'

'You inflict misery wherever you go. It's sadistic and inhuman.'

The grin was back, and she knew she'd hit home. Not that he was ashamed. He was pleased. Proud.

'But I think it comes from a place of damage,' she said now, knowing she was right in front of the nearest glass jar. She lifted a hand and placed it on the counter beside her, as if to support herself.

'Damage? What damage?'

'I think your father's death affected you. I think you grew apart from your mother in your uncle's big draughty castle. I think you're frightened of your uncle and you're obsessed with gaining his approval.'

'Do go on.'

From somewhere she heard the sound of a car. Its engine cut and she heard the door bang. How long had Elaine said it would be before officers came in a car? No, it was far too soon. It must be a neighbour returning home.

'I feel sorry for you,' she said, making his eyebrows go up in amusement.

He stepped back, mock-offended. It gave her just enough time to twist her torso and grab the nearest jar and bring it round and up, flying into his face.

Except he was quick. His arm shot out and he blocked it, knocking the lid. Spaghetti flew everywhere.

Craig's face twisted into a snarl and he grabbed for her. Lola writhed as he gripped her upper arms — and then the doorbell rang.

'Get off!' she screamed, hoping she'd be heard.

Craig was behind her now. He had a muscly forearm under her throat, while he clamped her mouth with his free hand.

The doorbell went a second time. Lola roared through the clamping hand, while Craig pinned her tightly.

They grappled silently like that for several seconds. The doorbell didn't sound again. Suddenly Craig let her go, and threw her hard against the counter so that she cried out.

He snatched at the holdall. Seconds later he was cradling a gun.

Lola went very cold. Her insides threatened to give way.

He reached into the bag again and this time drew out a can of petrol, a handful of rags and a lighter.

'You don't have to do this,' she gasped, holding her arm.

'Don't I?' he said.

A movement by the back door. She reacted and Craig saw her. He went very still, looking at the glass.

'Out of here,' he said, motioning with the pistol towards the hallway.

She took her time, making more of the pain in her arm than she needed to.

'Go!' he hissed from behind her. 'In there.'

She went ahead of him into the living room.

'Draw the blind,' he ordered.

She went to the window and looked out. Sandy's silver Lexus was parked outside.

He was here. Had Elaine called him, or Frankie? But no, there couldn't have been time.

'Sit down,' Craig instructed, pointing at an armchair. Sandy's armchair.

She obeyed.

Oh, Sandy, be careful.

From somewhere in the house, she heard a tinkle of breaking glass.

Craig swore, eyes darting.

Outside, tyres screeched and engines cut. Car doors slammed. There were voices.

Someone was beating at the front door.

Craig was panicking now. He scrambled at the petrol can.

'Stop,' she implored him. 'Be sensible, for your own sake!'

The top was off the can and he was shaking stinking petrol out of it, splashing the couch, the walls, the blind.

Another crash from somewhere in the house, then stomping feet.

Craig let out a snarl of frustration and threw the can down. He lifted his lighter and cracked a flame, then turned, grinning at Lola again.

'Ready?' he asked her.

'Are you?' she asked him, then screamed and flew at him with all her rage and strength, fists flying, so that she struck his chin and knocked him off balance.

He staggered. Suddenly Sandy was in the room, eyes full of fury. A uniformed officer was behind him, then another. They brought Craig to the floor.

'Get the lighter,' Sandy cried at Lola.

She fell on it, grabbed it and threw it through the archway into the dining room.

Then she stood over the writhing mass of men, including the one she loved, and said, breathlessly, 'Carter Craig, I'm arresting you for possession of a handgun and for threatening behaviour.' Under her breath, she muttered, 'And all the rest.'

Craig was cuffed. Sandy stood and came to her. He held her arms and pulled her away, into the dining room.

'What are you doing here?' she asked.

'I got an alert,' he panted. 'On my phone. The doorbell camera I set up while you were away, remember? I linked it to my phone because you weren't here. It pinged to say someone was going down the side of the house. I saw it was Craig. I did try to call to warn you. I called 999 as I drove here. Thank God I wasn't far away.'

'Oh, Sandy.'

'It's okay,' he said, and pulled her into an embrace. 'They've got him now. You're safe.'

CHAPTER FORTY-FIVE

Tuesday 19 August

7.47 p.m.

Lola hung about in the reception area of the Golden Jubilee Hospital in Clydebank, feeling like a bad smell. A nurse saw her pacing and asked her if she was all right.

'Fine,' she responded jumpily. 'Just . . . just waiting on somebody.'

Joe had had his operation and it had gone well. Kev had kept her informed.

I don't know if I'll be there, she'd texted Kev earlier, in response to his third message of the day. *I'll need to see. Work's gone a bit crazy.*

He knew what she was talking about. The encounter with Craig at her house was all over the news.

She'd swithered all day about whether to come, but here she was. There was no chance Marie, Joe's wife, would turn up. She was on nights this week, according to Kev. She'd been in to see Joe in the afternoon and would be back in the morning.

So why was Lola here? She didn't know. Guilt? Love? Or to remind herself of how her life had been — of how unhappily she'd lived her life for thirty years, in hock to this man?

She checked the time and paced some more.

Kev was taking his time. He'd said he'd be out by a quarter to.

She thought about Joe and how he might look. Ill, no doubt. Thinner. Weaker.

Oh God, stop it . . .

She thought about love and its capacity to make you miserable: the sort where you prostrated yourself before other people and their needs. That was what Aileen Mackinnon had done with her sister, going full-on martyr, to the point where she'd nearly launched herself into the Atlantic. It was what Irene Rossiter had done for Carter Craig too. She wondered how Rossiter felt about that now, sitting in her cell. She wondered if anyone had let her know yet that Craig had been charged anew with the murders of Alex Sanderson and Xena Mitchell three years ago.

And Lola thought about herself. And the love she had for Joe. The love she'd always had — that she expected would never really go away. And how utterly wretched and powerless it had made her feel.

Could you ever fight that off and escape?

No escape. Never any chance.

Panic rose in her chest, like a bubble that might burst from her mouth in a scream.

She thought about what she'd done to Sandy. Validating Izatt's insinuations by asking Sandy if they were true, then by having Mairi Marshall ask about on her behalf.

He'd forgiven her. He'd told her that, late last night, after everything had calmed down.

'It's the thought of the jealousy I couldn't stand,' he'd told her.

'I know. I'm sorry. But the thought that what you and I have — that it might not be real . . . I thought it was going to drive me mad.'

Now, in the reception of the hospital, she took out her phone.

'What's wrong?' Sandy asked the moment he answered.

'I've changed my mind,' she said. 'I'm not going to see Joe. I'm coming back out.'

'You sure?'

'Aye, I'm sure.'

She dropped the phone back in her bag and hurried for the exit. Sandy's Lexus was already pulling into the pick-up zone.

She got in and put her belt on.

'Are you—?'

'I'm okay,' she said. She slumped back in the seat. She could message Kev later. Joe was in her past and he could stay there. 'I really am.'

At the lights Sandy eyed her with concern.

'What are you thinking?' he asked.

'Lots of stuff. Too much stuff.' She started to laugh, and was surprised to find tears bubbled up with it. Exhaustion washed over her. 'But right now I'm thinking I'm starving.' She wiped her eyes with a tissue.

'So am I,' he said as the lights changed. He turned right. 'Don't suppose you fancy a curry, do you? There's that place in Bearsden we went to. We both liked it. It's slightly out of the way, but—'

'Let's do it,' Lola said, and smiled at the thought of a hot and steaming balti.

And of Sandy, her future, sitting opposite her.

THE END

ACKNOWLEDGEMENTS

Once again, a big thank you to Chief Inspector Kirsty Lawie of Police Scotland for her assistance with the policing elements of the plot, and for linking me with others who could advise me on specifics of the story (noted below!).

I want to acknowledge the late Hon. Lord McEwan for considering various legal scenarios and helping me to choose the right one for the story.

Victoria Drew guided me with regard to Joe's ongoing cancer treatment.

Kev Paterson talked to me about his experience volunteering for HM Coastguard and pointed me towards information about Coastguard helicopters. He advised me on the scenes involving the chopper.

Georgina Fraser, MD of Jeffreys Interiors in Edinburgh, kindly immersed me in the world of interior design for an hour. Thanks to Campbell David Parker for putting us in touch.

Elaine Gardiner, Programme Lead MSc Medical Ultrasound in the School of Health and Life Sciences, Glasgow Caledonian University, helped me to understand diagnostic imaging and confirmed that my plot would work! Thanks to Deborah Hill for introducing me to Elaine.

Daniel Fenn at the Scottish Criminal Cases Review Commission helped me to understand appeals and how juries work and provided guidance for me to read.

I also received fascinating advice from the Crown Office and Procurator Fiscal Service.

Superintendent David Ross of Police Scotland talked me through the policing set-up on Skye.

I've been writing in cafés again. My current favourites are the Perch Café in Garelochhead and Skoosh Café in Drymen. Special thanks to the Perch for selling signed copies of the books.

Thank you to Simon and Chris for once again letting me stay at their cottage in Kintyre to write bits of the book. Simon helped with some medical stuff. He still hasn't read a single page I've written, but hey . . .

Thanks to writer pals for their ongoing support and wisdom. Shout-outs to Sally-Anne Martyn, Linda Mather, Marion Todd and Allan Radcliffe — all brilliant writers too. A special thank you to the star-in-human-form that is Margaret Murphy. Her advice on key parts of this book really helped to strengthen it. I value our chats so much!

My beta readers were immensely helpful this time round — and very speedy. A huge thank you to my mum, Julie, as well as to Alison Winch, Allan Radcliffe, Astrid Reid, Janice Fraser (who read it twice), Jill Crawford, Joanne Welding, John and Rowena Gregory, Katharine Bradbury, Laura Hamilton, Linda Mather and Margaret Murphy.

Special thanks to my brother Alex for information about cars.

Emma Grundy Haigh oversaw the writing and structural edits of this book, before moving on to a new company. My new editor Siân Heap picked up the reins and brought it to completion. Thanks to both of them.

Thank you, finally, to my wonderful agent, Francesca Riccardi, who is always there, and for bossing me about in the nicest possible way.

THE JOFFE BOOKS STORY

We began in 2014 when Jasper agreed to publish his mum's much-rejected romance novel and it became a bestseller.

Since then we've grown into the largest independent publisher in the UK. We're extremely proud to publish some of the very best writers in the world, including Joy Ellis, Faith Martin, Caro Ramsay, Helen Forrester, Simon Brett and Robert Goddard. Everyone at Joffe Books loves reading and we never forget that it all begins with the magic of an author telling a story.

We are proud to publish talented first-time authors, as well as established writers whose books we love introducing to a new generation of readers.

We won Trade Publisher of the Year at the Independent Publishing Awards in 2023. We have been shortlisted for Independent Publisher of the Year at the British Book Awards for the last four years, and were shortlisted for the Diversity and Inclusivity Award at the 2022 Independent Publishing Awards. In 2023 we were shortlisted for Publisher of the Year at the RNA Industry Awards.

We built this company with your help, and we love to hear from you, so please email us about absolutely anything bookish at feedback@joffebooks.com

If you want to receive free books every Friday and hear about all our new releases, join our mailing list: www.joffebooks.com/contact

And when you tell your friends about us, just remember: it's pronounced Joffe as in coffee or toffee!